The Wealth of Kings

By

Sam Ferguson

The Wealth of Kings

Copyright © 2016 by Sam Ferguson
Published by Dragon Scale Publishing

For A.F.

CONTENTS

Other Books by Sam Ferguson

Other Books by Dragon Scale Publishing

The Protector of Esparia by Lisa M. Wilson
Kingdom of Denall Series by Eric Buffington:
The Troven
Secrets at the Keep
The Changing

Tales from the NoWhere and NeverWhen
Wisp the Wayfinder
Puck the Pathwinder
Nobb the Nightbinder

ALSO
Check you some great short fantasy stories on our website like:

Tharzule's Tome of Wishes
And
Orcs and Elves

CHAPTER 1

Year 3,201 King's Era.
2nd year of the reign of Sylus Magdinium, 5th King of Roegudok Hall.

Sylus watched the line of trees to the south. He couldn't yet see the orcs from his vantage point on the hill, but he knew they were there. Dwarven spies had already warned him of the danger posed to the humans in the north. Sylus was determined not to let the orcs ever reach the humans.

A single captain waited atop his mount on Sylus' right hand side, waiting for the king's order. Sylus' own cavedog shifted restlessly beneath him, and Sylus leaned forward slightly in his saddle to run his hand over the rough, black scales of the beast's neck, clicking his tongue quietly to soothe her.

He didn't have to wait long before the first orcs emerged from the trees. The main body of the army was comprised of footmen. They carried spears, swords, and axes. Their armor clinked and clanked as they marched, reflecting the sun off their grease-stained metal. Sylus took in a breath and waited patiently until the first goarg riders appeared on the western flank of the army. The goargs were a giant breed of shaggy coated goats with massive, curled horns they could use to batter down soldiers and weak doors alike. The orcs had long ago found the secret to domesticating them, but no other race in the Middle Kingdom was capable of replicating their success. The goarg riders were among the fiercest orc warriors known in the Middle Kingdom. Within minutes, King Sylus counted a total of four thousand orcs. Three thousand footmen, and one thousand goarg riders. Their focused march to the north told Sylus that none of the orcs had spotted him or his captain yet. A low profile was yet another advantage to the cavedogs.

The dwarf king couldn't help but smile when he saw the enemy army. Though he abhorred the notion of losing dwarf life, deep within himself he couldn't help but relish a good challenge.

"Prepare the others," Sylus told the captain. "Upon my signal, charge over the hill and follow me into the eastern flank. We will cut them down here."

"By your command," the captain replied dutifully. Sylus watched as the captain turned his cavedog, and directed the massive lizard down the opposite side of the hill to where the three thousand dwarf soldiers waited.

Sylus surveyed the enemy army, letting his black eyes scrutinize them until his gaze fell upon the enemy general.

"Borgnat," Sylus whispered as his smile widened. His spies had already told him that Borgnat was leading the assault, but that did nothing to spoil Sylus' pleasure at seeing the orc general for himself. Borgnat was large for an orc, rumored to pull the arms off of prisoners taken in battle with nothing but his bare hands. There was more to the orc general than rumors, however. In the last three years, he had razed seven human settlements farther to the south. He had also destroyed a city of elves near the border with the orcish lands, and that was to say nothing of the conquest he had already completed among the orcish tribes themselves as he rose to power by cutting down other orc chiefs and generals.

To let this orc through to the north would spell the end of the sapling human settlements.

Sylus looked to the sky, wondering whether Tu'luh the Red would return in time to join in the battle. When he failed to spy the great dragon, he sighed and tugged on his left gauntlet one more time. Dragon or no dragon, the fight was upon him.

The Wealth of Kings

King Sylus pulled his hammer, affectionately known among the dwarves as Murskain. The mighty weapon felt good in his hand, perfectly balanced and sized specifically for Sylus' body. The spike on the back side of the hammer glinted in the sunlight as Sylus held it out to the side and urged his mount down the hill, letting out a mighty cry as the massive black lizard burst into action. His dramatic hailing of the orcs had the desired effect, as the orc army turned in unison to face him.

A group of twenty spearman broke off from the army and knelt down at the base of the hill. Sylus almost pitied their foolishness. Just as he closed in on the spearmen, the orcs all looked up as the rest of the dwarf army crested the hill and the sound of thousands of feet announced the ambush. On the opposite side of the orc army, the goarg riders were shouting and pushing their way through the throng, but their help would not come soon enough.

Sylus swept aside five spears with his hammer as he charged. This might have left him exposed had he been a human knight riding upon a horse, but a dwarven cavedog was not without weapons of its own. The giant lizard snapped forward and ripped the arm off an orc on the left, then it spat the limb out in time to lunge up and rake the face and neck of the spearman directly in front while the lizard simultaneously struck out with its jaws and bit the orc just to the right on the shoulder. The teeth didn't penetrate the metal armor, but they didn't need to. The force of the cavedog's bite was enough to crush the metal, and the shoulder joint. Blood oozed out from the spaces between the pauldron plates, and the orc howled in pain as its arm bones cracked and splintered.

By this time, Sylus had brought his hammer back into play. He finished the orc on the left with a deft blow to the head that toppled the warrior backward to the ground. Next he swung in a horizontal chop, taking two heads clean off and dropping another pair of bodies. The other spearmen regrouped and tried to enclose him in a circle, but a tail lash swept the feet out from under two orcs, and a savage bite severed another orc's leg just below the knee, ripping the armor along with the limb. Sylus put another two orcs down as well.

The remaining spearmen were swallowed by the dwarf army which pushed through them as though they had been made of paper.

Sylus urged his steed on, looking through the chaos of bodies and blood to find Borgnat. He drove in behind a trio of dwarves that formed a wedge for him. They split the army's flank open and drove their weapons into any orc foolish enough to square off against them. The dwarves used their momentum to push the orc army out to the side as they cut them down, mercilessly punishing them for their trespass. The cavedogs all fought as violently as the dwarves. Even when a dwarf warrior fell by the enemy, the cavedog would fight on until it too was slain.

Had this been an army of goblins, or even humans, the battle would be over by now. The sheer ferocity of the assault would have sent most rational enemies fleeing for their lives, but orcs were another matter. They lived for battle. They relished it, worshipped it even. It was bred into their being as the only way to prove themselves worthy of a better station in the afterlife.

Sylus had often doubted that any station in Hammenfein would ever compare to the Heaven City of Volganor, but even he could not deny the conviction and fervor with which the orcs fought.

Shouts went up through the enemy ranks. Orcs snarled and put up a ferocious defense.

Continuing to push his way through to the center where he had seen Borgnat riding surrounded by his personal guard of goarg riders, Sylus flinched away suddenly as blood sprayed across his face. A second later he noticed a glistening spear point protruding out the back of the dwarf in front of him. A moment later he saw a massive, white-furred beast leaping out over the line of orcs immediately in front of him. The strong, thick horns blasted into the dwarf on the left side of the wedge. The crunching bone all but overshadowed the dwarf soldier's muted groan as he crumpled backward. The goarg's hooves landed square upon the cavedog beneath the slain dwarf, driving the lizard into the ground and snapping its spine in several places.

The cavedog underneath the dwarf slain by the spear lashed out and ripped the goarg's hind left leg off. The sinew and flesh made a sound not unlike parchment being torn by hand as the meat and bone came free from the goarg's body and the beast stumbled. Sylus charged in, one hit to the orc rider on top, who was struggling to maintain his balance on his gravely injured mount. The orc's helmet broke inward and blood spurted out the bottom.

Sylus then expertly flipped his hammer over and drove the spike down into the base of the goarg's neck. The beast grunted and fell to the ground.

"Sire!" a dwarf called out from the right.

Sylus turned just in time to see a dwarf leap from his cavedog to place himself between an orcish crossbow and the king. Sylus heard a loud, metallic thump, and then the dwarf fell to the ground. The cavedog he had leapt from, however, wiggled as it sprinted forward and lunged into a trio of orcs. It killed one and managed to topple a second before spears and swords took it down.

The dwarf king pressed forward as more dwarves arrived to guard his flanks. The fighting was much fiercer now as the orcs were fully turned to face the dwarves. More than that, goargs were breaking through the footmen and pressing the dwarves back. Sylus narrowly dodged a spear jabbing toward his chest, turning to the side slightly and then clamping his left arm down over the shaft to catch it in place. His cavedog responded to the slightest of Sylus' commands, this time stepping back and helping Sylus pull the orc forward. Sylus came in with an overhead chop that drove the orc to the ground in a heap atop other corpses.

Sylus ripped the spear free and flipped it over. Now he had a weapon in either hand. He squeezed his saddle between his thighs and urged his cavedog forward. He jabbed out at a sword-wielding orc, then came in with the hammer to finish the assault, driving the spike through the orc's armor and into his chest. An orc lunged in from the right then, but Sylus' cavedog snaked in and bit the orc in the tender flesh of the inner thigh. The lizard's teeth sank into the flesh just above the cutout in the greaves, and stopped the orc cold as he howled in pain.

A dwarf on Sylus' right helped the cavedog by driving a sword through the orc's neck.

Suddenly, the orcs in front of Sylus shrank away.

"Steady!" Sylus called out. He knew the orcs better than to think they might be routing. As the wall of orcs split apart, a mess of goarg riders confirmed Sylus' suspicion. "Bow-sticks!" Sylus commanded. The king threw the spear haphazardly, and with his now empty hand reached for a metal cylinder hanging from his belt. The dwarves nearby likewise pulled for cylindrical objects hanging from their belts. Sylus pointed one end of the shiny weapon at a goarg's chest. His thumb then found the button near the back of the bow-stick, and depressed it. A metallic click was followed by a *whoosh!* A small, but deadly bolt with a razor-sharp broadhead sailed through the air and sank deep into the goarg's chest. Dozens of similar shafts followed only an instant later as the other dwarves fired their bow-sticks.

The rushing wave of goargs fell to the ground, the nearest animal crashing a good ten yards away and stranding its rider. Sylus turned his bow-stick over in his hand, his thumb eagerly sliding around the shaft and looking for the second button.

"Fire two!" Sylus shouted.

The next volley dropped many orcs as the flying missiles easily penetrated the metal armor. Small, and powerful, the bowstick's only flaw lay in the fact that it was a very limited use item. The inner springs and triggering mechanisms required precision to manipulate, making it impractical to reload on the battlefield. Still, it fulfilled its intended use. It broke the goarg charge, and slew many orcs besides.

Each dwarf warrior let their bow-stick fall, kept in place by the chain attached to their belts, and followed their king as they began a short range charge at the stunned enemy.

The cavedogs tore at the ground with their claws, propelling the dwarves forward as clumps of dirt and turf were flung up into the air behind them. The scent of dirt and grass mingled with the metallic stench of blood hanging over the battlefield. Everything moved as if in slow motion. Sylus' brain worked faster than ever. He calculated the steps until his mount would reach the nearest orc. At the same time, he noted how the orc was moving. Scowling beneath an open-faced helmet with yellow bottom tusks protruding out from dark green lips, the orc warrior raised both hands overhead, preparing a chop with a mighty axe which was glistening brightly in the sunlight.

Sylus grinned. His cavedog moved in toward the orc's right side. The axe began slowly arcing downward toward the dwarf king. Shouts and groans erupted all around Sylus as other dwarves collided with orcs and the battle continued. His cavedog made straight for the orc's right side, head down and wagging in perfect counterbalance to its tail as the body swerved and moved. Then, the cavedog darted left at the last possible instant. Sylus struck up with his hammer, not at the orc, but snagging the axe just under the blade and breaking the shaft. Splinters exploded out under the pressure as the orc's weapon broke. Then, a fraction of a second later, the dwarf king brought the spike down and cut back toward the orc's unprotected neck. The orc never stood a chance.

All returned to normal then as the battle swarmed around him. Quick thrusts and swings blocked and parried, resulting in both orc and dwarf bodies falling to the ground. From what Sylus could see, there were far more orcs dying than dwarves.

Then he saw Borgnat.

The mighty orc was pressing his goarg through the fight at a methodical, tempered pace somewhere between a trot and a walk, allowing the goarg enough time to lash out with its sharp hooves while Borgnat brought death down with his mighty, black sword.

Sylus issued a command in Peish, the language of the dwarves, and instantly a group of twenty dwarves formed a wedge before him and pushed through toward Borgnat. They cut down as many orcs as they could, and pushed others aside. A few of the dwarves fell by spears or swords, but Sylus was easily able to follow the large, clear swath the dwarves left in their wake.

Then, the wedge reached Borgnat and everything changed.

Two dwarves went down in one swing.

Borgnat's goarg smashed in the heads of two cavedogs, one under each hoof.

A group of orcs rushed in to defend their general.

The fighting turned quite fierce as the dwarves traded blow for blow with the orcs. Neither the orcs, nor the dwarves easily gave up their ground. Sylus rushed in to help, but even he had to hit each orc multiple times before they would fall to the ground. Not surprisingly, only the strongest orc warriors had been placed near Borgnat.

Sylus took a glancing shot to the back. A warhammer came swinging in and collided with his chest, but he shook it off and pressed the attack. He broke the right hand of an orc swordsman and then smashed the orc's knee inward. The bone crunched, but the orc barely fell to his knee before pulling a short sword from his belt and launching a counter attack that nearly stabbed Sylus' cavedog in the face. Luckily the lizard pulled back in time. Sylus then brought Murskain down upon the orc's head, arresting the inexorable will of this warrior as his neck was crushed beneath Sylus' hammer.

A great spray of blood arced in front of Sylus then as a dwarf arm spun end over end to bounce onto the ground. Sylus couldn't help but feel a stab of pain in his heart as he watched his now one-armed captain struggle against Borgnat. He lashed out at the goarg with his remaining arm, but the animal dropped its head and easily deflected the captain's hammer with its horns and thick skull.

The captain's cavedog lunged out, but Borgnat drove his greatsword down through the lizard's neck with lightning-fast reflexes.

The goarg then lurched forward and connected with the captain's chest. To his credit, the dwarf captain was not dislodged from his saddle, but the attack had opened a clear shot to his chest. Borgnat seized the opportunity and the captain hung limp from the orc general's blade before sliding off and slumping to the ground.

Sylus had charged in when he first saw the severed arm, but he didn't reach Borgnat until seconds after his captain was slain.

The dwarf king let out a feral yell and rose out of the saddle to launch his attack. Jumping is not a dwarf's strong point, but Sylus had this particular maneuver down to an art form. He stood upon his cavedog and shouted a single word in Peish. Immediately, the cavedog leapt straight up into the air. Just before the cavedog reached the apex of its jump, Sylus launched off from the lizard's back, coupling the momentum of his mount with his own effort. The maneuver succeeded. Sylus managed to clear the charging goarg's horns by mere inches, and direct his attack at an incredulous Borgnat.

The two collided with what must have sounded like a clap of thunder to everyone around them. Borgnat's sword was caught on Sylus' hammer, but the dwarf's feet drove into the orc general's chest and the two went tumbling off the backside of the goarg to crash onto the ground below.

Sylus was the first to roll to his feet, but Borgnat was able to muster a defense from his knees, stopping Sylus' horizontal chop by planting the point of his sword into the ground and presenting it as a barrier. The metal rang out over the field, but the sword held firm. Borgnat then jumped to his feet and twirled his sword over as he ripped it from the ground and twisted his arms into a diagonal chop of his own.

Sylus stuck Murskain's head up in the sword's path. As

the two weapons collided, the dwarf's sturdy, muscled arms shook and trembled under the force of the blow. Borgnat then launched a kick that landed high on Sylus' chest, just below and to the right of his neck. From the weight of the kick, the king knew instinctively that he would stumble if he tried to stay on his feet. So, he let himself roll backward with the momentum, somersaulting away from a heavy chop that scarred the ground, but fell short of cutting Sylus as the king rolled out of the way and back up to his feet.

"Igaze furge, de megollek," Borgnat snarled.

Sylus hadn't the slightest idea what the orc had said, the orcish language was not something that he had ever bothered to study. The king figured knowing how to put the brutes down was the only thing he needed to learn about orcs.

Sylus charged in, raising his hammer up and to the left. Borgnat prepared a perfect parry, as Sylus expected. The two weapons collided, but Sylus stiffened his shoulders and lunged in under the weapons, releasing Murskain as he sailed in to collide with Borgnat. Their armor clanged, and Borgnat grunted as he fought against the dwarf's momentum. Sylus hadn't expected to bring the large orc down, he had only wanted to throw him off guard, and that had worked.

Borgnat came down with his arms. One hand grabbed Sylus' hair and pulled back as the other arm brought the pommel of the sword down onto Sylus' helmet. It was a heavy blow, but if there is one trait all dwarves have in common, it is their extremely thick skulls. Sylus ignored the sting and reached for a pair of small, scimitar-shaped daggers at his belt. With incredible speed he plunged the twin blades up on either side of Borgnat, slipping through the joint between Borgnat's breastplate and his greaves, just over the thick belt. The blades found soft tissue underneath and bored deeply into the orc's flesh.

Sylus twisted the daggers as he rolled around to the left, pulling the orc's torso along with him.

Now Borgnat was ready to strike properly. He let go of Sylus' hair and prepared to chop down mightily. Sylus then did something Borgnat had not anticipated. The dwarf king picked his legs up and, hanging from the two knives, dug deep into the orc, and swung himself under the orc's legs. Borgnat swung down, and stumbled forward as he lost his balance. The dwarf king let go of his knives and wasted no time clambering up Borgnat's back as the orc fell to his face. Sylus pulled a large knife from Borgnat's own belt and then leapt up to add extra momentum as he aimed for the back of Borgnat's neck.

Sylus came down hard, snapping the orc general's neck bone as he simultaneously drove the orc's knife through the flesh.

Borgnat let out a short wail, and then his body twitched twice before going stiff.

Sylus had no time to relish the victory, though. The fight was still raging around him. He let go of the knife and sprinted for his hammer. A moment later his cavedog stopped in front of him and he mounted the great lizard once again. Dwarves swarmed to him, shouting out the great victory and calling the battle for themselves.

The remaining orcs disagreed. They fought fervently. Not until the last orc was surrounded by twelve angry dwarves and put to death with a series of chops and stabs did the battle end.

"Stubborn lot," Sylus spat as he saw the final orc fall.

Cheers went up through the ranks and Sylus turned about in his saddle, making a mental guesstimate about the casualties. Fortunately, dwarves were also a stubborn lot. Many of the wounded began rising from the ground, drastically reducing Sylus' initial fatality estimate. Still, the fight had been costly. Including the wounded that were not beyond saving, Sylus had little over half his army remaining.

It had been a terrible cost for the dwarves to pay. Sylus said little as he helped his remaining officers tally the dead and arrange for care of the fallen bodies. He said less as they made their march back to Roegudok Hall.

Yet, even while in the depths of sorrow for his fallen kin, he knew that the price would have been much higher if

Borgnat had been allowed to reach the humans unimpeded.

When the dwarves reached the outer gates of Roegudok Hall, they were greeted by a score of the Home Guard, the mountain's defensive army. They opened the thick, brass gates leading into the outer tunnel and stood silently saluting their kin as Sylus marched the cavedog riders through the tunnel.

Sylus led his army through a long, upward sloping tunnel. The walls were smooth, with small holes in the low hanging ceiling every dozen yards or so. To those not of the dwarven race, the construction of the tunnel seemed strange, but Sylus appreciated the purpose behind its unique design. Roegudok Hall was built on the inside of a great mountain. The sheer cliffs and impassable peak forced all guests, both invited and uninvited, to use the tunnel as the main entrance. Tu'luh, and other dragon lords known as Ancients, had helped the dwarves design the entrance when the dwarf kingdom was first established some three thousand-three hundred years ago in the year nine hundred of the Ancient Era. The tunnel's slope allowed the dwarves to defend against invading armies by unleashing molten metal, burning oil, or any other deadly liquid they deemed appropriate to scourge the invaders. The defense was so effective that no invader had even seen the gates of Roegudok Hall itself. A few orcish armies had tried over the years, but they did so at great peril, and were either sent scurrying for the south, or were utterly destroyed before they could reach the end of the three-mile-long tunnel.

Even the height of the ceiling was specially designed to aid in defending the great inner palace. With the tunnel only six feet tall, it hindered taller soldiers, yet allowed for the almost comfortable passage of invited guests, so long as they walked. Furthermore, no invader could ever ride a horse or goarg through the tunnel. This fact rendered enemy cavalry useless against the dwarves. Beyond this, Sylus knew of one additional secret defense that could be unleashed.

In a large aquafer above the ceiling was a great reservoir of millions of gallons of water. With a few levers, the aquafer could be drained into the tunnel. At the same time, a great door of iron would slide over the front entrance to the tunnel. The bottom of this door was a razor sharp blade, which was terrible enough for any foe caught underneath, but its true purpose was to block the released water from escaping and draining from the tunnel. Meanwhile, the great gates on the opposite end of the tunnel were also water tight. It created an effective trap that would work if all else failed to stop an invading army.

Sylus and his army reached the main gates and found them slightly open, allowing a wall of golden light to reach out from the extremely tall, arched doors of iron. Sylus needed only to signal by raising his hand. A series of horn blasts echoed through the tunnel and the doors creaked and groaned as they were pushed open to allow the army to ride through.

Even with the many losses suffered, and the foul mood Sylus was in, there was something about crossing that main threshold that always invigorated and cheered him. The sense of returning home, to a place that was wholly his and felt as comfortable as anything in the Middle Kingdom could. He had lived as a prince in Roegudok Hall for over two hundred years before taking his place as king when his father passed on from the plane of the living, yet even still he marveled at the beauty and exquisite craftsmanship that had forged the main hall from the once solid interior of the mountain. The vaulted ceilings almost disappeared well over two hundred feet above Sylus' head. The ceiling was covered in a layer of gold and platinum plates that reflected the light of the torches and oil lamps hung in exact intervals of fifteen feet up each of the massive columns. Each supporting column had been hewn and worked to perfection. The pink granite stone was smooth as silk and polished so that one could almost use it as a mirror.

Off to the left of the entrance stood stone buildings; a guardhouse and a barracks for the Gate Patrol. These buildings were created with etchings and carvings into the stone bricks, and held in place by a scarlet red mortar that had also been polished to a high shine. The roof of each of these buildings consisted of gold and green shingles that glimmered in the light of the main hall.

A pair of dwarves sitting at a granite table outside the guardhouse rose from their game of cards and saluted their king upon sight. Sylus returned the salute and they returned to their cards after he passed.

There were many more ornate buildings of stone along the western wall of the chamber, but Sylus was now busy counting the great columns as he led his army through them. It wasn't that he needed to count them, he would have known his way through the main hall if he was blindfolded, but he enjoyed counting the columns. It was almost as if each one was a dear friend welcoming him back from the outside and stretching out warmth from their lamps and torches.

After he had passed ten columns, and several smaller craftsman shops, Sylus turned to the right and led his army through the main pathway through the market. There were tables with trinkets of all shapes and sizes strewn over them. There were also a few tables that offered vegetables, both the kinds that grew inside the mountain as well as those grown in a secluded valley nestled near the top of the mountain. Other vendors offered clothing, books, weapons and armor. A few dwarves had carts pulled up around the back of the shops and tables, filling orders that they would transport to the various settlements outside Roegudok Hall. The hustle and bustle barely paused as the king rode by and the throngs of dwarves watched the first part of the procession.

Sylus knew they meant no disrespect to the fallen warriors. Those working in the market district were extremely busy. They could afford Sylus a moment of respect, but after that they had to return to their work to fill the orders they had. The dwarves within Roegudok Hall had everything they could ever wish for, and all indicators pointed to an era of unprecedented prosperity under Sylus' reign. That also meant that they were the largest supplier of goods for the settlements outside the mountain. Armor, stone, metal ore, and all manner of dishes, jewelry, and other fine goods were shipped from the mountain as soon as the goods were produced. The great quantities of goods upon the tables for sale within the mountain were only a fraction of what the dwarves of Roegudok Hall produced.

As the army crossed through to the other side of the market, the warriors turned off to the north, eager to corral their cavedogs and unburden themselves. Tonight the wounded would be cared for by physicians and healers. Those without injury would rest. The fallen would be placed in a cool chamber and prepared for their final rites. Tomorrow the mountain would halt its production. None of the miners would lift their tools. The craftsmen would abandon their work benches. All would come together to honor the fallen and begin the funeral rites. As busy as the mountain ever was, the dwarves could never forget to honor their kin who had sacrificed their lives.

Sylus turned and watched the army ride by him, already thinking about the morrow's activities and what he would say during the services for the dead. He swung a stiff leg over his cavedog and slid off as the lizard bent slightly to ease his dismount. The cavedog then turned and followed the others.

The king made his way to a small building at the base of a grand set of stairs. Inside, a trio of body servants helped him remove his armor. He then left the building and ascended the stairs, winding his way up the spiraling steps cut right into the stone of the eastern wall. The way was long, and would be tiring to all but the dwarf folk, who were built for climbing up and down long tunnels in the mountain. The staircase was twenty feet wide, adorned with stone engravings and murals along either wall. Some depicted historical events, battles, coronations, deaths and births of kings. Others were ornamental designs created by the greatest of dwarven masters. The stairs themselves were hewn right out of the black mountain stone, polished to a high sheen and inlaid with gold that crisscrossed diagonally and glittered under foot as the great chandeliers above burned bright and cast their light down.

Thirty minutes passed before Sylus reached the top landing in front of the throne room. The landing itself was forty feet long and flanked with four sets of armor on display atop pedestals of solid gold. Each pedestal had the name of a previous king carved into it. Those kings were Sylus' father, grandfather, great grandfather, and great-great grandfather. Sylus went to his father's set of armor and gently brushed the left pauldron. He then looked a few feet beyond it and saw the empty pedestal that would one day hold his armor.

Sylus concealed the condescending grin that tried to worm its way across his mouth as an idea struck him suddenly. Would they honor Sylus' armor even if it was dented and scarred from his battles with orcs, or would they recreate armor that would glorify his victories but omit the memory of the injuries and wounds that had come along with the battles?

CHAPTER 2

Year 3,711 Age of Demigods, Late Spring.
2nd year of the reign of Aldehenkaru'hktanah Sit'marihu, 13th King of Roegudok Hall.

Al stood on the landing atop the spiral staircase leading up from the barren market in the main hall. His tired eyes were fixed upon a highly polished set of armor standing upon the fifth pedestal. The golden plaque upon the pedestal read, "King Sylus Magdinium, fifth king of Roegudok Hall." Al admired the black metal the armor was made from. A silver and gold inlay was set in a weaving pattern at each joint and edge, and a mighty dragon was embossed over the chest. The gauntlets had fierce spikes protruding from the knuckles, and a large ruby was set into the back of each hand. The pauldrons protruded out in a very pronounced way, almost mimicking wings as they tapered down into sharp blades that reminded Al somewhat of the dragon-slayer armor he had seen Master Lepkin wear in recent weeks. In Al's estimation, all of the armor paled in comparison to the mighty hammer fastened to the wall above the pedestal though.

"The great weapon, Murskain," Al whispered reverently. "The hammer by which King Sylus forged the greatest and most prosperous generation of dwarves to ever grace Roegudok Hall." Al smiled and nodded respectfully to the hammer, as if it still housed a piece of Sylus' soul. "Would that I knew your secret to wealth now," Al said as his shoulders slumped and he turned his gaze to the floor. "The tables in the market are bare, save for a few trinkets left over from before the war with Tu'luh. We have no ore, no stores of weapons or armor. My brother squandered all of the wealth left by our father. Whatever remained was consumed by the war."

Al sighed and stretched a hand out to the breastplate before him. "That is to say nothing of the loss of kin we have suffered." Al looked to the helmet, half expecting Sylus to appear and rebuke him. Still, despite his grief, he had known the risk. There had been no other way to stop Tu'luh the Red. The dragon was far beyond reason, and the army he led would have ravaged the entire Middle Kingdom.

The dwarf king sighed once more and patted the breastplate as he turned and walked toward the golden double doors that separated the stairs from the throne room. Diamonds, emeralds, and sapphires sparkled and shimmered in an arch around the doorway as Al approached. Normally, there would have been a pair of guards before the doors, but Al had sent them away upon returning to Roegudok Hall a few days before so they could help with the burial rites.

When he left Roegudok Hall sixty years ago, he never would have guessed that he would have become king, and then led the dwarven army to fight off an orc invasion from the south after Ten Forts was conquered. Though, even that particular series of battles paled in comparison to the height of the war when he led the full might of the dwarven army to Fort Drake in an attempt to stop Tu'luh the Red, one of the nastiest dragons to darken the skies of Terramyr, and cull the zombie army that the dragon commanded.

Al stopped and leaned into the open doorway as the memories came flooding back to him. So many had been lost. Nagar's Blight had threatened the entire Middle Kingdom, but even in defeating it, Al had lost nearly each and every dwarf soldier that had gone on the campaign with him. Those who had not been slain, had been captured by magic, and then killed when the magic of Nagar's Blight was destroyed once and for all.

There were good memories too, though. He thought of his most unlikely of friends, a young teenage boy named Erik who had become the Champion of Truth. There was also Master Lepkin, and his wife Lady Dimwater. Even with how many friends and kin were slain, Al knew that he and his companions had fought on the right side of the war. What they did, they did to protect their freedom and their homelands.

His only true regret was the fact that he had not stuck around Fort Drake long enough to meet with Hiasyntar'Kulai, the Father of the Ancients. Seeing the massive, golden-scaled dragon land within the Middle Kingdom once more was something akin to a miracle for Al. It had been centuries since the Ancients had been seen in the Middle Kingdom.

Al sighed and pushed off from the doorway and brought his thoughts back to the mountain and the issues at hand. He had a kingdom to rebuild, and he had to do so during a time of great grief and loss for his people.

Two days after returning, Al had stood at the pulpit, addressing the whole of the dwarven folk in Roegudok Hall and praising the fallen warriors. The tradition was sacred, heralding all the way back to the first king, Persais Magdinium. Al turned his thoughts away from the funeral rites. It was not something he could think about without feeling the sadness that accompanied such loss. He pushed on to the throne room, steering his mind to topics of commerce and trade.

When he spied a group of dwarves seated at the long, wooden table in the center of the hall, he sighed. He had hoped that he would have at least a few hours of privacy before the others would come to him. He hated council meetings almost as much as he disliked the funeral rites. Of course, he didn't mean to compare the two events, as one was so obviously worse than the other, but he couldn't help it. Every time he saw the council waiting for him, it was almost as if he was preparing to give his own funeral rites.

It wasn't purely the weight and responsibility of being king that pulled his soul down, though that was certainly part of it. It was the lack of belonging he felt since returning home.

Home. He wasn't even sure he felt that it *was* his home. He had left Roegudok Hall seventy years ago, before his father had passed away. Though he had been the first born, Al had always rejected his father's intent to crown him king one day. The smithing hammer that hung from Al's belt even now had been the cause of a great rift between him and his father. A prince who would prefer a forge to a throne. Al had been the cause of much of his father's worry, but Threnton had been there to step into Al's position. In all the years since Al had left Roegudok Hall, he had only returned for his father's funeral.

Al looked to the table, seeing the new wood that held it together now and sighed. There had been one other time when Al had returned. He had come to ask his brother for the golden scale given to the first king by the Ancients. Threnton had not only refused, but had Al thrown into a pit and left him to die. The rebuilt table was a reminder of the battle that had occurred in this very room. Al had escaped from the pit, challenged his brother for the throne, and he had won.

Had he known the extent to which Threnton would have depleted Roegudok Hall, he might never have left in the first place, or at least, that is what he would like to think would have happened.

"Sire, we have given you the first week to recuperate, as you asked, but now we must convene. There is much to discuss," Alferug said.

Al forced a smile and moved to sit on the bench next to Alferug, his advisor in the ways of the Ancients, and a trusted steward who had also served Al's father. Al's choice of seat was met by four disapproving frowns. Al sighed and looked to the high-backed chair at the head of the table.

Dvek, a silver-haired dwarf with bushy brows and narrow-set, dark eyes, was the first to break the uneasy silence. "Perhaps, you should take your seat at the head of the table," Dvek suggested with a slight deferential nod.

Al grunted and slapped the table as he rose back to his feet. He shuffled away from the bench and moved around to sit in the high-backed chair, scooting it clumsily across the stone floor toward the table. "Thank you for meeting me here," Al said. "I know that protocol dictates we should hold council in the council chamber, but inasmuch as we are effectively reorganizing the court, I thought it fitting that we meet in the throne room."

Al looked up and saw that the painting of his father was hung over the entrance, next to a portrait of Sylus. From both the table, and the throne, Al would be in clear view of the two kings he revered most. He had hoped that the paintings would give him inspiration. However, as he sat at the roughly repaired table in the middle of the throne room now, he couldn't help but feel the weight of their gaze in more of a scrutinizing light.

"Yes, I believe the symbolic nature of the choice is fitting," Alferug said quickly. "I also appreciate that the repaired table we find ourselves at is the same one destroyed by the fight with your brother, Threnton. It gives a sense of duty, but also shows the hope of renewal."

If Dvek or the other two dwarves present agreed with Alferug, they didn't show it. Dvek merely grunted, and the other two were silent.

Alferug cleared his throat and turned to matters at hand. "My king, we have much to discuss, but we propose to settle the matter of who will fill the vacancy left by Faengoril the Bull first."

Al nodded. He glanced at Dvek, who was quietly looking down at the table, and then looked to the other two dwarves. Captain Benbo was a stout dwarf, fiery red hair worked neatly into a single plait fastened with a silver band at the bottom. His arms were large, even by dwarf standards. However, unlike most dwarves, he was rumored to be unable to grow a full beard. At least, that was what others said when discussing the single braid coming down from Benbo's chin that was almost identical to his plaited hair. Facial hair notwithstanding, Benbo was very much a dwarf in all the right ways. Al had heard Faengoril praise Benbo on several occasions as well, which carried significant weight.

Opposite Benbo sat a stoic dwarf with jet black hair that frizzed out in all directions, somewhat resembling a lion's mane. A heavy purple scar ran from left eyebrow to the tip of this dwarf's nose, and was the cause for the dead, white eye. Captain Kijik had more than made up for his lost eye, though. He was as tough as they came, and, unlike Benbo, he sported a full, thick beard that nearly passed his belly button.

These were the only two dwarves recommended for the position of Minister of Defense.

Al cleared his throat and all eyes fell upon him. "Captain Kijik, I have heard great things about your service in the north with the Lievonian Order. From what I have been told, you slew a great number of Tarthuns and fought in a way that would make any dwarf proud to call you brother. Truly, a hero of such renown and ability is a rarity."

Dvek and Alferug rapped their knuckles on the table, signifying their agreement with Al's assessment. Captain Kijik nodded his appreciation, but remained silent.

Al then turned to Captain Benbo. "You were with Faengoril for his last battle." Al paused and took in a breath. Since he had heard of Faengoril's heroic sacrifice, he had a hard time putting the image of the warrior being buried alive out of his mind. "What Faengoril did brought about the destruction of many Tarthuns who would have otherwise attacked the Lievonian Order from behind. I have the utmost respect for Faengoril the Bull. He knew not only strategy, but also how to make the tough command decisions. Not only that, but he never shied away from danger. I personally fought beside him at Valtuu Temple when we found Tu'luh the Red there. He was a magnificent warrior, and he was an excellent advisor." Al shook his head and studied Benbo's eyes.

"I bring this to your attention, because Faengoril praised you, Captain Benbo. He told me how he felt about you. That was why he assigned you to his army when we set out from Roegudok Hall after the last council I held here. Truth be told, the decision is an easy one in that Faengoril already made a recommendation for his replacement."

"He did?" Alferug cut in. "I was not aware of that."

Al nodded. "It was something between me and him," Al explained. "I have his note here." Al pulled a folded letter from his pocket and set it on the table. Captains Kijik and Benbo both turned to stare at the folded letter. Al slid his fingers under the fold and opened it to reveal a short letter. "He asked me to make Benbo the next Minister of Defense in the event of his death," Al said.

Captain Kijik did his best to hide it, but the disappointment flashed across his face and his shoulders dropped just a hair for half a second before he rose to his feet and saluted Benbo.

"A wise choice," Kijik said. He then turned to Al. "If that is all, sire, I shall return to my station."

Al nodded. "That would be well," he said. Kijik turned to leave, but Al held up a hand. "Do you know the way?" Al asked.

Kijik frowned. "Of course, sire."

Al waved his hand and shook his head. "No, I mean, do you know your way to the Home Guard offices?"

"Sire?" Captain Kijik asked.

Al pointed to Benbo. "This is my new minister of defense. He will work on rebuilding our army. However, I have been thinking that the Home Guard needs a revitalization as well. I am appointing you as the General and Commanding Officer of the Home Guard. I want you to take the Home Guard, and make each one of its members as fierce and fearsome as you were on that battlefield in the north."

Kijik smiled and nodded. "Yes, my king."

"What of General Grubo?" Alferug asked.

Al nodded knowingly. "Grubo is retiring from the Home Guard," Al said.

"I didn't hear of this either," Alferug said with a frown.

"Both of his sons died at Fort Drake," Al explained. "He approached me after the funeral rites and asked to be released."

Alferug nodded understandingly.

"General Kijik, you may go. If you have any questions as to your duties, you will find Grubo's lieutenants eager to help acquaint you with your new responsibilities."

Kijik bowed low and left the throne room.

Al then turned to Benbo. "Your first order of business will be to report on the status of the cavedog breeding program. After you have ensured that we can replenish our stock of cavedogs, then you can begin recruiting new soldiers."

"If I may," Benbo started somewhat timidly.

Al arched a brow and nodded.

"I thought in addition to soldiers, I could expand our ranks of healers and surgeons."

Al furrowed his brow and reached up to stroke his gray and red beard. "Expecting more trouble that soon?" Al asked.

Benbo shook his head. "No, my king. But, I thought that perhaps if we could expand in those areas, as well as commandeering some engineers, we could venture out into the Middle Kingdom and offer assistance rebuilding from the war."

Al nodded and smiled. "That is an excellent idea. It will not only help take the burden off of King Mathias, but it will also show a continued solidarity with him. I see now why Faengoril chose you. Do what you need to, and coopt as many engineers as you need."

Dvek interjected, "With respect, I will need most of the engineers here."

"Our buildings have sustained no damage," Al said quickly.

Dvek nodded and continued. "True, however, since you have been gone, our mines have dried up entirely. We have not been able to produce enough ore for the smelting facilities for months."

"You have full command of the miners," Al said. "You can dig new tunnels as you need."

Dvek nodded again. "I appreciate that, sire, but there

is more to it than that. The shafts we are digging now go through a strange mixture of rock and soil. I have needed to assign engineers to the mines to help stabilize them. Normally the miners could do it themselves, except I split the miners into many smaller groups in an effort to cut the time needed locating a productive mine. Usually we run only two shafts at a time, but I have them drilling and cutting six shafts."

"Six?" Al repeated. "I have never heard of that many being mined at once."

Dvek sighed. "The mines all dried without warning," he said. "They also ran dry within days of each other. Seeing as we have little food reserves, I thought it best to maximize the search for gems and precious metals to enable us to purchase food from outside sources."

"What about the valley near the top of the mountain?" Al asked. "Isn't it producing yet? It has been well over a year since I left. I told you to focus on farming."

Alferug cut in. "Sire, it is not his fault. The fields of Two Peak Valley that sit near the top of Roegudok Hall were abandoned by your brother, and turned to pasture for sheep."

"We always raised sheep there too," Al said. "How did that become a problem?"

Alferug sighed and pointed back to Dvek.

Dvek nodded and tapped his right hand nervously. "Your brother commanded me to abandon our crops in the valley in favor of raising more sheep. By his reasoning, if we raised enough sheep, we wouldn't need to hunt outside the mountain. So, in obeying his orders, we multiplied the sheep until they overran the valley. They ate everything, and became so numerous that they polluted the lake there as well, and the fish have suffered. We have culled the sheep back to manageable numbers, but the valley has not yet produced crops. I do believe it will produce this year, but I am afraid it will not produce enough to supply for the winter."

"What about the cave-rice and the fish growing in the reservoirs?" Al asked. "There are three separate reservoirs managed in Twin Peak. Do you mean to tell me that none of them are producing cave-rice anymore? We have grown cave-rice there for as long as I can remember, and there was never a shortage. It may be that it's hard to boil and tougher to chew, but it is food."

Dvek sighed again. "The spring that provides culinary water throughout Roegudok Hall has also run dry. I have assigned dwarves to find a new source of water, but until one can be located, the reservoirs are now used for culinary purposes."

"It seems my brother has left me many problems," Al said.

"Actually, sire, there is more," Dvek said slowly. He worked his thumb on the table in front of him, digging into the wood with his nail as he took in a deep breath, obviously hesitant.

"Spit it out, Dvek," Al commanded. "I may as well hear all of the bad news."

"Have you heard of the Greenband?" Dvek asked.

Al frowned and glanced to Alferug. With a shrug he replied, "Sure, they are one of the most powerful merchant guilds in the Middle Kingdom. They are also fairly hostile to anyone who borrows money from them. What do they have to do with us?"

"As you said, sire, they are hostile to individuals, or groups, that have borrowed money from them."

Al thumped his hand down on the table and narrowed his eyes on Dvek. "You didn't?"

Dvek shook his head quickly. "No, no, I didn't, but your brother did. The mines were producing less and less over the last decade, to be honest. Your brother went into deep debt with the Greenband."

"And now they are calling their debt due?" Al guessed.

Dvek nodded. "So you see, we need to expand the mines below for more than just the ability to buy food. If we don't pay the Greenband back for every bit we owe them, they will levy sanctions against us. If they do that, there won't be a merchant in all of the Middle Kingdom that will be able to do business with us until the sanctions are taken off."

"What do we owe them?" Al asked.

Dvek shook his head and sighed. "I have tried to gather everything we have on hand. We have twenty tons of marble, another three tons of iron, as well of stores of zinc, and a few other minerals. In addition to this, I have separated a couple hundred head of sheep, several crates of wool, porcelain, and pewter crafts. Still, when I totaled everything we have, it doesn't cover a fifth of what your brother owes them."

Al leaned forward and let his forehead thunk on the table. "Stonebubbles and beetle spit," he swore. "We are that far in debt?"

Dvek nodded. "I didn't know the extent of it until I received the list from a Greenband collector just a couple of weeks before you returned."

Al shook his head. "Save the iron. We can perhaps fashion it into arms and armor. That will sell for more than raw ore. Keep the sheep back as well. We need the food. Send the rest of it as a good faith payment and let them know that I will do what I can to repay my brother's debt."

"Of course, sire."

The king shook his head. "Alright, do what you can. Take what engineers you truly need for the mines, Dvek, but do try to spare any engineers for Benbo that you can. Perhaps we can barter services for food, if it comes to that."

"As you command." Dvek said.

"Actually," Alferug said as he turned his body to Al. "Do you remember when we first came into Roegudok Hall together, we found that library?"

Al nodded. "I remember."

"Your father often referred to it as the wealth of kings. Perhaps we can find answers there."

"Why haven't you looked in there already?" Al asked, his tone taking on a sharp edge.

Alferug patted the air with his left hand. "I tried," he said. "If you recall, the entrance through that mirror sealed upon our exit. I have not been able to find the way to open it."

"My father never told you?" Al asked.

Alferug shook his head. "As I told you before, he never told me about it. I was unaware of its existence until we walked through it together."

"I do remember seeing a chest inside," Al said as he recalled his brief moments in the library. "If it has gems or coins, then it could help us buy what we need until we find productive mines."

"I have gathered a few clues for you, sire, and placed them in your study," Alferug said.

"Then I will continue mining while you work on that puzzle," Dvek offered.

Al nodded. "I wanted to ask one more thing," he said as the others started to leave. They stopped and turned back to him. "My grandfather reinstituted our traditions and relationship with the Ancients. My father kept that tradition. My brother did not. Alferug, now that you are again fulfilling your role as Advisor on Tradition and the Ancients, what has been the people's reaction to resuming our traditions and religion?"

Alferug frowned and shook his head. "I am afraid that it has not gone as well as hoped. Another reason for our lack of productivity, which pains us to talk about, is the fact that many of the previous officers and dwarves who held authority under your brother's rule have left the mountain."

"They left?" Al asked incredulously.

"You seem surprised," Dvek said. "Yet, you yourself left the mountain."

Al shook his head and leaned into the back of his chair. "It is true that I left, but before that, very few dwarves had ever left the mountain permanently who weren't exiled. In fact, I think that if we count from the time of the first king, we are only talking about a handful of dwarves. However, what you are saying is that a group of dwarves have left together, am I correct?"

"Not just the officers," Alferug said. "They took their families with them. We are missing, in total, in excess of three hundred dwarves."

"WHAT?!" Al shouted as he sat up rigid in his chair and slammed a fist on the table. "Three hundred dwarves have left?"

Dvek cut in. "Your brother ran a very different kingdom, sire. His officers were able to grow fat off the work of others. Their pockets deepened while the majority of our people worked longer shifts. When the people became unruly, your brother altered the supply of food, basically making the people dependent upon him and his officers. Before the mines ceased producing, he controlled all production also. It was a very different time."

"Why didn't anyone say anything?" Al asked.

"A few tried, in the beginning," Alferug said. "After the first couple of protestors disappeared, the others learned to be quiet."

"Why didn't you tell Master Lepkin?" Al asked. "I know he was here. He came here shortly after finding me in Buktah."

Alferug shook his head. "That was also the day I was exiled," he said.

"You have to understand," Dvek chimed in. "Your brother cut ties with the outside world. The humans were our enemy. He blamed them for our diminishing lot. He kept promising to find a great treasure digging in the mines." Dvek chuckled. "He actually called it 'the wealth of kings.' I suppose had he known he was chasing your father's library, he might have done things differently. As it was, after the first fifty years of fruitless searching, he ordered the mines closed. I suspect it was nothing more than childish bitterness that prompted him to do it, but as I told you when we met before you challenged Threnton, we weren't given a choice. He ordered the mines closed from that point on, and I knew better than to defy him. Given how he had you secreted away to a forgotten pit and left you to die, I suspect you know where most of his enemies ended up better than I do."

Alferug folded his arms. "Things were manageable up

until the last year or so of his reign. You might have thought the dwarves would rebel, but he had the younger generations convinced that he was providing everything they needed. Those of us who knew better weren't free to get word out of the mountain for help. Even if we could have, by the time Lepkin and Senator Bracken came, it was apparent that King Mathias was facing his own dangers. Besides, you know as well as we do that no human army is going to pass through the entrance tunnel unless they are invited, and Threnton was not the type to send out invitations."

Al closed his eyes and let his head fall back to thump against the back of the chair. "Well then, let's get to work. I'll go to work on solving the puzzle of the library. Hopefully that chest has what we need. In the meantime," Al turned and pointed to Dvek, "you keep working on finding a good mine shaft."

"What of appointing new counselors to the other vacancies?" Alferug asked.

Al grunted and shook his head. "That can wait." Al rose from the table and dismissed Dvek. Alferug walked with him through a side corridor that led from the throne room to the royal quarters.

Neither of them spoke until they stopped by the large mirror that hung in the hall a short distance from Al's room. Al reached out and slid his hands around the edge of the mirror, checking for any sort of lever or mechanism.

"I tried that," Alferug said with a shake of his head.

"Of course," Al replied as he gave the mirror one last tug. The frame was solidly in place. "You said you had clues for me?"

Alferug nodded. "I placed some books on your desk in the study. Nothing directly speaks of the wealth of kings, but there are some veiled references to it."

Al nodded and turned to walk on, but Alferug remained standing before the mirror. "My king," he called out.

Al stopped and twisted around to regard the old advisor. "Is something else troubling you?" Al asked.

Alferug nodded once and clasped his hands in front of his waist as he took in a deep breath and steeped forward. His eyes gazed down at the floor. "Your grandfather reinstated our religion and traditions," he said flatly. "Before his time, the Ancients were shunned by our people sometime around King Sylus Magdinium's reign."

"Yes, I am aware of this," Al replied evenly. "I may not have gone to King's College, but I know a bit about our history."

"My thought is that perhaps our trials are a punishment," Alferug said directly. "Your father continued the traditions and religion that your grandfather reestablished, but your brother did not. He allowed some semblance of our connections with the Ancients to exist up until he exiled me, but even then the level of worship waned throughout the mountain. Perhaps Roegudok Hall has dried up because of our lack of faith. When we turned our backs upon the Ancients, then maybe the mountain decided it was time to rebuke us."

Al nodded thoughtfully. "If that is the case, then Hiasyntar'Kulai, the Father of the Ancients, will restore us. I will send a message to him, and ask for his help."

"He lives?" Alferug asked. His eyes lit up as a child's might when presented with a large gift. He stepped forward and placed both hands on Al's shoulders. "Why didn't you tell me this immediately upon your return?"

Al shrugged. "I have a lot to work through," he said matter-of-factly. "I was not trained to be the king. I didn't mean to keep it from you, I just didn't think about it until now."

"The Father of the Ancients lives, and you didn't think it worth mentioning to me?"

Al snorted. "I spent a great deal of the last couple of years surrounded by dragons. By the time I saw Hiasyntar'Kulai, the war with Tu'luh the Red was over. I didn't get a chance to speak with him before he took off again from Fort Drake. I assume if he had intended to reestablish links with Roegudok Hall, he would have said so then."

Alferug frowned. "I see." The advisor turned and mumbled something under his breath as he shook his head and bit his lower lip. "So, then we are on our own?"

Al shrugged. "As I said, I will send a message to him. If he is able to help, I am certain he will. Until then, I need to find the way in." Al thumbed at the large mirror.

*****

Hiasyntar'Kulai, the great Father of the Ancients, soared through the sky, propelled through the cool clouds by his massive, supple wings. He scanned the ground far below, watching the trees and fields pass by beneath him until he came to Valtuu Temple. His heart saddened when he saw what was left of the once mighty temple that had towered over the valley.

The outer citadel wall was intact, but the ground below and around the temple had sunken in. The tower itself had collapsed into the tunnel. It was obvious that the priests had spent their time salvaging what they could since the terrible catastrophe that had destroyed the temple, but all they had managed to create was a single-story building thirty feet by sixty feet made from brick and stone that had once been part of Valtuu Temple.

The dragon landed lightly upon the ground and peered into the great hole. A couple of priests called out, announcing his presence as they ran toward the building.

Within moments, seventeen priests exited the building and approached him.

"Is this all that remains?" Hiasyntar'Kulai asked as he looked to the priests.

A shorter, pot-bellied priest came forward and spoke for the group. "Many of our order died in the war with Tu'luh and the orcs," he said. "Others abandoned our order when news of the prelate's death reached us." The short man turned and swept his arm out toward the others. "We stand loyally, ready and willing to rebuild the order, my king." The short priest and all the others knelt on both knees and bowed so that their heads touched the ground.

"What is your name?" Hiasyntar'Kulai asked.

"I am Magdon Sorent," the priest said. "I have been with the order for thirteen years."

The dragon nodded. "And who is the new prelate?"

Magdon frowned and shook his head. "The Keeper of Secrets has not appointed one to take the old prelate's place."

Hiasyntar'Kulai smiled. He had already known of Master Lepkin's intentions to seek seclusion with his wife, Lady Dimwater, and their newborn son. His question was meant more as a test of these priests, to see whether there had been any struggles for power, or if they had abided by tradition. He was pleased that the latter was the case. "I am here now, and I shall appoint a prelate."

Magdon nodded and bent his head low to the ground.

Hiasyntar'Kulai let out a low, throaty growl as he focused his mind. As an Ancient, he had two different types of vision he could use. There was the normal kind of vision that all intelligent beings had, albeit his sense of sight was far more acute than any humanoid's, and then there was another type that was called true sight. True sight allowed Hiasyntar'Kulai to see into the auras of living things around him. He could see the green and white energies of the grasses and trees and other plants around them, but more than that, he could decipher from the priests' auras exactly how they felt and what kind of character they had deep within their hearts. The priests each had a lesser degree of true sight given to them. Their natural eyes had faded into gray orbs, for they no longer saw as other humans did. The dragon's gift, however, was one he could use at will, changing between the two types of vision as he needed.

He scanned Magdon first. He saw blue energy swirling around yellow, with a small, marble-sized ball of green and white toward the center of the man. The dragon turned and studied the rest of the priests together. He saw several men with orange hues, red streaks, blue waves, and yellow cores. He saw darkness in none of them, but he was not entirely pleased with any of them either. None of them appeared to have the wisdom and brightness he was looking for.

Hiasyntar'Kulai scrutinized them for several moments, his gaze falling upon each man in turn and then moving on to the next. He repeated the exercise three times, but was still unsatisfied.

The door to the building opened again and a person stepped out with a bright aura that eclipsed all of the others. A core of white swirled within the person's center. As the light radiated out, there was a bright, warm layer of golden yellow. The outer shell was green, the color of birth, growth, and life. This person had the traits he was searching for. More than that, the traits were far brighter than any counterpart currently bowing before the dragon.

Hiasyntar'Kulai changed back to his normal vision. "I have chosen," he said.

The priests pushed up to a kneeling position, but did not rise to their feet. They watched expectantly as Hiasyntar'Kulai reached up and pointed a single talon. They glanced around each other, confused for a moment before they turned and looked behind them.

The brown-haired woman near the building stood and stared at the dragon with curious brown eyes.

"My king, she is not a member of our order," Magdon protested. "She is a volunteer from a nearby village. She helps us with cooking and cleaning."

The dragon shook his head. "Yet, each of you can see her potential."

The woman reached up and put a hand to her throat. "What do you want with me?" she asked the dragon. Her voice was cautious, but Hiasyntar'Kulai detected no fear. The woman was as confident as her aura was bright.

"You shall lead this order," the Father of the Ancients said. "If, you will accept the position as prelate of Valtuu Temple, I will have these priests train you in what you should do."

"Will I lose my vision, like they have?" the woman

asked.

Hiasyntar'Kulai shook his head. "No. The gift of true sight was given to these priests because we Ancients had to leave the Middle Kingdom centuries ago. The gift of true sight allowed the priests to help find the Champion of Truth. However, the Champion of Truth has already been discovered, and Nagar's Blight no longer clouds the Middle Kingdom. Now that I have returned, I no longer require assistance of that kind. I would have you keep your natural sight, but you would be the steward of this temple and everyone in the order."

The woman nodded thoughtfully.

"What is your name?"

"Sissil Varone," she said.

Hiasyntar'Kulai stepped forward and bent his head low to hers. "Sissil Varone, I will form a connection with you now, and endow you with the authority and power necessary to be the prelate. Afterward, you shall go in and rest for a day. Tomorrow, these priests will begin to train you in your new duties. All of them are faithful, and will help you grow into your new position. With your stewardship, you shall make this temple great once more."

The dragon locked eyes with the woman and formed a telepathic connection between them. Sissil's shapely body went rigid and still as the dragon used the mental conduit to grant her the powers needed by a prelate of Valtuu Temple.

When he finished, a pair of priests were quick to help Sissil back into the building. They emerged a few moments later and bowed their heads.

"The prelate is sleeping," one of them said.

"Good, she will need her rest," Hiasyntar'Kulai commented. He then turned to Magdon. "Is there any addorite left within the temple?"

Magdon scrunched up his brow and shook his head. "No, my king. There has been no addorite here for more than a century."

Hiasyntar'Kulai nodded. He knew there had been a store of addorite in Valtuu Temple before. He now understood that Tu'luh had likely taken in sometime after the Battle of Hamath Valley. That was the only possible explanation. The dragon sighed and looked back to the ruined temple. In his mind's eye, he could see the temple rebuilt, but that did little to lessen his current sadness at seeing the destruction wrought upon the once mighty temple by his son, Tu'luh the Red.

"What shall we do, master?" Magdon asked.

The dragon turned and said, "Help the new prelate learn of her role. She has great power inside of her. Serve her as you would serve me. I shall return from time to time, but she will have authority to rule over the temple and direct its reconstruction as well as have oversight for recruiting new priests and acolytes."

"Where will you go?" Magdon asked.

Hiasyntar'Kulai needed to find addorite. However, that was not a concern he was ready to fully disclose to the priests yet. Instead, he bid them farewell without answering the question, but promised to return soon. He then beat his massive wings and sailed through the sky.

CHAPTER 3

Year 3,711 Age of Demigods, Summer.
2nd year of the reign of Aldehenkaru'hktanah Sit'marihu, 13th King of Roegudok Hall.

Al sat at his large, ebony desk. He leaned back in his chair and wiped a hand down his face and over his beard. He had read through each of the highlighted passages Alferug had given him. There were no obvious answers in front of him. He sighed and slumped down in his chair, frustrated and ready for a break. Then, his eyes saw a green leather book leaning against the wall on the farthest side of his desk. Without even reading the Peish rune emblazoned on the front, he knew the book.

"Well, Sylus, perhaps you will have some wisdom for me?" Al said as he leaned forward, stretching out for the book. He took it in his hands and then unceremoniously flopped back into the chair. He opened the cover and skipped the first chapter. As was customary with any historical text left behind by a king of Roegudok Hall, the first chapter was an account of the king's heritage and ancestry. One might have thought that since Sylus was only the fifth king, the first chapter might have been small, but this was not so. Dwarven customs demanded an accounting of each king's major accomplishments as well as their name and genealogical information.

The first chapter on Sylus' book was well over one hundred pages.

Al shuddered to think how thick his first chapter might have to be if a book was ever written about his reign. He was the thirteenth king of Roegudok Hall. He pushed the idea out of his head and moved into the second chapter. If there was any advice to be found on how to make the mountain prosperous again in the face of such tragedy, Sylus would have the answer in his book. It was well known that Sylus had ushered in an age of unprecedented wealth for the dwarves of Roegudok Hall. The kings who came after him managed to extend that success, but none ever achieved the same status Sylus had created. This was not to say that Roegudok Hall had ever been poor after Sylus' reign, however. Up until Threnton's time as king, the dwarves had always enjoyed abundance and wealth.

King Al spent the next several hours scanning the book for insight into Sylus' process. While the endeavor gave his mind a much needed break from straining to unlock the Wealth of Kings, it shed little light on the subject of prosperity. Sylus had expanded the mines much in the same way Al and Dvek had agreed to expand the mines now. However, there was no secret formula for success. It seemed that it was luck as much as expert mining that resulted in the windfall of gems and ore Sylus extracted during his reign.

It soon became painfully obvious to Al that Sylus had hidden the secret of Roegudok Hall's wealth, instructing the historian to leave it out of the book. It puzzled Al at first, but then he landed on the idea that perhaps it was because each chapter detailing Sylus' battles with the orcs of his time was so vivid and painstaking in its accuracy, that perhaps Sylus wanted to be remembered as a warrior-king, and not as a king who labored in the pits below the mountain. Chapter seven opened with the battle against an orc general named Borgnat. The account was so descriptive that Al was able to picture each moment of the battle in his mind as his eyes studied the runes.

He read through until the moment Borgnat was slain, and then Al flipped to chapter eight. It too, was an account of a great battle. So were chapters nine through thirteen. Al grumbled and tossed the book to the desk. Learning of battles long forgotten was not going to help him help his people. Al was already an accomplished warrior-king in his own right, having survived the battle at Fort Drake, and before that, having fought against the orcs in the south.

Al groaned and lifted his head to the ceiling. In that moment, he almost wished that he was back upon the battlefield once more. It wasn't that he liked violence, or the grief that came with war, but there was something about it that made him feel more alive. It gave him a sense of purpose. An all-encompassing reason to exist.

He looked to the green book lying haphazardly upon the desk. "Is that why you focused on your battles?" he asked Sylus. "Maybe you didn't care to focus on mining and farming because it wasn't what gave you your value, is that it?" Al reached out and grabbed the book again, deciding that must be the reason the warrior-king had left such an exhaustive account of his wars while barely glossing over the general points of commerce in his time. "There is something about the crown that dulls the spirits in creatures who yearn for action," Al said with an approving nod to the book.

He flipped through the last two chapters, scanning the runes just enough to know that chapter fourteen was a treatise about weapon types and the best metals to use in their creation, and that chapter fifteen was a short account describing Sylus' death. He grabbed the back cover to close the book, but as his hand brought the cover up, something caught the light just right, shining ever so slightly.

Intrigued, Al bent his nose to the book and narrowed his eyes. It was an ink smear. The writing was old and much of it was faded. He turned and looked at the runes on the last page. They were written with black ink, and the writing there was not dimmed by time. Furthermore, the faded runes on the inside back cover appeared to be made by a different hand. Al held the book up to the light at an angle to better see, and discovered that there was a message there. There wasn't much that was visible, but Al did see a distinct line of runes that made his mouth drop.

Al set the book down and called out to a servant to

find Alferug. "Tell him to bring something to restore ink!" Al added as the servant scurried off down the hallway.

Alferug was quick to answer. An excited smile on his face told Al that he was expecting a breakthrough. The wooden box in his arms, filled with various bottles and brushes, showed that Alferug was prepared for any kind of restoration that might be needed.

"Have you found something?" Alferug asked as he set the box down on the desk.

Al pointed to the back cover. "Did you notice this before?"

Alferug bent down close to the book. "I don't see anything," he said.

Al gently pushed Alferug back and raised the book to the light. "Look again."

Alferug's mouth fell open and he nearly jumped with excitement as he turned to the box. "Tell me, is it red or black ink?"

Al paused as he brought the book closer. "It appears to be red."

"Very well, set the book down. Move all the others. We don't want to have any accidents."

Al did as he was told and stepped aside.

Alferug brought out a thick cloth and set it on the last page of the book. "Don't want to damage any of the intact pages," he explained as he stretched the edges around the rest of the book. "Give me a moment." Alferug went to the box and pulled a large stone bowl from the bottom. Next he pulled a cube of soap and three bottles. Each of the liquids in the bottles were clear, but the bottles were different shapes and were each stoppered with a large cork. "Water, ammonia, and muriate of tin," Alferug announced as he indicated the bottles. Without waiting for a response, Alferug went to work shaving off an amount of soap from the cube and then grinding it into a powder inside the stone bowl. Next, he poured precise amounts of each liquid into the bowl and mixed thoroughly.

Al covered his nose and took a step back. He never

did care for the smell of ammonia. Mixed with the other items, it was even worse.

Alferug then took a brush and held his breath as he dipped it into the mixture and then lightly applied it to the back cover. "Watch carefully. We may need to transcribe the writing to a new paper. This mixture is highly acidic, and may eat through the writing after a while."

Al grunted as he fished for a piece of parchment from the drawer in the desk. He then set it next to the green book and marveled as the runes became clear, changing from an almost imperceptible, faded red to a greenish color that contrasted well against the aged book.

"The Wealth of Kings shall be found again when the bloodgrass springs up from the mountain," Al read aloud as he quickly scrawled an identical set of runes on his paper. He then turned back to the cover.

"Find the book written by mine own hand, and you will understand the Wealth of Kings," Alferug said as he read the last line of runes aloud.

Al transcribed the entire message and then shook his head as he looked to the signature at the bottom of the secret message. "This was written by Sylus," Al said.

"But why would he hide the Wealth of Kings?" Alferug mused. He then took his brush and applied a thin layer of the mixture to other areas of the cover. In doing so, he revealed a smaller line of writing near the bottom. "Beware that you do not squander…," Alferug said.

"Squander what?" Al asked.

Alferug shrugged. "The rest of the writing is too deteriorated to bring back. I can't recreate the entire message."

Al set his pen down and pointed to the book. "The Wealth of Kings," he said. "Maybe he was afraid the mines would run dry one day, and he was cautioning us not to squander our wealth."

Alferug sighed and set his brush down across the rim of the stone bowl. "What we need to do is find this other book that Sylus wrote."

"Did my father ever tell you of it?" Al asked. Alferug shook his head. "He never told you anything about it?" Al asked again incredulously.

Alferug again shook his head. "As I said before, he never mentioned it to me. I never knew of the library's existence until we found it together."

"But surely you knew of the back door in the mountain, yes?"

Alferug frowned. "Your father told you about it, but he did not tell me."

Al snapped his fingers. "We don't need to find the book," he said excitedly. "We just need to go back through the rear door. We have been wasting our time when all we had to do was retrace our steps." Al smiled widely and moved to retrieve his cloak. "Come, you should be there with me. We will open the mirror from the inside, as we did before!"

The two made haste through the mountain and within the hour were outside, climbing the slope as the afternoon sun slowly made its descent in the west.

Al pushed on, ascending the mountain side as the loose dirt gave way to patches of gray shale and round pebbles. His thick fingers easily found the niches in the stone wall as he started up a sheer cliff, scurrying up the face like a squirrel climbs a tree. Alferug was only a few feet behind him until they reached the top and stood on the first shelf.

They made their way along the same path they had traveled together once before. At times the flat shelf gave way to steep drops where rockslides had occurred over the years. A man might have easily fallen down any one of the dangerous slopes, but Al was a dwarf. His feet were in tune with the mountain and the rock. He often joked that when it came to climbing mountains, dwarves were more akin to goats than to their taller human cousins.

They walked for the space of an hour before Al stopped to scan the ascending slopes, looking for the best route up the mountain. It didn't take him long. He pointed a sausage-like finger at a jagged crevice and went straight to it.

His hands found purchase quickly and his feet propelled him up. The rock felt cool and strong to the touch. A part of him began to come alive as the mountain seemed to welcome his ascent. A great smile stretched across his face and he increased his pace, scrambling up the mountain as though he were a strong summer wind, bending up to crest over the peak.

Once they arrived at the second shelf, Al led them on a winding trail to a place near the back of the mountain. They were about two thirds of the way up the great peak, exactly in the same area where they had found the door before.

"We'll rest over there," Al said, pointing to a flat area recessed in a small nook where the mountain curved into itself, hidden by a patch of scrub oak. The two dwarves knew they would need to wait for nightfall, for the door was only revealed by a blue moonstone set in the mountain.

"If you recall, the last time we were here, we were discussing how you brother had expelled the Keeper of Secrets from Roegudok Hall," Alferug pointed out.

"I remember," Al grunted.

"Fortunately for our people, Master Lepkin's assertion that Threnton would not be king for long held true. Whatever hardship we face now in the mountain, I am glad you are here to guide us through it."

Al took the compliment and offered a half smile. "And I am glad to have you by my side to guide *me*." Al smiled and looked down below the mountain, taking in the sweeping view of valley floor and green forest. "It's interesting how history unfolded," Al said as he changed the subject. "To think that during Sylus' time, Tu'luh the Red was the Patron Ancient of Roegudok Hall. He fought beside Sylus in many battles. The dragon even helped advise Sylus."

"And then he turned on us," Alferug said with a wistful nod. "There is not much written about the first rift between Ancients and dwarves," he added.

"My father told me that it happened either during Sylus' reign, or shortly thereafter, for his was the last king's book to mention them until my grandfather restored our traditions."

Alferug nodded. "Even then, the Ancients did not restore their relations with our kind until your grandfather stood with them in the Battle of Hamath Valley."

"I wonder what caused the first rift." Al said.

The two of them then drifted silently into their own thoughts as they waited for nightfall.

As the sun set and the moon began to rise, Al and Alferug walked to the edge of the slope and looked out. To the east they could just make out the great, jagged snowcapped mountains that separated the Middle Kingdom from the lands of the Tarthun barbarians and raiders. As they surveyed the land and moved their gazes west, everything appeared so still and peaceful. With the sky ablaze with pink and orange hues, Al couldn't help but comment on the beauty they saw.

"Give me my tunnels," Alferug replied. "I wouldn't trade my home for a vast, empty sky. It feels so cold."

Al laughed. "Spend a few nights under the stars, and you will change your mind," Al said.

"I spent time sleeping under the stars, when your brother exiled me," Alferug said curtly. "No, I prefer to have a roof of stone over my head. I want the forges burning hot beneath my feet and I want walls of stone so thick that dragons themselves couldn't claw through."

Al smirked and slapped Alferug on the shoulder. "Come, the moon should be high enough soon."

The day ultimately yielded to the dark, thick blanket of night. Stars began to appear as the last colors of the day faded away. Twinkling blue and green dots littered the sky, adding their lights to that of the bright crescent moon. Al scanned the rocks in the same spot where he had found the moonstone before. It barely took more than a minute to locate the glowing stone. "There," Al said.

"As impressive as it was the first time," Alferug commented.

Al rushed over and placed his hand below the moonstone. "I Aldehenkaru'hktanah Sit'marihu, command the door of kings to open and allow entrance to Roegudok Hall."

The mountain groaned. Shale and pebbles bounced and vibrated away from the landing they stood upon as the rock itself came alive, sliding and scraping as it writhed before them. A massive, arched slab of slate and granite removed itself to the side and revealed a shallow cavern that covered a glowing blue doorway, covered in runes and designs of stars and moons.

Al walked inside without hesitating. He reached up to the side of the cavern, grasping a brass tube. As Al twisted the brass tube, a stream of light emerged from the end and shone upon a small spot on the door. Satisfied that he had adjusted the light correctly, Al walked forward to the door.

"It appears the jewel is missing," Alferug pointed out.

"No, we left it here after we entered," Al said. He moved toward the door and slid his fingers along the edge of the hole where he had placed the pink gemstone. "It should be right…"

"What is it?" Alferug asked when Al didn't finish his sentence.

Al didn't answer. He turned and started frantically searching the floor of the cave. "It was here. It was here!"

Alferug dropped to his knees and the two of them searched everywhere for the gemstone they had used to open the secondary barrier the first time they found the secret library.

"It's gone," Al said. "The key is gone."

"How could that be?" Alferug asked.

Al shook his head. Then his face soured as it dawned on him. "Threnton must have taken it after catching us."

*****

On top of a snow-capped granite peak which rose high above the clouds in the sky, Hiasyntar'Kulai was stretching his wings as he surveyed the land before him. The sun was just rising in the east, throwing its pink and orange hues through the sky and starting to warm the world as it shook off night's blanket. He had flown thousands of miles to the west of the Middle Kingdom, traveling over oceans and nations to arrive last night upon the eastern most edges of Svatal Island, which was inhabited by Svetli'Tai elves.

It was also the last known resting place of Gorensikdar, a mighty Ancient who had also been the cause of much mischief and grief in Terramyr. This particular dragon had been slain in battle at the hands of elves, and a human king who rode upon a great white dragon.

Hiasyntar'Kulai threw his mighty head back and let out a roar that caused the mountain upon which he stood to tremble, and scattered the clouds from before him. His terrible voice echoed around him several times after he finished. His great, golden eyes scanned the lush, verdant valley below, searching for any sign of life. What he was about to do could not be witnessed by any mortal.

Seeing that he was alone, he stretched out his right foreleg and gathered a ball of silver energy between his talons as he uttered an ancient incantation that only the gods and a handful of Ancients knew. Then, he released the sizzling, crackling ball into the air below him and it tore through the fabric of the mortal plane, opening a passageway to the plane of the dead.

The golden dragon continued to repeat the incantation until the rift was large enough for him to pass through. He floated down into a world that looked very much like Terramyr in shape and size, but there were no trees or plants to speak of. The rocks on this plane were dark. The sky around him was also black, showing silver streaks through the air at times that offered light to the land below.

He flew over the plane of the dead, ignoring the silvery spirits that looked up at him and whispered in hushed tones. He was not hear to speak with the elven dead. He was here to find Gorensikdar, his treacherous son.

He found the spirit of the mighty black dragon after searching for nearly the space of an hour, and covering hundreds of miles in this place of spirits. The great beast was sitting upon a floating island of stone that hovered over an expanse of nothingness.

"Ah, father has finally come to visit his son," Gorensikdar said in a mighty voice that rumbled through the void.

"I have come to ask you where the addorite has gone," Hiasyntar'Kulai said.

Gorensikdar laughed, lifting his head and swishing his ethereal tail. "And what makes you think I would tell you anything about that?" the black dragon asked. "You may have been a ruler in Terramyr, but I am king here!" Gorensikdar stood and expanded his wings as if to display his strength in the plane of the dead. "Look around you and see the chaos I have brought to the plane of the dead! I have created the black void which you see here."

Hiasyntar'Kulai lashed out and grabbed the top of Gorensikdar's head, then he slammed it down onto the floating stone island as he landed in front of the squirming spirit. The golden dragon roared terribly, sending beams of light out from his mouth and causing Gorensikdar to quake. "I am still the Father of the Ancients," Hiasyntar'Kulai said. "You may think you are safe from me in spirit form, but I have the power to cause you great pain even now!"

The ghost dragon squirmed, whimpering and trying to pull away.

Hiasyntar'Kulai squeezed and then pulled Gorensikdar up so he could look his son in the eyes. "Where is the addorite I had stored at Valtuu Temple? You know that I need it!"

Gorensikdar relented. The golden dragon released his grasp on the ghost and the black dragon shook his head as if he could still feel the golden dragon's talons upon him. "Alright, father, I will tell you." The black dragon sat back on its haunches and the haughty, proud arrogance was gone from its countenance. "Before I came to this land, Tu'luh sought me out."

"What did you tell him?" Hiasyntar'Kulai pressed.

"My brother was displeased with how slow events were transpiring. So, I gave him a push. I explained to him how to use the addorite. I convinced him that he might be able to create a secret supply of his own."

"You told him *everything* about the addorite?"

The black dragon grinned. "I am the Patron of Chaos, father. Of course I told him everything, otherwise it would not have been as much fun for me. If your store of addorite is missing, then go and see Tu'luh, for he is the one who has it. Does he also have The Infinium?"

Hiasyntar'Kulai reached out and back-slapped Gorensikdar. A terrible thunder resounded through the area as the Father of the Ancient used his powers to strike the ghost. Gorensikdar's head jerked to the side and his body shuddered as the pain rippled through him.

"Tu'luh is dead," Hiasyntar'Kulai replied. "He is dragged down to Hammenfein, and serves there as a slave."

Gorensikdar seemed to take pleasure in hearing that. He grinned wickedly and turned narrowed eyes on Hiasyntar'Kulai. "How many sons is that now that have been lost?"

Hiasyntar'Kulai raised his foreleg to strike again, but then stopped short as Gorensikdar began to laugh.

"What, will you remain here forever and slap me for every sin I have committed?"

The golden dragon knew there was no more point to speaking with the black dragon. He had gotten the information he needed. He started to leave, but issued a warning to his wayward son. "Remember, Gorensikdar, I can still reach you. Be careful that your love for chaos does not anger me beyond my limits. I have the power to rend your soul apart."

Gorensikdar stopped laughing, but the evil smirk remained. "Why Father, do I detect a lie coming from the blessed Father of the Ancients? You and I both know that only the Aurorean had the power to destroy a dragon's spirit. You should be cautious not to provoke me, for I too can still reach the mortal realm."

"What do you mean?" Hiasyntar'Kulai asked.

Gorensikdar laughed. "When you go to Hammenfein to speak with Tu'luh, ask around about Basei, the demi-god of war. I think you will uncover that interesting events have, in fact, transpired by my hand. I too, have power to reach out and wound."

Hiasyntar'Kulai had heard enough. He flew up and started to leave the plane of the dead. However, he had one more punishment for Gorensikdar before he left. A warmth built up in his chest. It churned and rolled within him as it grew. It felt very similar to the sensations of gathering flame to spew out of his mouth, but this was something far different. The golden dragon's chest began to glow and the elven spirits below began to point and whisper.

Then, as the intensity built up beyond what Hiasyntar'Kulai could contain, he opened his mouth and issued forth a searing white beam of light that scattered the darkness. A great, high-pitched melody rang out through the plane of the dead as the beam shot out to the farthest horizon. A great flash, like an exploding star, erupted when the beam of light hit the edge of Gorensikdar's darkness. That explosion rippled through the vast expanse and chased away the chaos that the black dragon had brought to the area.

The sky was now as bright as if the sun were hanging in the heavens above. Grass shot forth instantaneously from the barren rock below, as did flowers of every color. Trees began to sprout and reach upward. In the void beyond the mass of rock, water appeared.

Hiasyntar'Kulai could hear the terrible, angered roar of his son as the darkness was chased away and replaced with a brilliant paradise. The elven spirits below cheered and praised Hiasyntar'Kulai for restoring the beauty that had filled the plane of the dead before Gorensikdar had come.

"That is better," the golden dragon said to himself as he disappeared from the plane of the dead, leaving his crazed son to rant and wail as he lost his powers over that portion of the plane of the dead.

CHAPTER 4

Year 3,711 Age of Demigods, Summer.
2nd year of the reign of Aldehenkaru'hktanah Sit'marihu, 13th King of Roegudok Hall.

Deep in the eastern hills, set within the thick forests nestled at the base of the mountain range that separated the Middle Kingdom from the Eastern Wilds, Threnton sat inside an old, dilapidated cottage. A clay bowl of long-cold soup sat before him untouched. A pewter goblet of wine was half full. The deposed former king of Roegudok Hall was alone, sitting in the dark as bits of starlight filtered into the room through sizeable holes in the roof. His gray hair, a byproduct of his battle with his brother Al, waved in the wind as the door swung open.

A tall man in a light cloak stood in the doorway, peering into the dark room. Threnton noted the rapier dangling from the man's left hip. The man stepped into the room and pulled back the hood of his cloak, yet his face remained covered by the shadows of night until he moved in close enough for Threnton's eyes to pierce the darkness.

"I didn't expect you to be alone," the man said as he moved to sit at the table opposite Threnton.

"Robert Delmecian," Threnton said in a low voice. "I have heard that you know how to contact individuals who are willing to hire on for, shall we say, delicate matters. Is this so?"

Lord Delmecian removed his black gloves and set them to his left, as if preparing to eat a meal with the deposed dwarf king. "It is not common, to see a dwarf working in the shadows and lurking about the surface at night," he said in his annoyingly nasal voice. "I, of course, know what you want from me, but my question is what do you have to offer in return?"

Threnton smiled. He was not overly fond of the tall folk. He thought humans only marginally better than orcs. Still, he appreciated Delmecian's brevity. It was a welcome departure from a human's, especially a noble's, tendency to ramble on, prattling the night away without ever accomplishing any significant business. Now, Threnton would see if he had something to entice the good noble with.

"I can offer revenge," Threnton said flatly.

Delmecian laughed aloud and shook his head. "Revenge?" he echoed. "I have no quarrel with the dwarves of Roegudok Hall. For all of my life, they have been silent inside the mountain. Why should I care if you murder your brother?"

Threnton tapped his solid knuckles on the table and reestablished silence. "No, you have no quarrel with the dwarves, but you do have a quarrel with King Mathias," Threnton said evenly.

"You offer to kill Mathias if I help you murder the king of Roegudok Hall?"

"He is NOT the king!" Threnton hollered as he slammed his fist down on the table.

From the shadows emerged seven other dwarves, each armed with swords and ready to pounce on Delmecian. The nobleman took in a breath, but mostly ignored the dwarves. With a calm voice he asked, "I was under the impression that I was to come alone, was that not the arrangement?"

Threnton sniggered. "My scouts told me a long time ago that you brought four men with you," he said evenly.

Delmecian beamed from ear to ear and slid his hands onto the table. "Ah, what has happened to the trust in the world, huh?" Delmecian then cocked his head to the right and held up a finger. "I am afraid, however, that your scouts are mistaken. I brought five men with me."

Threnton narrowed his eyes on Delmecian. The noble grinned even wider and snapped his fingers. From the shadows to the left, emerged a man clad in black. The nearby dwarves startled and turned to face the new threat, but Threnton knew on sight who the intruder was.

"Stand down," Threnton said decisively. "This is our other guest."

"A guest?" Delmecian repeated. "I am not sure I would ever count a Blacktongue as a guest, but then again, I never thought I would be doing business in a ruined cottage with a dwarf."

"Name your price," Threnton told the Blacktongue.

The warrior moved to the table and slowly slid a wickedly curved scimitar out, the blade glinting in the moonlight as he set it upon the table. "To kill a dwarf king is a great undertaking," the assassin said in a low voice. "I will require a share of Roegudok Hall's treasury."

"How much?" Threnton asked as he arched a brow. Spies on the inside had already informed Threnton that the mines had dried up months ago, but that was not a fact he was about to share with a mercenary.

"As you are certainly aware, most of our kind have been slain. Normally, I would not even speak with a dwarf, but desperate times have presented me with few options."

"You seek to rebuild your order then?" Threnton asked. The Blacktongue nodded. "How much of the treasury will you need?"

"Training Blacktongues is a very expensive ordeal. I will need fifty thousand bars of gold and five pounds each of refined diamonds, rubies, and sapphires."

Threnton whistled through his teeth. Even if the treasury was full, that would be a staggering price to pay. "Why not ask for gold coins?" he fired back.

"Coins are no good," the assassin replied. "The coins used in the Middle Kingdom will be of no use to me where I will go."

"Where is that?" Threnton pressed.

The Blacktongue shook his massive, shaved head. "I will tell you where to deposit the treasure, but that is all. After this job is completed, then we will go our separate ways."

This job. Threnton smiled and nodded. "I have spies on the inside. My brother has squandered much of my people's wealth, but I believe there is more than enough left in our coffers to fulfill your demands," he lied. Then he turned back to Delmecian.

"Your money does me little good," the nobleman said. "I have more than I could spend in this life as it is."

"My original offer still stands," Threnton said as he shifted in his seat. "I know Mathias is out of reach, but I also know that your southern estate was sacked by the orcs as they moved into the Middle Kingdom."

Delmecian's self-assured smile disappeared and the man stiffened as he took in a breath and set his jaw. Threnton knew he had hit the right nerve.

"Help me retake the throne, which is rightfully mine, and I will assign my cavedog riders to you. I know that you were summoned to Drakei Glazei before your estate was attacked. I also know that the captain left in charge of the guard assigned to your estate fled when he saw the orcs."

"This is common knowledge," Delmecian snarled hastily.

Threnton held up a finger. "Ah, but I know where the captain is now. I have his location, as well as the location of each of the men that fled with him, written down."

"How could you come by this?" Delmecian asked incredulously. "I, myself have spent much treasure to find this information. Even today I have only found three of the fifty names on my list."

"There are officers in Roegudok Hall who are still loyal to me," Threnton said. "Many of them fought in the war that my brother forced them into. They mingled with Mathias' army. You know how soldiers talk."

"You know where all forty-seven of them are?" Delmecian pressed.

Threnton nodded eagerly. "I knew where all fifty of them were, until you reduced that number to forty-seven by the point of that fancy sword hanging from your belt."

Lord Delmecian wrinkled his nose and looked to the Blacktongue. Then, he looked back to Threnton. "When this is done, what will you do?"

Threnton smiled widely. "After my brother's body is pinned to the wall above my mantle, I will claim my throne and make Roegudok Hall strong again. My brother has failed as a commander, and allowed too many precious dwarves to die."

"But you offered me the use of your cavedogs," Delmecian reminded him.

Threnton nodded. "Forty-seven cowards who ran from orcs instead of defending their home will not stand a chance against my warriors. I will give you the information, and command of my cavedog riders. Then, when they have helped you exact justice, they will return to Roegudok Hall and we will close the gates, never to emerge again except under the auspices of war."

"You would sever the dwarves' alliance with Mathias?" Delmecian pressed.

Threnton grinned evilly. "That should make it easier if there were any aspiring, ambitious nobles who thought they might like to remove Mathias from power."

Delmecian's arrogant smile returned to his face. "Now, you are speaking my language."

"Excellent," Threnton said. "Then we are agreed?"

The Blacktongue nodded.

"We have a bargain," Delmecian said as he stuck his hand out. Threnton shook the nobleman's hand and then pointed to a door on the far side of the room. A dwarf opened it, revealing a steep stairway leading down.

"Then come into my office. We can plan our assault," Threnton said as he left the table and made his way for the dimly lit stairs.

The nobleman and the assassin followed.

Threnton led them down into a musty room, where

they were greeted by a dozen well-armed dwarves. They saluted Threnton as he walked beyond them and pressed a section of brick wall. It swiveled open to reveal a well-lit tunnel. The dwarf walked the two men through the tunnel and into a chamber shooting off from the left of the tunnel some fifty yards in. In the center of the chamber stood a table with a model of Roegudok Hall sitting upon it. There were a few cots and small desks in the room as well.

Threnton stepped in and waved his arms out to the side as he turned to show off the chamber to his guests. "This has been my home since my exile began," he said. "It is simple, I know, but it is hidden well and has kept us safe despite all the action happening up there," he said with a jab of his finger to the ceiling.

The Blacktongue was the first to stop and take notice of the two severed heads set in large jars of amber-colored liquid. "Servant who failed you?" the assassin asked.

Threnton laughed. "Something like that," he said. He turned back and looked upon his cousins' heads as he laughed once and shook his head. "They were my cousins, once."

"What did they do?" Delmecian asked as he moved to stand near the table with the model of Roegudok Hall.

"They betrayed me," Threnton said evenly. "After my brother exiled me from my own throne, those two false dwarves took it upon themselves to deposit my unconscious body in the forest deep within the mountains to the east. They left me with only the clothes upon my body."

"What did you do?" the Blacktongue asked.

Threnton shrugged and turned back to Delmecian and the assassin. "I hunted them down and beat them to death with my bare hands," he said. That last bit wasn't entirely true. Threnton had woken before his cousins left. They had given him a knife and provisions as well, but that wasn't the kind of story he needed right now. He needed Delmecian and the Blacktongue to believe he was a very capable warrior in his own right. Anything less might force them to rethink their involvement in this plan, and he knew he needed them.

"Seems a bit cold," Delmecian said as he turned and pointed to the model. "This is the mountain, yes?"

Threnton moved to it and pointed to the eastern slope. "Near the top, high above the cliffs that make up the bottom third of the entire mountain, there is a balcony. It opens directly into the king's chamber. That is where you will attack," Threnton said as he pointed to the Blacktongue. "Are there any others who can go with you? My brother is a tricky fighter."

The Blacktongue nodded. "I have one brother who will go with me."

"One?" Delmecian echoed sharply.

"One Blacktongue is worth five dwarves. My brother is worth two Blacktongue assassins, and I am better still."

"Good, good," Threnton said as he nodded and moved around to the northern slope. He grabbed Delmecian's arm and pulled his attention to a small ledge high up on the mountain. "There is a secret door here," he said. "My father never told me about it, but this is how my brother gained entrance into the mountain. You and I will use this entrance to make the secondary assault."

"Won't it be guarded?" Delmecian asked.

Threnton shook his head. "No," he said flatly. "When I caught my brother, I knew there must have been a secret entrance. He and one of the other traitors had just appeared in the hallway a short way off from my bedroom. The guards said that my brother and the traitor had emerged from a mirror in the wall. After a day of searching for clues, I figured out how to open the mirror to reveal a secret passageway. I followed it through until I found the entrance they used to steal their way inside the mountain. I also found instructions tucked away in an old ledger for how to use the doors."

Threnton produced a small, pink gem. "This is our key. The first door will open to any prince or king of the mountain, and the gem will get us in the rest of the way."

"But, again, won't your brother have guards there if that is how he snuck in?"

Threnton shook his head. "My spies tell me that he has not used the passageway, or sent anyone out to guard the entrance. From all accounts, it seems that he has not revealed the secret door to anyone."

"So you and I will assault from the secret back door and the Blacktongues will attack from the balcony?"

Threnton nodded. "I will take the crown without raising the alarm, and then you will earn your pay, Lord Delmecian."

Lord Delmecian nodded. "Once I see your brother, I can use my magic to make you appear in his image."

Threnton grinned wickedly, basking in the beautiful simplicity of his plan.

"Can you do such magic?" the Blacktongue asked.

Delmecian winked and then a mist rose around him. Several seconds later, the mist fell away and the Blacktongue jumped back and instinctively reached for his sword. Where Delmecian had been, a mirror image of this Blacktongue assassin now stood. The large, shaved head was identical to that of the real assassin. The tattoos on his cheeks and chin matched in the minutest detail.

The Blacktongue stepped forward and grabbed Delmecian's hand. He slid back the sleeve of the cloak and smiled when, instead of Delmecian's fair white skin, the assassin saw dark tattoos weaving up the man's arm. Not only that, but there were matching scars, and the very shape of the arm was the same.

Delmecian snapped his fingers and returned to normal in the blink of an eye. "If you continue to hold my hand, I may have to insist you buy me dinner," he said with a wink.

The Blacktongue nodded and stepped back, releasing the nobleman's arm.

"How long before we can set out?" Threnton asked, grinning ear to ear.

*****

Sam Ferguson

Hiasyntar'Kulai flew high above the desolate plains of Nahktun Valley. It was a place the dragon had hoped to avoid forever after the Great War of the Gods. The land was brown, cracked, and still held the scars of battle from that terrible war that resulted in the Old Gods sealing off the rainbow bridge to Volganor, the Heaven City. Not only was the land itself dark, but there was a permanent layer of filth and dust in the air that blocked out most of the sunlight.

The golden dragon thought it might have been a place well suited for Gorensikdar, except for the fact that there were creatures here that even the black dragon would not want to provoke. The Father of the Ancients only came here because he knew of no other way to reach Tu'luh. If Tu'luh the Red had been dragged down to hell by Khefir, one of the gods of the underworld, then Hiasyntar'Kulai would have to travel to Gaia's Tear, the only known conduit that physically connected Terramyr to the planes of hell called Hammenfein.

Still, the mighty dragon was careful to stay high in the sky. Even he did not want to risk being attacked by the vile monsters that called this part of Terramyr home.

As he approached the magnificent volcano known as Gaia's Tear, he circled higher into the air and inspected the area around it. Lava flowed out from several places on the mountain, running down in red, hot rivers that meandered out into the gray-brown lands beyond. There were no trees here, but there were strange cacti that reached up to thirty feet tall and formed wicked tines that could pierce through a steel plate of armor.

Other than those cacti, there were no signs of life.

Hiasyntar'Kulai flew over the volcano and looked inside. Chills coursed through his spine as he saw the stairway to hell circling the inner walls inside the volcano. A churning, smoking pool of orange lava sat at the bottom. The dragon knew that the gates to hell were near that pool of lava.

He also knew that any being besides Icadion, who freely entered Gaia's Tear, was considered a willing prisoner in Hammenfein, and both Khefir and Hatmul, the brother-gods

58

who ruled Hammenfein, would come out with their armies to collect their victim.

The dragon roared down in his mighty voice, "Khefir, Collector of the Damned, come without the gates of Hammenfein and grant me an audience."

Nothing happened for several minutes. The dragon circled the opening high above the volcano and waited. Then, he heard a great commotion, and deep within the volcano he saw an army march out from the gates. They took up a defensive position near the lava pool and stopped, turning their gazes upward and looking directly at him.

The Father of the Ancients called out again. "Khefir, I come alone, and with no ill intent. I only wish to speak with you."

A line of blackness rent the sky over the volcano and a pair of skeleton hands reached through and then stretched the line into a hole. Hiasyntar'Kulai could see Khefir standing inside the portal. A dark hood covered most of Khefir's bony face, but his ghastly, yellow eyes glowed brightly as they watched Hiasyntar'Kulai. As the dragon circled in the air to remain in flight above the volcano, so did the portal spin, allowing the dragon to see the god from any direction.

"You cannot have your son," Khefir said. "He made a deal with me, and then he broke it. I have proper claim on his soul."

"I have not come to ask for his soul, mighty Khefir," Hiasyntar'Kulai said. "I have come only to ask for an audience with him. He has stolen something from me, and I need it back."

Khefir chuckled softly, his jaw clicking and clacking as it gyrated up and down. "Tu'luh the Red has betrayed many, it would seem."

Hiasyntar'Kulai said nothing as he soared around in a circle, watching the portal as it kept pace with him.

Khefir nodded and pointed at the golden dragon. "It is not every day that an Ancient needs my help. Surely, this must be worth a favor from you in return if you would venture all this way."

Hiasyntar'Kulai had expected as much from the collector of evil souls. "What would you demand as payment to speak with my son?"

Khefir pulled his hood back and revealed a yellowed skull. His glowing, yellow eyes were nothing more than a magical manifestation of where his physical orbs had once been. "Not just to speak with him," the god corrected. "I will also demand he give you the answers you seek. As you have likely heard, I have power over the souls here; they must obey my command."

"Very well," the golden dragon said. "What is your price?"

Khefir glanced around and then came close to the portal. He spoke in a soft voice. "Not now, but later I may come to you with a proposal."

"You wish me to agree to a favor that you will only name after I have sworn? That is not acceptable."

Khefir flashed a bony arm across the portal. "No, my price is that when I have a proposal for you, you will afford me a fair audience and give my future proposal proper consideration. That is all."

"What if I hear it and decide it is a favor I want nothing to do with?" the dragon asked.

"Then you shall be bound to hear any proposal I think of after the fact, until you hear one that you will agree to."

Hiasyntar'Kulai nodded as he flapped his wings and then flattened them out to soar. "Agreed."

Khefir nodded and left. The next image the gold dragon saw was that of his son.

Tu'luh had a large, golden spike placed through his snout. The spike was attached to fiery reins made of golden chains which were held by a powerful orc spirit. Hiasyntar'Kulai could not help but feel shame and sorrow for his son's current situation. Though the golden dragon knew that Tu'luh had done many reproachable things, the love he held for his son was still there, pulling at his soul.

"Speak," the orc riding Tu'luh told Hiasyntar'Kulai.

The golden dragon looked to his son's sad, broken eyes and then asked his question directly. "Where is the addorite you stole from me?"

Tu'luh grunted, but didn't answer.

The orc riding him lifted a mighty, golden whip and cracked it down on Tu'luh's brow. He then yanked upon the chains and Tu'luh groaned in pain. "Khefir has ordered you to answer the Father of the Ancient's questions fully and honestly. Now answer him!"

Tu'luh complied. "The addorite was taken to a cave to the west of Roegudok Hall, but it is no longer there."

"What do you mean?" Hiasyntar'Kulai asked.

"I used some of it. Gorensikdar, my brother, was the one who told me how to create the spell that later became known as Nagar's Blight. Its creation required a great amount of addorite."

Hiasyntar'Kulai growled angrily. "And where is the rest?"

"Taken," Tu'luh replied. "A band of goblins stole the rest. I tracked them farther west, into a small network of tunnels and caves, but I never found it. Go west from Roegudok Hall for two hundred miles, then turn south from the dark forest where the funnel spiders live. In a pine forest you will find three small mountains. The entrance to the network of caves is in the middle mountain, but I do not think the addorite still remains."

"Why not?" the golden dragon pressed.

"The goblins who took it used its power to augment their magic. They had no understanding of its toxicity. It warped them into something different. Now they are a strange, vile tribe that hardly resemble goblins at all. Unless I am mistaken, they died from their use of addorite, and the addorite has been entirely consumed."

"Any more questions?" the orc shouted out to Hiasyntar'Kulai.

The golden dragon replied, "No, that is all."

The orc yanked on the chains and Tu'luh walked away. Khefir returned for a moment and reminded the golden dragon of their deal, then the portal vanished. Hiasyntar'Kulai stopped circling and flew away, making a direct line for the Middle Kingdom, which was many thousand miles away.

CHAPTER 5

Year 3,403 King's Era.
203rd year of the reign of Sylus Magdinium, 5th King of Roegudok Hall.

Dvek stepped into the miner's hall as they were finishing their supper. Normally the hall would have been filled with tobacco smoke and flowing with ale, but that was not the case now. The miners sat around wooden tables playing cards and betting with toothpicks instead of anything that had real value. A few of the miners looked up at him, but none of them said anything. They knew well enough that he hadn't come to speak with them.

The Minister of Commerce made his way to the left side of the hall and pushed through a swinging door to find thirty dwarves standing around and talking with each other in hushed voices. When he stepped inside the room, they all turned and fanned out to face him.

"I have the orders from the king," Dvek said. "We are in a tight spot, so I won't mince words, and I am not going to make this a long, drawn out meeting. You are some of the best team leaders Roegudok Hall has ever known."

"Tell me something I don't know," said Brugg, a brown haired dwarf with a burgeoning belly and thick, scarred arms.

A couple of the others laughed.

Dvek arched a brow and continued. "I have a list for each of you. It details how many crews will be assigned to you, as well as who is on each crew. We are changing tactics so we can spread out to explore as many mines as possible. Each of you is going to have a team that consists of seven crews. Each crew is going to have four miners and one explosives expert. The senior-most miner on each crew will be the crew leader. In order to keep the mines working around the clock, we have given each team three shafts as assignments. That means your teams will have two crews per mine. One crew will take a shift of several days, and then the second crew will take their place and work a shift of three days also. The seventh crew will work in wherever you like. Use the extra crew to relieve injured miners, or to add extra hands if you find a promising mine."

Dvek looked around the room. "Any questions?"

None of the team leaders said anything.

Dvek nodded, pulled a leather satchel up and opened it. He pulled out one rolled parchment at a time, calling out the names written on the outside. As each team leader was called, they would walk forward, take their assignment, and then exit the room.

When Dvek had finished, a young, green-eyed female dwarf stood alone in the room. Her eyes were fixed on the satchel.

"What about my assignment?" she asked. "I am as good as any other team leader that was here."

Dvek patted the air and smiled. "Easy now, Akmei, the king has an assignment for you, but it isn't to run a team this time."

"Why not?" she asked as she stamped a foot on the floor and folded her arms.

Dvek laughed. "You still do the foot stomp when you're angry," he said.

"Father, I won't stand for any of your meddling. I am a miner, and that's what I love—"

Dvek cut her off. "This is out of my hands," he said. "The king has asked me to appoint you as the Mining Advisor."

Akmei took a few steps forward and shook a finger at

Dvek. "Well, you can tell the king that I..." Akmei stopped and the anger vanished from her face. "What did you say?" she asked.

"I said, the king would like you to accept the position of Mining Advisor."

"He wants me to sit on the council?"

Dvek nodded.

Akmei smiled and started to turn around, but then she stopped and turned back to her father. "Wait, what did you do to get me the position?"

Dvek shook his head. "I did nothing. The king went through the list of qualified candidates and he decided to offer the position to you. He didn't even ask what I thought about it."

Akmei smiled. "I'll be the best Mining Advisor Roegudok Hall has ever had."

*****

"You sure this is the tunnel we are supposed to work in today?" Trynt asked as he shifted his pickaxe on his shoulder.

The lantern Haggart held swayed with each step he took down the newly formed mine. "Yep," he answered for the hundredth time. "King Sylus said that Tu'luh told him we would find the addorite in the shaft that has bloodgrass growing in it." Haggart stopped and held the lantern close to the wall on the left as he turned a sour look over his shoulder. "See, bloodgrass."

Trynt looked at the bony stems of the strange plant and grimaced. The round, flat leaves hung vertically from small branches shooting off the main stem of the bush-like plant. True to its name, the plant was bright red.

"Still, you have heard the rumors about these lower tunnels, right boss?" Jasper asked.

Haggart growled and turned around to point an accusing finger in Jasper's face. The younger dwarf backed away instinctively as the crew leader laid into him. "You will keep such talk to yourself, you hear? The king wants us to open up the lower mines and that is what we are going to do. We are dwarves, hewn and formed from the very rock this mountain is made of. There ain't nothin' down here that can best the five of us. We are going to find the addorite, and we are going to fill the coffers with more gems than has ever been seen, you hear?"

Trynt nodded, but his mouth opened, letting his doubts tumble out. "If the addorite is so important to Tu'luh, then why doesn't he come into the mountain and dig it out for himself?"

A swift back-hand shut Trynt's mouth.

The others stiffened and shared a glance, but none of them moved to intervene.

"You don't bad mouth the Ancients," Haggart warned. He looked up from Trynt and eyed the other dwarves in the group with his piercing, blue eyes. "If not for them, we wouldn't exist. I shouldn't have to tell you that. If they want us to dig to the bottom of Terramyr, then we'll do it."

"Haggart," one of the other dwarves began in a gruff, yet pleasant voice. Trynt looked up to see Rikker, the explosives engineer, stepping forward. "Trynt is only an apprentice. He hasn't the same experience the rest of us do. He is on loan to our unit due to his strength, since Finorik is down with a broken arm from the cave in yesterday."

Haggart scratched his bald head and shrugged. "You have a point," he said. "Trynt, listen up, cause I am only saying this once. The Ancients need us to dig for the addorite because it is formed deep within the mountain, where geological and magical pressures combine to create a very rare, very powerful, crystal. Think of it like a diamond. You know how they form deep within the ground where pressures and heat are optimal for their creation, it's like that, only throw in the magical nexus that exists below Roegudok Hall and you have an extremely rare crystal. Tu'luh told King Sylus he needs it, however, Tu'luh can't mine it himself because the same magical pressures that create the addorite are harmful and toxic to dragons. It would be like me throwing a gold coin into a lake that is a hundred feet deep and asking you to go swim after it. We aren't built for the water. Sure, you might be able to dive down a few feet, but you'll struggle to reach the surface again. Go down a hundred feet and you can forget about ever seeing your home again."

Haggart drew a line across his neck with his finger. "Doesn't matter how strong you are, the water would swallow you up. Same thing for the Ancients. They are mighty strong creatures, but they can't survive the magical pressures below this mountain."

The crew leader turned and waved his arm for the others to keep up as he stormed off.

Rikker moved in next to Trynt. "Don't worry, he is grumpy with everyone. In fact, he has a fuse shorter than any of my explosives," Rikker smiled widely.

Trynt returned the smile and moved to keep up with the others, but Rikker held him back just long enough for Del and Jasper to move ahead.

"You aren't wrong about the rumors, though," Rikker said. "Haggart would never admit it, but there are dangers down here that we should be wary of."

"Have you seen them before?" Trynt asked.

Rikker shook his head of black hair and frowned. "No, but you can feel it, that sensation like something is watching you."

Trynt went silent.

"Don't worry," Rikker said. "I have been working with Haggart for decades. He is as tough as he is cranky. I'm sure he can handle anything that comes our way. More than that, I will watch over you until Finorik is healed up."

Trynt nodded, unsure if he believed Rikker's statement about Haggart. He looked back to the black haired dwarf and noticed something in the explosive engineer's eyes. The words had sounded confident, but the cloud of fear was visible in Rikker's eyes. Trynt reached into his pocket and felt for the silver charm his wife had given him several weeks before upon graduating from the mining guild university. His thumb rubbed over the flat shape of a dragon as Trynt whispered a prayer in his mind.

He followed the other four miners for hours as they walked down the freshly carved tunnel. Trynt studied the grooves and holes in the wall. There were veins of gold and silver left nearly untouched in this shaft. He wondered how much addorite might be worth by comparison if Haggart was ignoring the gold and silver entirely.

After a while, he found himself wishing that they had mining carts to speed the journey along. He wasn't sure why there were no tracks set in this shaft. It was certainly long enough to warrant them. Pushing handcarts was much more difficult than mining carts on tracks. He quick-stepped up to Rikker and elbowed him to get his attention.

"Why are there no tracks down here?" Trynt asked.

"Dvek said we don't have enough metal to build them," Rikker replied.

"Can't we take old tracks from other mine shafts?"

Rikker shook his head. "All the other shafts are being expanded as well. So, other teams will be using the old tracks as much as they can."

"Shut up back there," Haggart called out. "I am tired of listening to your questions, Trynt."

Trynt blushed and moved away from Rikker.

The deeper the tunnel went, the warmer the air became. The bloodgrass plants grew larger and thicker also. Trynt couldn't be sure if it was just his imagination, but he thought he heard a low humming noise from the walls of the black tunnel. Perhaps this was the effect of the magical pressure Haggart had spoken of. He stopped and bent over to touch one of the leaves protruding out from the wall. The leaf was stiff and brittle. He barely pinched it between his thumb and forefinger before it crumbled and fell from the stem.

The light dimmed in the cavern and Trynt jerked his head up. He could see light dancing upon the wall in front of him. The others had followed the cavern around a downward sloping curve to the left.

Trynt brushed off his hand and started to jog to catch up.

A rumbling sound rolled through the tunnel, and a cool breeze flew up from around the curve. The hairs on the back of Trynt's neck and arms rose to stand on end. He couldn't explain it, but something felt very wrong.

The shadows on the wall in front of him stopped moving. Trynt watched the shadows of the other miners for a moment, and then a scream erupted from the tunnel and the lamps went out. Trynt felt his heart flutter up into his throat and stop

Another scream.

Trynt heard the clattering sound of metal falling to the floor. Someone shouted and then everything went silent.

Trynt was a miner, not a soldier. He turned tail and sprinted up the shaft to escape. As he ran, something pounded the ground behind him. Whatever it was, it had far more than two feet and it was closing fast. He didn't bother looking back. He pulled his pick-axe down into both hands, just in case it managed to catch him. Being a dwarf, his eyes adjusted to the dark quickly enough for him to navigate through the tunnel without tripping or running into a wall, but he was not a fast runner.

Something clawed at the back of his shirt.

Trynt yelped and the burst of fear was turned into a boost in speed for a few seconds as his feet seemed to nearly fly over the stone floor. Something grabbed his arm. Without turning, Trynt swung around with his pickaxe.

The tool was ripped from him and something hit his left leg. Trynt went down onto the ground and slammed his face onto the stone, sliding to an unceremonious halt as he huffed and gasped for breath. He turned over onto his back and struck out into the darkness. Something caught his hand.

He struggled with everything he had in him, but soon all of his limbs were seized and held to the stone floor. Trynt heard a growl and felt a steely talon slowly drag its way up his torso. Trynt shut his eyes and turned his head, accepting his fate.

Instead of a death-blow, a match was struck and a lantern was lit. Trynt looked up and saw the smiling, laughing dwarves standing on and around him.

"Maybe strong as a miner, but he's a bit short on courage if you ask me," Haggart teased as he spat to the side.

"Just a friendly bit of hazing," Jasper said as he released his grip on Trynt's left arm and leg.

"You should see your face," Del said as he backed away from Trynt's right hand and leg. The red-haired dwarf contorted his face and shrank away, mocking Trynt's terror.

"You'll watch my back?" Trynt huffed as he spied Rikker standing over him with a pickaxe in hand. The point was lightly resting on Trynt's chest. There had been no talon. There had been no beast.

Rikker shrugged. "Can't help it," he said. "It's tradition."

"Besides," Haggart cut in. "You fell behind. You didn't think I would let you get away with it did you?"

Trynt pushed away from them and up to his feet. "Not funny," he said.

"Oh, don't worry," Haggart said. "No one has seen any beasts down here. They are just rumors and stories to tell around the fire."

Trynt brushed himself off and shook his head. No sooner had he bent down to brush the front of his pants than the lantern went out again. Another burst of cool air rushed around him as something snarled in the darkness.

"I'm not falling for it," Trynt said as he stood up. He crossed his arms, furious that they would continue the prank. Then, something wet and warm splattered onto his face. "Cut it out!" Trynt yelled. His eyes finished adjusting in that moment and he saw Haggart standing right where he had been. However, the lantern was no longer in his right hand. In fact, Trynt wasn't sure he even saw Haggart's right arm at all.

A whimper sounded in the dark and something streaked behind Haggart.

Then the crew leader fell to the ground.

Trynt couldn't help but jump.

"Watch out!" Jasper shouted.

Trynt turned just as something leapt up from the ground and ripped the miner's head clean off his neck. Jasper's body fell forward and Trynt caught what was left of Jasper.

A scraping sound scratched along the stone floor.

Rikker pulled a hatchet and swung through the air, yelling ferociously. "It's true!" he said as he swung in all directions around himself. "The legends are true!"

Trynt cried out as a strange form seemed to lunge out from the wall and grabbed Rikker. Trynt heard squishing flesh and cracking bones as the explosives engineer was taken.

Del rushed in and pulled Trynt out from under Jasper's body. "Come on, we have to get out of here!" Del hooked his arm under Trynt's left armpit and pulled him along.

The two ran, but they didn't make it very far.

Something seized Del and the miner called out in agony. Trynt tried to pull on Del's arm and wrench him away from their stalker. A terrible growl sounded in the darkness. Then, Trynt heard a *pop!* Del's arm came free, but only the dwarf's arm.

Trynt screamed and dropped the limb as he continued to run.

He didn't hear feet pounding the ground as he had when the other dwarves had been teasing him. This time the cave was silent. Trynt could only hope that whatever the thing was, it had been sated by taking the others.

For the longest time, he heard nothing. His legs burned from the exertion, but his fear would not let the dwarf's feet stop.

Then, he felt that eerie rush of cold wind from deep within the tunnel. The faint sound of scratching on the stone barely reached his ears.

Trynt redoubled his efforts, ignoring the knot in his

large stomach and sprinting up the sharp incline.

A low growl rumbled through the cave. The scratching sounded closer.

"No!" Trynt whispered to himself as he thought of his wife. He was going to make it home. He was going to see his wife again. He would tell the guards about the attack and then King Sylus would eradicate the monster with the cavedog riders.

Trynt was not going to die. Not here. Not like this.

The sharp scratches grew closer, tearing along the stone floor as the stalker closed in.

Trynt's lungs burned beyond anything he had ever experienced before.

His mind threw doubt at him.

It had taken the group of dwarves hours to walk this deep into the mines. There was no one close by to help. Could he really run all the way back?

No! Trynt said within his mind. He forced out the doubt and replaced it with the image of his loving wife's face. They had been married only two years. They had many hundred years left to enjoy. He couldn't leave her now.

The scratching stopped.

Trynt thought perhaps the beast had given up pursuit, but he didn't dare slow down to look. He was determined not to die in the tunnels.

Something black sailed along the ceiling over him, drawing Trynt's eyes up.

It stopped just a few yards in front of Trynt and dropped from the ceiling.

Trynt's eyes shot open wide and his mouth fell.

A gleaming, white claw slashed out from the thing and Trynt felt himself flying through the air. He tumbled to the ground, scraping along the stone until his body came to a stop. He was face down, mouth full of dust and body aching. His head rang sharply. He pushed up with his hands, purely surviving on will at this point. His lower back burned, but he couldn't feel his feet or legs.

My back! Trynt thought to himself, *Please don't be broken. I didn't hit the ground that hard.* He pushed up enough to turn around. Nothing could have prepared him for what he saw.

His legs and waist were lying several yards back in the tunnel. The great, shadowy monster was moving toward them. It reached out and picked up the severed legs, devouring them whole, clothes and all.

Then it turned to face Trynt. The ghastly, glowing yellow eyes drained what remained of Trynt's will. The dwarf gave up the ghost as the monster closed in.

CHAPTER 6

Year 3,711 Age of Demigods, Summer.
2nd year of the reign of Aldehenkaru'hktanah Sit'marihu, 13th King of Roegudok Hall.

Al placed his hand on the cold, iron door and pushed it open. His nostrils pulled in musty, damp air as he stepped into the well room. Four sconces, all placed evenly around the chamber, sparkled vibrantly as they lent their light to the area.

Alferug stood at the edge of the well, on the opposite side of the room from the entrance, looking down.

Al pushed the door closed behind himself and then walked to the well. He looked into it and whistled through his teeth. His eyes traced the large, copper pipes leading out from the side of the well and disappearing into the right hand wall.

"Normally, the water level in the well would exceed the height of the pipes, and the well would pump endless water through for our culinary use," Alferug said from the opposite side of the well.

Al nodded. He had been here before, with his father, many decades earlier, and seen the well working in its full glory. At that time, the clear, cool spring pushed up to rest just inches below the rim of the well, and the pipes could barely pull enough of the liquid out to keep the well from overflowing.

It was not so today.

Al placed his hands on the smooth stone rim of the well and leaned over to peer down inside. There was no water that he could see. "Did something shift inside the mountain?" Al asked. "It seems strange that this spring would run dry when it has lasted for thousands of years."

Alferug placed a book on his side of the well's rim. "I was reading about this subject. I won't go over all of the details, but it appears that this spring is not the first of its kind. Apparently, it was discovered during King Sylus' reign, after he expanded some of the mines below."

"Artesian wells require pressure to drive the water up. How could expanding mine shafts below increase pressure? Shouldn't it have had the opposite effect?"

Alferug held up a hand. "I have found some vague references to something the Ancients called Maaginen or Mystinen, depending on which historian you read. Apparently, it is a type of energy that exists below the mountain. Mining can at times shift it, and the presence, or absence, of this force can be measured in two ways."

"What is that?" Al asked.

"The sudden appearance of new wells, as the Mystinen drives water from aquafers and bores holes for it to escape. The other evidence is the sudden disappearance of wells, but to ensure the disappearance is due only to the Mystinen, then there must be another sign present."

"What other sign?" Al asked.

Alferug motioned for the king to join him on the other side of the well.

Al walked around the outer edge of the well and stopped as he came around Alferug's side.

A strange plant grew out the side of the well. Its stems were stiff like bones, and it had round, thin leaves hanging from smaller branches.

"Is that the bloodgrass mentioned by Sylus?" Al asked breathlessly.

Alferug nodded. "It took me some time to identify it for sure. So, I waited to call for you until I knew I was correct."

Al nodded and moved in close to the plant. He bent

down and took one of the brittle leaves in his fingers. It cracked and crumbled instantly. "It's a very fragile plant, isn't it?"

Alferug nodded. "If we could find Sylus' book, then I might know a bit more about it, but I have at least found enough evidence to be sure what it is. In *Hermek's Herbal* there is a drawing that fits this plant, but other than the name, there is no information."

"*Hermek's Herbal*, wasn't that also written in Sylus' time?" Al asked as he smoothed his beard.

Alferug shook his head. "No, it was before Sylus. Hermek did most of his research during the second king's reign. I am not sure if the lack of information comes from the plant's rarity, or if it was perhaps thought dangerous to experiment with. Either way, he is the only one who refers to it by name, and has a drawing to accompany it. Other Herbals name it obscurely, but most of them claim the plant is a myth, or a bad omen."

"Well, it certainly isn't a myth," Al said. "They might have been on to something with the bad omen part though. If it only springs up when the wells dry up, then that is as bad an omen as I have ever seen before."

"Yet Sylus would have claimed it a good omen," Alferug pointed out. "Remember, he claimed that the Wealth of Kings would be found when the bloodgrass was seen again."

Al smiled. "If we can find the mines he used to build up Roegudok Hall's coffers, then that would be swell indeed."

Alferug nodded knowingly. "We have enough water from the other reservoirs for now. Besides, you are expanding the mines like Sylus did. Perhaps it will shift the Mystinen enough that a new well will spring up somewhere."

"I am afraid that we ran into a snag trying to send a message to Hiasyntar'Kulai," Al said, changing the subject.

"How so?" Alferug inquired.

Al sighed. "No messenger bird can reach the place he is at currently."

"What about the Champion of Truth? Doesn't he know where to go?"

Al nodded. "Erik has been there, but Erik is no longer in the Middle Kingdom. No one seems to know where he went either."

"And there is no one else?" Alferug pressed.

Al held up a single finger. "There is one, a gnome named Jaleal. However, I have just received word that he is missing. Apparently he returned to his village and then after he went into his house no one has seen him since."

"Curious," Alferug said. "And you have no idea where the Father of the Ancients is?"

Al shook his head. "I know where he is, I just don't know how to get there."

Alferug frowned and clasped his hands in front of his waist.

"The officers at Fort Drake tell me he has gone back to a palace in the east, the residence of the Immortal Mystic."

"I take it they did not know how to find it?"

Al shook his head. "Hiasyntar'Kulai told no one. It appears that unless we could find Jaleal, or Erik, our best chances to find the Father of the Ancients is to mount an excursion to the east."

"That would take far too long," Alferug said.

Al nodded. "I know. I came to that conclusion as well. I just thought that, since you are the advisor for everything revolving around tradition and the Ancients, perhaps you might know a different way to contact him?"

Alferug shook his head. "If I did, I would have mentioned it before. I can only guess that perhaps one of the priests at Valtuu Temple may know something I do not."

Al groused and kicked at the dirt. "No, they don't."

"It's alright, my king," Alferug offered. "We have a plan. We'll stick to it. I am sure something will turn up in the mines."

*****

"Pass the beans," Tareggh said.

Kirrik, a stout dwarf with a bit of gray peeking out from his otherwise black beard took the small pot in hand and offered it to Tareggh. The crew leader grunted, and spooned out some beans onto his tin plate. He then shifted closer to the fire.

The other three miners were working on clearing rubble out from the tunnel. It was long, unforgiving work, but the dwarves were used to it. They had been working on this particular tunnel for weeks. Just the day before, they had almost started dancing in celebration when they had found a vein of silver in the wall, but that had dried up after yielding only four pounds worth of quality material. Hardly enough to smile at, given the current state of affairs in Roegudok Hall. They needed something ten or even one hundred times that amount before they could celebrate.

"Dvek was sure he wanted us to clear this mine?" Kirrik asked as he took the beans back from Tareggh and set them down.

Tareggh nodded. "Yep. He handed assignments out to all the crew leaders in person." Tareggh fished a piece of paper out of his pocket and held it out for Kirrik. "We drew mine thirty-seven."

Kirrik nodded. He had seen the numeral designation over the entrance to this mine. But, he had also seen the boulders near the entrance. "This is the deepest mine," Kirrik said. "We are two miles beneath the surface, and this shaft is rumored to go down for several more miles before branching out into different tunnels."

Tareggh nodded and choked down his mouthful of beans. "And that's why you see things you have never seen before, like that plant." Tareggh pointed to a blood-red plant with round leaves. He then pointed a finger back at Kirrik and narrowed one of his green eyes on him. "This is also rumored to be one of the mines from King Sylus' days. You know how well he did for himself. It would be nice to get a taste of that action."

Kirrik offered a half smile and took a bite of beans himself. They were horribly bland, not to mention overcooked. The skins fell off and the beans turned to mush without even chewing. Kirrik might have chastised the chef, except in this case that would mean he would be yelling at himself. He managed to force the bite down and then he set his plate beside the pot that was very likely full of beans that were not going to be eaten.

He cleared his throat and then glanced to the three working on clearing the rubble. They hadn't been tasked with clearing the mine entirely. That would waste too much time. Their job was to reach the deeper tunnels, and then to look for signs of gems or precious metal.

Kirrik doubted they would find any. Why else would Sylus, or any king afterward, allow the tunnel to remain blocked off unless it had been emptied of its treasures? There was, however, something else that bothered Kirrik. He hadn't mentioned it to anyone, but it was always there, in the back of his mind, nagging and pulling at him.

Still, he kept it to himself, as he had for the duration of their shift in the mines. As it was, they only had three more days' worth of food. They would soon be going back up to the main hall, and another mining group would take their turn in this forgotten tomb of a tunnel. So, for the next two days, Kirrik continued to hold his tongue when time for sleep came and they gathered around the fire. There was no need to upset anyone.

On the third day, during the final four hour shift before they would pack everything in, Kirrik was called over to help move a particularly stubborn boulder. It was several yards across, and nearly as high as the tunnel, stopping just short of the ceiling.

Kirrik hefted his large, canvas backpack up and moved over to the boulder. The other four dwarves moved a safe distance back, taking cover behind a pile of smaller boulders. Kirrik first took out a tin can filled with lard. He set it on the ground and then pulled a small, wooden box containing fuses out of the bag and set it down as well. He then pulled three additional bags out from inside the large backpack. He opened the drawstring on each bag and then bent his head back to look at the large boulder. There were no obvious fissures, but a vein of quarts did split the rock on one side, running horizontally with the floor and connecting with the wall.

Kirrik took the lard in hand and placed a copious amount in the thin space between the wall and the left side of the boulder. He then went to the backpack and pulled a large funnel out. He set the can of lard back into the backpack and picked up the first smaller bag. He pushed the end of the funnel as far as it would go into the space and then he poured a large amount of powdered charcoal into the funnel. A heavy, black dust flew up around his face, but Kirrik didn't mind. He was more than used to it. Once all of the powder was situated on the lard, he repeated the step with the other two bags. The second bag contained saltpeter, and the last contained sulfur.

He then put away the ingredients and took out a long, wooden spoon. He gripped it by the bowl and used the long handle to mix his powder together. Some of the explosives engineers chided him for not mixing his explosives before setting them, but there was something about mixing it in place that always pleased Kirrik.

When he had satisfactorily mixed the black powder, Kirrik placed the fuse and then packed lard on top to hold it all in place. It was an oddly shaped explosive, but it was custom fit for this boulder. It was only an inch wide, not counting the lard shell, but it was nearly two feet deep and several inches tall. That was why he never mixed his powder first. Pre-made explosives never fit the way his custom mixes would.

He took a moment to smile at it and then he carried the backpack, containing all of the ingredients, back to the barricade where his colleagues were waiting.

"Anyone care to do the honors?" Kirrik asked.

They all shook their heads.

"Get on with it Kirrik," Tareggh shouted. "I don't

want Jesep leading the next crew right behind us and finding something in the first few minutes just because we did all of the hard work."

Kirrik knew none of them would offer to light it. If he thought they would ever say 'yes' then he wouldn't offer. For him, only half of the fun was making the bomb. The other half was setting it off.

He nearly skipped back to the fuse. It was three feet long, dangling out from the bomb and running along the floor. Easily enough to ensure Kirrik got back in time.

He lit the fuse and that old, familiar spark ignited with a *soowish!*

He admired the leaping, golden sparks for just a moment before turning to hurry back around the barricade.

He sat down and smiled at the others. He held up one hand with three fingers up. He dropped one, then two. As the third finger dropped, he rushed to cover his ears before a terrible explosion rocked the cavern. The blast wave was hot and smelled of burnt sulfur. Dust flew over and around the dwarves for a long time after the last bits of rock settled upon the floor.

As things settled, Kirrik peered around the side of the barricade and saw that the boulder had split exactly the way he wanted. The bottom half had been separated along the quarts line, and the top half was now lying in five parts across the stone floor. Several of the smaller boulders that had been wedge in by the large one were now loose as well.

Kirrik got up and went to inspect the blast mark.

He didn't need to. He had given the miners more than enough to work with, but that wasn't the point. Each blast mark was different, and Kirrik liked them all.

"The men in Drakei Glazei may paint or write sonnets, but I make magic," Kirrik said quietly, more to himself than anyone else as he spied the telltale scorch marks and smiled. He approached them and breathed in deeply as he rubbed his hand across the boulder.

That was when he felt a strange, cool breeze.

At first he thought it came from behind the boulder. He moved next to the wall, trying to look deeper into the tunnel, but he couldn't see anything. The breeze felt stronger on his cheek. Kirrik turned and saw a hole in the wall where the blast had gone off. This was not entirely unusual, of course. His explosions often created holes and craters. However, this hole was different. The wall was not solid as he had expected. The hole had blown through fifteen inches of rock and provided a window into a strange chamber. Kirrik placed his face close to the hole and wrapped his hands around his face to shield from the lanterns his colleagues were bringing closer.

His dwarf eyes adjusted to the dark quickly and he saw a large, dark room. There appeared to be no way in or out of the chamber. The floor, curved walls, and ceiling appeared to be made of stone. Stalagmites, stalactites, and columns obscured the view, but otherwise the room appeared empty.

Then he saw something else. A strange, pink sparkle. He wasn't sure he saw it at first, but as he adjusted his position and a bit more light slipped into the chamber, he confirmed it. There was some sort of crystal formation growing on one of the columns.

"You are going to want to see this," Kirrik said.

Tareggh was already most of the way to him, pickaxe and lantern in hand.

Kirrik glanced back to the crystal, and then something moved in the shadows. He opened his mouth to speak, but Tareggh pulled him out of the way.

"What is it?" he asked in a gruff voice. "Did you find gold?"

"I...I'm not sure," Kirrik said. "But I—"

"Jumping horny-toad, he found crystals!" Tareggh shouted over Kirrik. The crew chief turned and started barking orders. "Forget the tunnel. Burrow through this wall. Sarep, Red, break out your picks and go berserk. If it's anything we can sell, then we'll be the heroes of Roegudok Hall!"

The other dwarves hopped into place, nearly shoving Kirrik out of the way.

Kirrik took a moment to regain his senses, and then he pulled Tareggh aside.

"What is it?" Tareggh asked. "Want to blow the wall with some more of your powder?"

Kirrik shook his head. "I think I saw something move in there," he said.

Tareggh's green eyes narrowed on Kirrik and then the crew leader glanced over his shoulder at Sarep and Red, who were both already chopping away at the wall. "You saw what?"

Kirrik shrugged. "Not sure, but I saw *something.*"

Tareggh nodded and called for the others to halt their work.

The crew leader moved to the hole and peered inside. Kirrik watched him for several moments. Flint, a muscular dwarf with a brown beard and no hair, moved up next to Kirrik.

"What is it?" Flint asked.

Kirrik shrugged. He wrestled with whether to tell Flint what he had seen. What if he was wrong? He didn't want the others to think him afraid just because of some rumors and stories his grandfather had told him when he was young. Kirrik turned and lied. "The boss just wanted to reevaluate the chamber inside. Wants to make sure its stable before we go in."

Flint took the lie with a thoughtful nod and walked off closer to Sarep and Red.

A minute later Tareggh came away from the hole and slapped Red on the shoulder. "Back to work, the chamber is good."

Fortunate choice of words. Kirrik thought.

Tareggh marched over to Kirrik and poked him in the shoulder, hard. "I know what's in yer head," he said in a harsh whisper. "You keep it to yerself!"

Kirrik frowned. "I wasn't trying to spook anyone," he said. "I swear I saw something."

"Bah!" Tareggh huffed. "You saw what your mind wanted you to see. You think I haven't heard the stories? Any miner who has been down here for more than a century or two knows em all. That doesn't mean they're true."

"The shaft was sealed off," Kirrik replied evenly.

Tareggh shook his head and thunked Kirrik again. "Enough! There are no scary monsters down here in the shadows. Next, you'll be telling me that the main drain has demons living at the bottom of it. Rubbish!"

Kirrik nodded and kept his mouth closed. He had, in fact, heard the story about the main drain as well. It was Roegudok Hall's strangest shaft. A hole dug straight down some two hundred yards behind a secret gate of stone and iron. Its true purpose was to drain the water if ever the entrance tunnel needed to be flooded in defense, but of course there were rumors that the hole was a shortcut to Hammenfein itself. Still, Kirrik knew that that particular story was a child's fable. The rumors of what lurked below in the forgotten tunnels, he was not so sure of.

With each strike of the pickaxes, Kirrik jumped. He watched the hole widen as chips and hunks of stone fell away from the wall. Tareggh watched while Sarep and Red hacked away and Flint cleared the rubble.

A rush of cold air came out from the chamber that made all the tiny hairs on Kirrik's neck stand on end. He didn't rest easy until a passageway was made and Tareggh went through. He took a lantern, and the others eagerly followed him. Shouts of excitement and celebration filled the air.

"Kirrik, you did it!" Tareggh shouted. "You did it!"

Kirrik smiled. He grabbed his backpack and rushed off to the chamber, relieved that it had only been his imagination playing tricks on him rather than some creature hiding in the shadows for them. He passed through the passageway and could hardly contain his smile. There were several pockets of the same pink crystal he had seen, but there was much, much more than that. A rich vein of gold sparkled under the lantern light on the north end of the wall. Off to the right of that by four yards was a round, smooth shaft that Kirrik had not seen before.

"Lava tube," Tareggh said as he pointed to the smooth shaft. "It goes in for several yards and then looks like it curves to drop straight down. Come here, Kirrik."

Kirrik nearly stumbled as Tareggh stuck his lantern into the tube. The glimmer was unmistakable. There were diamonds embedded in the walls of the tube.

"Diamonds and gold," Kirrik said breathlessly. "Doesn't get much better than that."

"Hey boss, what is this stuff?" Sarep called out from the southern side of the chamber. He had managed to loose a hunk of the pink crystal and he held it up in his palm.

"It's morganite," Red called out.

"No," Tareggh said quickly. "Morganite is a peachy-pink crystal. This is different." Tareggh and Kirrik moved over to take a closer look.

"Rubellite Tourmaline then?" Red guessed.

"No," Flint answered. "This crystal is far too pink. Rubellite Tourmaline, is a much deeper red."

"Could be tugtupite," Kirrik said as they came in close and inspected the deep pink crystals.

"That sounds right," Tareggh said as he took the hunk of crystal in his hand and held it up to the lantern light. The hunk of crystal was felt warm in his hand as he brought it up to inspect it. "It has the right color, the correct sheen on the outside." Tareggh cocked his head to the side and twisted the crystals around. "Now that is different," he said. "The translucency is wrong. Tugtupite is not like this at all. The color is right, but I can see into the center of these crystals with just the lantern light. If it was tugtupite, I wouldn't be able to do that."

"Well, whatever it is, I found it, so I get to name it if it is new!" Sarep said as he yanked the crystal back from Tareggh and placed it into his satchel.

Tareggh shrugged. "Fine, you take the pink rock. I'll claim the diamonds and gold."

They all shared a laugh and then Tareggh ordered them to work. They were to fill their packs with as much as they could carry and take it back tonight as proof they had found a new, promising mine for Roegudok Hall.

Kirrik pulled out his powder and other ingredients, setting them near the passageway leading out from the chamber. He ignored Tareggh's joke about Kirrik blowing the mine shut and sealing them inside to keep the treasure for themselves and picked up tools to start helping.

He moved to the north wall, but Tareggh was more than handling the gold vein while Flint crawled into the lava tube a ways and was gathering diamonds. Kirrik moved to one of the columns that had formed when a stalactite and stalagmite met, and started pulling the strange pink crystal out from it.

A cool breeze howled up from the lava tube that Flint was in, circling around the chamber and chilling Kirrik.

"Whew!" Flint said as he covered his nose. "Smells like sulfur!"

"Just don't go falling into the tube with my diamonds," Tareggh called out.

Flint laughed.

Kirrik looked up to Flint to make a funny face, making fun of the boss, but as he did so, he caught a glimpse of something beyond Flint, like a strange shadow lurking just out of sight. He pointed to it and was about to say something when Flint folded in half, let out a gargled groan, and was pulled back into the tube.

"FLINT!" Kirrik shouted.

Tareggh turned a warning green eye on Kirrik, but Kirrik pointed to the tube with a trembling hand while he raised his pickaxe in the other.

Tareggh moved toward the tube, but Red called out from the back of the chamber.

"Tareggh, get away, something is there!" he shouted.

Tareggh rolled away just as a two foot long, white claw struck out from the tube and stabbed into the wall next to where the crew leader had just been.

"For Flint!" Tareggh shouted as he leapt up to his feet

and swung his pickaxe. He hit the claw with perfect precision, but the metal tool ricocheted off and Tareggh staggered back. A hideous figure emerged from the tube.

It walked upon four legs shielded by a black exoskeleton. The back was covered by thick, wavy black fur. Two long arms stuck out from the top of the body, each tipped with a single white claw. It arched its front portion up, exposing an underbelly covered in rectangular, black scales and displaying its grotesque face. Two massive, spider-like mandibles unfolded to reveal a gaping mouth filled with circular rows of sharp fangs.

The beast snarled and stepped forward at an alarming speed, its claws and feet scratching the stone floor. Tareggh moved in and slammed his pickaxe into the monster's chest. The force of the blow was barely enough to penetrate the thick scales. The pick went in a couple of inches, but it was obviously not enough to do any real damage.

A split second later a white claw cut Tareggh in half at the waist.

Kirrik ran back for his powder, hoping he could create a mixture that would either kill, or scare the beast away.

Sarep and Red might have tried to run, but the beast went directly for them. A claw reached in, severing Sarep's satchel and pulling the pink crystal out as it snarled ferociously. Red jumped in, swinging at the monster's face, but the creature was too quick. It sidestepped Red and came up with a devastating kick to Red's chest that sent him flying away.

Sarep swung his pickaxe, but the creature leapt back, easily avoiding the attack. It then opened its mouth and spat a thick, sizzling gob of black ooze at Sarep. It hit the unlucky dwarf in the face and he cried out in pain as smoke rose from the goo and Sarep fell to his knees. The creature lunged in, thrusting the point of one claw through Sarep's chest.

Kirrik forced himself to concentrate as he mixed powder and prepared a short fuse. He finished one explosive just as the creature started to eat Sarep's corpse with sick, smacking sounds as bones broke and sinew was chewed. Kirrik lit the fuse and threw the weapon.

"Red, get down!" Kirrik shouted.

The beast looked up just as the explosive reached it and went off. A blinding flash of light erupted and the chamber echoed with a deafening boom. The creature shrieked and fell to the ground.

Kirrik smiled, but as the smoke cleared, he saw that the creature was not dead. There was a smoking hole in its side, and one of its four legs had been blown off, but the creature seemed to ignore the wound as it stood back up and howled at Kirrik.

It came speeding toward him.

Kirrik fumbled with the powder.

Red rushed in, yelling and jumping with a mighty swing that punctured deep into the creature's back. It screamed and arched upward toward the ceiling. Then, it leapt up, clinging to the ceiling and shaking Red from its back.

A thick mess of yellow gunk coated Red's pickaxe, but now the creature was cautious, scurrying away and snarling at the two dwarves.

"Hit is again!" Red yelled. "I'll keep it busy."

Kirrik put his head down and focused. Soon he made two more bombs. He could hear Red shouting and cursing at the beast as it snarled and lunged at him. Kirrik stuck the fuses in and prepared to throw one. "Move!" Kirrik yelled.

He stood to throw the bomb and saw Red's last moments as the beast dropped from the ceiling and drove both claws through Red. Then the creature looked to Kirrik and made a noise that almost sounded like laughter. Kirrik lit the bomb and threw it.

He didn't wait to see if it hit its mark. He had to act fast if he was going to stop the monster from escaping this chamber. If it had been sealed in here by the stone wall, then odds were it couldn't dig out. So, Kirrik did the only thing he could think of. He mixed all of his powder in the three containers and prepared one large bomb.

The explosion rocked the chamber. Shards of stone

flew around, bouncing dangerously off the walls, but Kirrik didn't slow. He didn't look up either. The screeching scrapes along the ground were enough to tell him the beast lived through the second bomb. Worse than that, it was coming for him.

The snarling grew louder and the seconds slowed while Kirrik's hands furiously worked the last bits of powder. He popped the fuse and lit it. He picked up the three containers, hugging them tightly to his chest. He didn't have any special casing to hold the bomb in place this time.

He was going to have to do that himself.

Kirrik leapt up onto the large bottom half of the boulder he had blown apart, drawing the creature closer to himself. Then, a moment before the fuse reached the powder, he turned and leapt into the hole. He felt something sharp rip through his back as the creature caught him, and then there was a flash of light and a terrible, thunderous explosion that shook the entire mine shaft. Hunks of rock and great granite slabs fell into the cavern, sealing the chamber, and closing off the tunnel for fifty yards beyond.

CHAPTER 7

Year 3,711 Age of Demigods, Mid-Summer.
2nd year of the reign of Aldehenkaru'hktanah Sit'marihu, 13th King of Roegudok Hall.

Al's cavedog moved almost effortlessly through the winding tunnels as he led the rescue group down to shaft thirty-seven. The explosion had been felt all the way up in the throne room. He had called for a group of volunteers moments after, but he had little hope in his heart that he would find anyone alive. Even the miners that had been on their way to replace Tareggh and his crew told Al it was a hopeless effort. They had been a quarter mile outside of shaft thirty-seven and they had still been assaulted with a wave of heat that coated them in dust from the explosion.

Still, Al was king. He could not sit idly by while others did work he felt he should be doing. After all, it was his command that had sent the crew down to the mine in the first place. In his mind he recalled the wreckage at Valtuu Temple. They had needed to dig out survivors there as well after the battle with Tu'luh. Yet, there *were* survivors. That was why Al was not about to waste precious moments. If he could get there and start the work faster by riding upon a cavedog, then perhaps it could make the difference between life and death for one of the trapped miners.

His determination burned hot as he and the others reached the point of the cave-in. Al leapt off from his cavedog and started calling out to the rescue group.

"Split into two groups. Fifteen of you will work the rubble. Clear it away as quickly as possible." Al turned to the cavedog riders farther to the back of the group. "You fifteen take the loose rocks and boulders out so we can clear a path. Let's get on it!"

Al moved in with the rest of them, pulling rocks free from higher up on a sloped pile and handing them down to the other dwarves that would shuttle the removed stone away from the cave-in site. It was hard, sweaty work, but none of the dwarves complained. They moved in perfect harmony with each other. The diggers grabbed the rocks and pivoted at the waist, hardly looking before they set them into hands already outstretched and waiting to take the stone away and pile it along the sides out of the way.

They worked for hours before the other mining crew arrived on foot. They dutifully moved in without being told where to assist and started adding their efforts to the rescue crew's own efforts. With the extra hands to help, it only took another ninety minutes before they cleared enough stone away to find the blast marks on the left side of the wall.

"Looks like they found another chamber," one of the miners said as they turned their attention to the charred hole.

Al moved through the others, taking a closer look. He saw dark brown spots on some of the stone. He knew at once that this was where the other miners had been.

"Hello?" Al called out as he pressed his face close in to the blocked passageway.

No answer came.

Al shook his head and smacked the wall with his fist.

"Shall we keep digging, sire?" one of the rescuers asked.

Al nodded. The others began removing rocks while Al moved to the back of the group and took a drink from the canteen hanging from his cavedog's saddle. "What next?" he grumbled to himself in a low whisper. "Empty mines, dry wells, emigrating dwarves that would prefer to live on the surface than under my rule, and now dead miners."

Al hung the canteen back onto his saddle and took in a deep breath of musty air.

"It isn't your fault," someone said.

Al turned around, but all of the dwarves were busy hauling stone away from the passageway.

The voice came again, more faintly this time. "It's not your fault."

Al looked up the tunnel, but no one was there except for the rescuers and miners.

"You are destined to find the Wealth of Kings," the voice said in a soft whisper.

Al spun around. *What in Hammenfein's name is going on?*

The voice disappeared without another word.

"You alright my lord?" one of the miners said as he walked by carrying a hefty boulder half again as large as he was.

Al nodded and wiped a hand over his face. "Just a bit tired," he answered.

"Well, take a rest then, Sire. We can manage."

Al shook his head. "That isn't the kind of king I wish to be," he said as he walked back to the blocked passageway.

He bent down and pulled a massive, oblong boulder out from the pile. He rolled it away carefully, letting the rough edges slam down to stop its own momentum before other dwarves hauled it away. He then pulled a black sphere of stone and tossed it to another dwarf. He continued working the front of the line until they broke through the passageway.

"By Icadion's beard," Al muttered as he broke through to see a large chamber. There were bags on the ground with gems and crystals spilling out of them. Unrefined hunks of gold and hunks of diamond sat on the ground on the northern side. Pickaxes littered the ground. But, there were no bodies.

Al turned around to face the others and shook his head. That was when he saw a streak of blood stretching across the wall beyond the charred stone. He pointed to it. "Can an explosion make the other miners disappear?" Al asked.

The mining crew entered the chamber and began

looking around.

One of them bent low, picking up a ragged piece of canvas. He smelled it and then looked to the blood on the wall. "I'm not sure what to make of it, sire, but there should be..."

"Should be what?" Al pressed.

The miner held up the ragged cloth. "Pieces," he said flatly. "Not to be crude, but the explosion should have left evidence of the others." He then shook his head and pointed around the chamber.

"I have blood here," another miner called out.

"I found some here too," said a third.

"Sire, over here!" another called out.

Al moved around a column to see a dwarf squatting inside of a lava tube. "What is it?"

"Blood, a lot of it." The dwarf turned and pointed to the bottom of the tube, slowly tracing a line with his hand and turning to point at the back of the tube. "There is a wide trail of blood that goes back down the tube." Then the dwarf pointed up. "Diamonds too," he added. "A big vein of gold off to the outside of this chute as well."

"Come out of there," Al said quickly. The miner did as he was told.

Without warning, Al's cavedog sprinted into the tunnel and started making clicking noises. Its pink, forked tongue flicked in and out as it licked the air and its muscles tensed. Then, the animal did something that Al didn't know a cavedog could do. It made a guttural sound that was something between a bird's cry and a snarl. All of the other cavedogs filtered into the chamber around the dwarves and formed a defensive wall between Al and the lava tube. Two of the cavedogs even pushed the miner farther away from the tube's opening.

"What are they doing?" one of the rescuers asked.

Al shook his head. "I haven't the faintest idea, but it seems they believe there is danger coming from that tube."

"They might be right, judging by the blood we see around the chamber," the miner with the piece of cloth said.

"I'm no expert with war, but if there is something in that tunnel, I could seal it off with explosives. My bet is that's what the others tried to do when they were attacked."

"Attacked by what?" Al asked. "There isn't anything down here but stone."

"With respect, sire, that isn't entirely true, if you believe the legends."

Al turned a curious eye on the miner. "Why would the others blow the tunnel while they were still in it?"

The miner sniffed the cloth again and shook his head. "I'm not for knowing that," he said. "But, I can tell you that Kirrik was one of the best explosives engineers we have ever produced. If his powder was set to detonate, you can be sure he did it on purpose."

"Could have been an accident," one of the rescuers put in.

"Ha!" the miner said. "Kirrik wouldn't accidentally set off his explosives even if he was sleeping with a torch in one hand and a bomb in the other. No, he set it on purpose."

Al sighed and moved toward the lava tube. The cavedogs fought against him, blocking his path and trying to push him back, but he pushed through all the same. He jumped up into the tube, followed a half second later by his cavedog.

"Stubborn lizard," Al snarked.

The lizard made a clicking noise in its throat and its tail went rigid as it zipped around Al and stared down the tube. Al shuffled forward, and put a hand on the wall to steady himself as he leaned over the edge. The light the others brought into the chamber was enough to penetrate a few feet of the darkness as the tube dropped into oblivion below. Al saw streaks of dried blood and knew that there had been something in the tube. He reached down and patted his cavedog on the head.

"Stubborn, but smart," he said as he offered the creature a smile. It didn't look at him. It kept its eyes on the darkness below and remained still. Not until Al was safely buffered by the other cavedogs did Al's lizard come out of the tube.

The others waited quietly for Al's assessment.

Al looked around the chamber. There was wealth to be had in here, but not enough to risk dying for. "Gather up the diamonds and other treasure they found and move it into the main shaft. Once that is done, blow the lava tube shut." Al pointed to the passageway. "Then start piling those stones in here and seal this place off. Hopefully the blast you drop in the tube will kill whatever it was. If not, then we will bury it inside."

The others hopped to work without a word. It took them little more than ten minutes to gather all of the gems and gold. What struck Al, though, was the fact that none of the cavedogs moved from their defensive positions in front of the lava tube. Whatever it was, cavedogs could sense it, and they hated it.

Even when they prepared to blow the tube, the cavedogs stayed in place.

The explosives expert, Rupit, pulled several long, cylindrical bombs and wound their fuses together. Unlike Al, he was not quite strong enough to push through the cavedogs and get into the lava tube, so he lit the fuse and then tossed the bomb to the back of the tube. It bounced off the back wall and then the sizzling sound faded as it descended into the mountain's depths.

"Back up," Rupit said as he hurried back through the throng of angry lizards.

Seven seconds later an explosion erupted and the tube was illuminated with hot, yellow and red light. A wave of smoke and dust blew out from the tube, shooting over the cavedogs and settling slowly in the chamber. That was immediately followed by a rumbling tremor as rocks clacked and smashed into each other deep within the tube.

"One more time?" Rupit asked.

Al looked to the cavedogs. They still stood rigid, guarding the dwarves. The king nodded. If the cavedogs still sensed danger, then best to be safe.

Rupit repeated the process, gathering several bombs together. "You all might want to go out and take shelter for this one," he said matter-of-factly. Everyone left but Al, who stood in the passageway so he could watch from behind cover.

Rupit lit the bomb and tossed it in. This time he didn't meander through the cavedogs to get away. He ran and hopped around them, scurrying for cover. He made it to the passageway with time to spare. Al was about to ask him why he had run, but the answer roared through the tube a moment later as flames and shards of rock exploded out and sprayed into the chamber.

Al ducked back, pushing Rupit out into the main shaft as a great quake shook the ground. Dust fell from the ceiling and everyone held their breath until the shaking stopped and the dust settled.

"I think that did the trick," Rupit said.

Al slowly inched back into the chamber and saw that the cavedogs were now filtering out into the hall as well. The lava tube was sealed, entirely caved-in. He smiled and nodded. "Alright, let's set the miners to work in here on extracting everything we can from that gold vein. Once this chamber is dry, then use this as a place to stack the stone from the main tunnel while we continue to expand down the original mine. I want a guard set as well, just to be on the safe side."

"Sire?" one of the miners asked.

Al pointed to the bags of wealth. "This will help, but it won't solve our food shortage problem. I need this mine cleared. However, if the cavedogs can sense whatever attacked the others, then the answer is to assign soldiers with cavedogs to each mining unit. That should ensure safety while also keeping our mining operations going at full capacity. Also, none of you are to speak of this. I don't want hysteria running through the mountain."

The miner nodded, but what else was he going to say to the king?

Al counted out ten soldiers from the rescue party and

sent them up to the main hall with the bags of treasure, and with orders for Benbo to set up proper shifts for guards in each of the open mines. The other twenty stayed to watch over the current miners, as their shift wasn't set to end for a few more days.

"I'll send some runners down with extra food and provisions," Al promised as he saddled his cavedog and started his way back to his chamber.

He felt confident that the cavedogs would make short work of anything that would dare come out of the depths again. Now he needed to solve the riddle of the Wealth of Kings. He needed a space to think. There was a balcony adjoined to his bedchamber that overlooked much of the valley beyond. It was peaceful and, best of all, secluded from any visitors or advisors.

*****

Hiasyntar'Kulai moved his tired wings just enough to maintain his altitude as he soared high above a deep chasm that scarred the land between great, forbidding mountains covered in lush vegetation and teeming with animal life. He followed the canyon's path for several minutes, propelling himself quickly over a dozen miles.

As he banked to the north and soared over the top of a rocky cliff, his eyes caught sight of a sparkling in the distance. It was hard to see at first, but the sunlight reflected off of it so brightly that he was sure he had finally reached his destination.

A large spire was the first shape Hiasyntar'Kulai made out clearly. It was green, with golden trim shining in the sunlight. Even with all the wonders the golden dragon had seen, this was his favorite construct in all of Terramyr, for it reminded him of his home on Kendualdern. As he flew up over another small incline that broke out into a wide plateau, the dragon roared and smiled at the magnificent castle of green glass before him. There were no walls around the structure, but the castle's keep itself rose up into the sky more than fifty feet.

The tops of the pointed towers ascended many stories higher still, with golden crests that reflected the sunlight with a fiery intensity that warmed the golden dragon's heart.

He flew to the castle and stopped to land in front of the grand double doors that boasted hinges made of solid gold. A long handle bar was affixed vertically to each door and was made of the same, bright yellow gold as the hinges. However, the gold was not what the dragon admired most. Of course the gold called to him, singing its healing melody, but it was the clear sheets of thick glass that he appreciated the most, for they were formed from a special crystal that added its song to the gold and literally invigorated the mighty dragon with its melodies. From a distance the glass appeared green, but that was only because each sheet of glass was so thick that the crystal panes appeared green if viewed from specific angles.

The dragon closed his eyes and a golden sphere of light enveloped him. He felt the strange, tickling sensation as his body shrank down into a human-like form. He was not human, but he had the power to assume a smaller shape while in this particular palace.

As he opened the doors with a wave of his hands and passed beyond the doorway, the doors swung shut, creating a vibration through the hallway that was felt reverberating through his chest.

From the inside, the glass was so thick that he could only see through one wall at a time, meaning that rooms deeper within the palace were hidden by a screen of beautiful green. There were no lamps, torches, or candles. The palace itself radiated with its own light.

He was surrounded by many people, or spirits rather, as they were all dead. Being a dragon, he could see the ghosts easily. They were all dressed in fine silk robes of white, red, green, blue, and yellow. They were all busy walking through the palace, some carrying books, others engaged in deep conversation. However, when they noticed him, they all stopped and looked at him expectantly.

"Go on about your business," Hiasyntar'Kulai

instructed. "I have matters to tend to down below."

The spirits obeyed silently, moving into rooms filled with bookshelves lined with books and scrolls, or sitting at tables as they continued their conversations. The dragon watched some of the people gather inside of a small room and grab a couple of books from the shelves. Then, the dragon saw the old, familiar light blue energy flowing through the glass, humming sweetly and creating additional light within the room where the spirits were reading from the books.

Hiasyntar'Kulai began to walk again, but was stopped by a stout dwarf spirit.

"My king," the dwarf greeted. "There have been stirrings in Roegudok Hall. Might I be permitted to go and lend aid to the king of the mountain?"

The dragon nodded slowly. "See that you do not interfere more than is necessary. We can whisper words of aid and subtly guide, but we cannot intervene in the lives of mortals."

The dwarf spirit nodded. "As you say, my king."

Hiasyntar'Kulai watched as the spirit of Al's father walked away quickly, disappearing around a corner. The dragon smiled then. The dwarves had had a long disconnect from the Ancients, but things were being put back together now. The Father of the Ancients felt a burgeoning hope that everything would work out in the end.

His mind returned to the current dilemma of finding the addorite. He knew he could go to Roegudok Hall and request the dwarves to look for it, but he wanted to spare them that fate if possible. If he could find the addorite Tu'luh had stolen, then at least he would have something to work with without risking the dwarves. He turned down the first corridor on the right. He walked for several hundred feet, passing chambers and rooms on either side of the hallway. As he glanced through the glass he saw groups, or sometimes individuals, deep in study. At the end of the hallway, he opened a door that led to a stairway spiraling down into the ground.

As he descended the stairs, the light from the light

blue energy flowed through the walls, the stairs, and the ceiling above to illuminate the area. That was why the dragon liked the crystal from which he had formed the glass slabs that made the palace. It was a perfect conduit for the energy that flowed through the palace, offering not only light, but actual wisdom and knowledge to those who sought it.

He descended deep into the mountain. The air remained warm and dry as he walked downward for nearly thirty minutes before finally reaching the bottom. He put his hands on the door, which had so much energy flowing through it that it appeared nearly solidly blue in color, and pushed it open.

The door moved silently as it glided open.

His eyes were assaulted by an exceedingly bright light, far whiter than anything he had experienced elsewhere on Terramyr. He raised his arms up to shield himself from the brightness while at the same time he felt an inviting warmth wrap around him.

He walked through the doorway and heard a powerful roar. He moved his arms enough to peer around them while still trying to adjust to the light. The giant chamber was so large that he could not see any walls except the one behind him. About thirty feet in front of him stood a massive dragon. Its legs were blue and gray. Its snout was covered in shiny scales that only accentuated the sharp fangs protruding out from under the lips. A thick pair of horns grew up and back from the rear of the skull, ending in sharp points that would put any spear to shame.

The dragon growled, but not in a menacing or threatening way. Then it turned aside and bowed its head.

"Garek, nice to see you again. Still keeping watch?"

The bowing dragon replied with a simple, "As always, my king."

There were dozens of dragons. All shapes and sizes mixed in together in the giant, seemingly endless chamber. There were blue and red skytes darting about through the air like sparrows. There were wingless drakes that walked upon all fours and breathed fire and wisps of smoke. There were greater drakes that had wings, larger dragons, and then there was a group far in the distance that appeared to be as large, or much larger, than Tu'luh the Red, but none were as large as Hiasyntar'Kulai's dragon form.

Hiasyntar'Kulai moved further into the chamber and transformed back into his natural form. He beheld the hundreds of dragons all bowing to him and addressed them in his loud, booming voice of thunder. "My fellow dragon-kin, over the last five centuries, we have been here, unraveling very threads of time and fate, interpreting them and creating prophecies of the future. Now that Nagar's Blight is no more hanging upon the Middle Kingdom, it is time to return to our full capacity. I would have you again spreading out through the world and giving your dreams and visions to good men and women who would use the knowledge for the betterment of Terramyr."

A mighty chorus of roaring dragons shook the chamber.

Hiasyntar'Kulai tapped his talon on the stone floor and then there was silence. "I will select three of you for a special assignment. Tu'luh has committed yet another crime against us. He has stolen addorite that was hidden away in Valtuu Temple. You all know how important that substance is for what we need to do. I ask for three volunteers who will search for a tribe of goblins who have taken the addorite from Tu'luh and hidden it deep within a network of caves far to the west. The rest of you shall resume the duties you performed centuries ago, helping to guide the mortals of Terramyr."

The first three dragon spirits to volunteer were given a vision of the conversation with Tu'luh and sent out to discover whether any of the addorite remained.

The rest of the dragons launched into the air and flew up through the high ceiling, disappearing from view and resuming their sacred work of guiding the blessed races created by Icadion and the Old Gods.

Hiasyntar'Kulai watched the great dragons leave, and

then he turned to the drakes and wingless dragons still in the chamber with him. He set them to be messengers and laborers throughout the palace, a station which they had occupied prior to the existence of Nagar's Blight.

Then he turned to his left and moved toward the far wall. He blew on the glass and the blue energy rippled through the wall until there appeared a doorway large enough for him to walk through. He entered his secret chamber where he read the signs and omens of the stars to help understand the future.

There, upon a black pedestal of stone sat The Infinium.

Hiasyntar'Kulai felt a nagging, persistent sadness whenever he saw the book, for he had personally known its author. The Aurorean, a dragon composed entirely of light that always shifted and changed, and who had held the total sum of wisdom and knowledge known by any being in the universe. He was the one who wrote The Infinium. The Aurorean was also the creator of all dragon kind. As mighty and powerful as Hiasyntar'Kulai was, he considered himself as nothing compared to The Aurorean.

He approached the book and sighed. The Aurorean had written it so that others might know the secrets of the universe. How it works, how it can be controlled, and how it can be saved. The problem, was Hiasyntar'Kulai had read all he could without suffering the damaging effects of its power. He opened the cover carefully with one of his talons. The blue light in the room intensified even more, sending actual tendrils out from the walls of the chamber to flow into him as he scanned the first two pages.

A green vapor rose up from the book and then formed into a thin, string-like column of light that waved and danced under the dragon's breath. A spark emerged at the top of the string of light. A second string, this one of violet light, extended out. A third one soon appeared and glowed bright orange. Hiasyntar'Kulai watched in wonder as four more limbs grew out from the spark. Each of the limbs was a brilliant color, and they shifted and danced in a slow, methodical rhythm. He watched for several moments, admiring the sliver of self that The Aurorean had managed to put into The Infinium, and then he closed the book.

"We must find the addorite," he said aloud. "Otherwise, I shall need to command the dwarves to reopen the mines, and that will only bring them death."

Unbeknownst to him, the stirring in Roegudok Hall mentioned by Al's father's spirit, was created by the fact that the dwarves were already doing just that, unaware of the dangers it would bring down upon them.

*****

Al stood on the jagged balcony overlooking the plains to the north and took in a deep breath of fresh, mountain air. Between the many meetings over the last several days and then the rescue operation that yielded some treasure, but was ultimately unsuccessful in saving any of the miners in shaft thirty-seven, he needed out. The weight of the crown was wearing on him.

Roegudok Hall was bustling with activity now. There was a lot of restructuring to do. There were vacancies to fill in the court, trade routes that needed to be reestablished, and mining to be started. Al took in another breath of air.

There was also the accident.

He had to settle that, and quickly.

The only problem was he wasn't sure what to do about it. The dwarves needed someone with more experience. They needed his father back. The dwarf king sighed and turned away from the view. He knew he had stayed out too long already. He needed to return to his duties. Chief among those duties was the riddle of the Wealth of Kings. If only he could solve that, then all of his problems would be solved.

That's when Al saw him.

A stranger standing between Al and the doorway that led back into the mountain.

He wore a green, shimmering robe and carried a long

spear. Al was put on edge immediately. How could a human have found him here? The tunnel was a secret that ran straight to this stone balcony from the king's chambers. No dwarf would be caught dead allowing a human to walk around freely through those areas.

That could only mean one thing.

An assassin.

Al pulled his war ax and held it up. "You won't find me an easy mark," Al warned.

The stranger held up his left hand and said, "I am not your enemy. I have come seeking knowledge." The voice was extremely nasal, which annoyed Al almost as much, or perhaps more than the stranger's presence.

"The court is where I consult with visitors, after the councilors deem the visitor worth talking to," Al said grumbling as much about the process of vetting a visitor in the stuffy court as he was protesting the stranger's request.

The stranger locked his fierce, blue eyes with Al. For a moment, Al couldn't move. His mind froze in mid-thought and his muscles remained still and calm as those light blue eyes held him in their trance. Then, a few seconds later, Al was released from the spell, and the stranger was gone.

Al pulled his axe and looked around.

His heart was racing and there was a dull ringing in his head.

Who was that, and what in the blazes of Hammenfein did he want?

Al rushed into his room and shut the door to the tunnel leading out to the balcony. He slipped the bolt into place and then went to his desk. Had the stranger been looking for the Wealth of Kings? Al breathed a sigh of relief as soon as he saw that all was as he had left it.

Still, having an intruder meet him on the balcony was beyond unnerving.

He went to the door and opened it.

The two guards outside saluted him silently.

"Did you let anyone through?" Al asked.

The two guards shared a puzzled look and then shook their heads.

"Nobody's been in there but you, my king," they said in unison.

"Go and get Alferug. I need his advice about..." About what? He wasn't even sure what had been down in the depths of mine shaft thirty-seven.

"'About', Sire?" one of the guards prompted.

"Just tell him to find the best bestiary for the Middle Kingdom and bring it to my chamber."

Al shut the door and went back to his desk. He poured over the books and clues about the Wealth of Kings once more. Nothing new jumped out at him. Worse than that, he hadn't found this secret book that Sylus mentioned in the faded note. At least some treasure had been found in mine thirty-seven. There had been enough there to buy provisions to help through the summer, but not enough to fully alleviate the problems facing Roegudok Hall.

The dwarf king lost himself in thoughts and theories about the Wealth of Kings. How could he get into the library again? As he thought about everything he had ever heard about it, he remembered the voice from the tunnel.

The words it spoke were perplexing to Al. First and foremost because it seemed a ghost had been talking to him, but also because of what the voice had said specifically. It hadn't said that Al was destined to reopen the library, which he assumed was the Wealth of Kings. It had said that Al was destined to find the Wealth of Kings. That made it sound as if the Wealth of Kings was not the library at all, but something else.

Could Threnton have been right all those years ago when he dragged me to the mines looking for the Wealth of Kings? Al wondered. Might there be some tunnel overflowing with riches? Is that what Sylus had hidden down below that had been the source of his prosperity? If so, then why hide it?

Knuckles rapped on the door three times. "Sire, you called for me?" Alferug's voice called out from the other side of the door.

"It's open," Al said.

Alferug pressed the door open and closed it behind himself. Al noticed that he was breathing a little heavier than usual, and his legs seemed stiff as he walked.

"Are you alright?" Al asked.

Alferug nodded and waved the question away. "Just age catching up with me, Sire. I'm afraid the trek up to your chamber is not as easy as it once was."

Al frowned.

The counselor pulled out a thick, brown book from a leather satchel hanging by a strap over his left shoulder. "I heard you found some treasure, but that the other miners were killed by something?"

"I asked them to keep it quiet," Al said.

Alferug nodded. "My nephew told me. He was one of the soldiers that accompanied you on the rescue mission. I doubt he will tell anyone else. He probably figured I needed to know."

Al shrugged. "Your nephew tells you, the others tell their families. Sooner or later it will come out, I suppose."

"He told me how you sealed the tube and set guards. The people will see you are doing the right things. We need treasure to fuel our economy, and we have guards now to protect the miners. It seems reasonable."

Al shook his head. "Nothing was reasonable about it." The king rubbed a hand over his weary eyes. "There was no trace of what attacked them. There were streaks of blood, but that was it. No clothing, no body parts. Nothing. Just pick axes and what they had managed to mine before they were attacked."

Alferug grunted thoughtfully and stroked his beard as he moved to lean against the desk. Al quickly pointed to the chair at the desk and Alferug nodded his thanks as he sat down. "I am afraid there isn't much in the bestiary that will help."

"Nothing about creatures that live in the

underground?"

Alferug set the book on the desk. "Plenty about that," he corrected. "I have a list of terrible creatures as well as some that are friendly to elves and dwarves. However, all accounts say that the depths below Roegudok Hall are a special place. None of the creatures listed in the bestiary can survive here. The one exception being cavedogs, of course. So, unless they smelled wild cavedogs, I am not sure what your animals found down there."

"Something provoked them," Al said. "They were as wary as if we were marching into battle. You could see it in their eyes, and the way they moved. They were ready to fight."

"It is a mystery I cannot solve, I am afraid."

Al nodded and sighed. "Then I hope the guards are enough," he said.

Alferug changed the subject. "What did you find in the way of treasure?"

"Diamonds, and a modest vein of gold ore."

"That is impressive," Alferug said. "Enough to help?"

Al nodded. "For a while. It wasn't a very large amount, and certainly won't go as far as six fully productive mines would in buying food for the winter and helping us get Roegudok Hall running properly again."

"It will come," Alferug assured him with a soft smile. "Every king has challenges to face, my lord. In fact, only the best of kings are given so much adversity in their days. Only under the weight of challenges can you become the great king you are destined to be. It's like producing a diamond. Without pressure, there is no gem."

Al shook his head. "My father was a far better king than I could ever hope to be, and he never had to face things like this."

Alferug shrugged. "One cannot know the plans of fate until they have traveled along the winding path," he said, quoting an ancient elvish proverb.

"Do you think the creature might have attacked because it is drawn to treasure?" Al asked, changing the subject to something more comfortable.

Alferug stroked his beard and hummed again for a moment before nodding slowly. "You know, that might be the case. From my knowledge of Ancients I have learned a great deal about dragons. For instance, did you know that precious stones and metal actually help them heal and reenergize? Most humans think dragons hoard treasure because of greed, but it isn't as shallow as that," Alferug said with a dismissive wave of his hand. "A dragon hoards wealth because he can regenerate while sleeping inside of it. The metals and gems actually sing to the dragon's soul. It heals not only physical, but magical and emotional wounds. It is conceivable that another creature may also seek treasure for a similar purpose."

Al nodded. "Perhaps that is why it attacked them. They were taking its treasure."

"You found no sign of the creature?" Alferug inquired.

Al shook his head. "None."

Alferug held up a finger and wiggled his head as he cleared his throat and then ultimately said, "Then I don't think it wants the treasure. If it did, it would have taken the wealth the miners dug up, but you say everything of value was still there."

"Yes, it was just lying on the ground. There was one bag that was lying on its side and empty, but I assumed it had always been empty for inside there was only a fine, pink dust. As if gems had been there before they started mining in the chamber and he hadn't yet filled the bag."

"Pink dust you say?" Alferug asked. "But there were no red or pink gems found?"

Al shook his head. "No. There was nothing pink in the chamber. Why do you ask?"

Alferug shrugged. "It may be nothing, but if all the other bags you found had something inside, but this last one had only pink dust, perhaps it did have something that the creature wanted. Maybe that is what it took, and it left the rest of the treasure in the chamber because it had no use for it."

CHAPTER 8

Year 3,407 King's Era.
207th year of the reign of Sylus Magdinium, 5th King of Roegudok Hall.

"So this is it," King Sylus said as he moved into the rounded tunnel sparkling with pink crystal formations growing upon several columns and walls.

"We have guards stationed in each mine, just like you asked," a stout dwarf officer said.

Sylus nodded and moved past him to break off one of the pink crystals jutting out from the column. The addorite felt warm to the touch. He turned and one of the miners held a large lantern up for the king. Sylus put the addorite close to the light and smiled. "Yes, this is it. A good find."

"We have mined forty pounds of the crystal just today," Didger said as he moved into the chamber and brushed his dusty hands on his stained, brown coveralls.

"Good," Sylus said. "Tu'luh wants us to send one hundred pounds to Valtuu Temple."

"Ah, we have much more than that, I assure you. You had better ask him where it all goes. Or, see if he would let us sell some of it."

Sylus shook his head. "Tu'luh was explicit. None of it goes to market. He said the addorite can be toxic to humans and elves if not handled properly."

Didger sighed and shrugged. "As you wish."

Sylus turned and tossed the bit of crystal into an open

basket and then moved in to inspect the rest of the chamber. In his estimation, there was easily half a ton of addorite, and that was just what he could see. If any more of it was hidden within the walls, then there would be a great payload for Tu'luh to take to Valtuu Temple.

"Any more attacks?" Sylus asked Didger as he slid a hand along the western wall of the rounded chamber.

Didger nodded. "We had one a couple days ago. More of those cursed lurkers. They are swift and deadly buggers, but we put them down."

"Not without loss on our side," the stout officer put in as he approached. "Two cavedogs and three soldiers. One miner was stabbed in the shoulder by one of the lurkers, but he should pull through after some time in the hospital."

Sylus nodded. He hated lurkers. Over the last several years since the first attack there had been several encounters. It was as if the addorite attracted them. The king studied this chamber once more, scanning the walls and ceiling for any sign of chutes or lava tubes that would let a lurker into the area.

"Don't worry, my king," Didger said. "When we found this section, we made sure there was no other way in. No lurker is getting in here except through the main tunnel, and we have sealed off all other known tubes in the area."

"Triple the guard," Sylus told the officer. "This is the most addorite we have seen. If we are right about the lurkers being attracted to the crystal, then I would expect them to try and come for it."

The officer nodded dutifully and turned to send a runner up for reinforcements.

"Now would be a good time to lay down some tracks," Didger suggested. "We could run carts up the tunnels."

Sylus shook his head. "From what I have seen, the cavedogs can sense when lurkers are in nearby tunnels. A system of tracks would take up most of the tunnel's width, and make it harder for the cavedogs to freely move. Let's stick with handcarts. Alternatively, we can bring more cavedogs down and those that aren't used to guard the mines can run bags of addorite up and down the shafts. They can move it faster than handcarts would in any case."

"As you say," Didger said with a respectful nod.

Sylus remained in the chamber for twenty more minutes, watching the miners work and ensuring that there was not going to be an attack. Should any more lurkers show themselves, he wanted to be there to personally send them to Hammenfein. His hands went down and slid over the handles of his twin knives. Despite his uneasiness, the workers continued to chip away at the stone with a rhythmic *ting-ting-ting*. Nothing attacked them. Even the cavedogs seemed at ease, most of them lying lazily on the stone floor and taking the opportunity to snooze.

So why couldn't he shake the uneasiness rising in his stomach like a churning knot of bile?

Sylus decided he would stay longer than originally planned. He had spent too much time on the battlefield to distrust his gut. He began to pace around the chamber. Some of the other dwarves glanced uneasily at him as he walked by. It was obvious that they could sense his wariness.

Good. It will keep them on edge in case I am right.

Sylus inspected the walls, placing a hand on the hard surface every few steps and feeling for… feeling for what? Did he expect the rock to tell him of impending danger? No, that wasn't it. He was looking for something. Perhaps there was a section of the wall that was thin. Maybe the miners would break through to another chamber, and there they would find lurkers.

Yet, every place he inspected the wall, the vibrations from the ceaseless pickaxes striking the stone was faint, hardly perceptible at all. It was exactly what he would expect of a solid area.

Sylus left the walls and turned to the columns. For a moment he wondered if one of them might be hollow, but he dismissed the thought as quickly as it came. These columns had been formed by stalactites and stalagmites reaching each other over centuries and forming a hard, strong bond. Besides, even if the centers had been hollowed out, they were far too small to conceal lurkers. Any dwarf could almost hug around the largest of the columns in this chamber. To think they could house anything that would give the soldiers or cavedogs any amount of trouble was laughable.

Eventually he eased his mind. Perhaps it was only the knowledge of the threat a lurker *could* pose rather than an actual imminent threat that had him worried. Many dwarves had lost their lives over the last several years in the mines, but it still wasn't a number nearly as high as those killed in battle beyond the mountain. Defending the humans was far more dangerous to the dwarf folk than mining in the depths below their mountain. Nevertheless, there was something about the dangers in the depths that kept Sylus awake at night. Perhaps it was the fact that lurkers were still so foreign and strange to him. They had never been able to take one alive, and those that died had either been burned to ash, ripped apart and consumed by cavedogs, or dragged away by surviving lurkers.

It made it nearly impossible to create a worthwhile entry in any bestiary. They had enough eye-witnesses to make rough sketches, but when it came to detailing precise information that would be useful, such as the length of their claws, what their scales were made of, or an anatomical description that could better point out weaknesses, there was nothing. They could only guess based upon haphazard battles, and that fact drove Sylus mad.

When he fought an orc, he understood his enemy. He knew that he faced a large humanoid with great strength, but a foe that ultimately resembled any other humanoid in aspects of anatomy. They had the same weaknesses. They had the same types of skills. They had a similar method of battlefield strategy. They even had the same blood.

Lurkers didn't have blood.

They had some sort of goo inside them that hissed and bubbled like acid before evaporating upon contact with the air around them. They had no discernable strategy, even when they attacked in packs. Their anatomy was a mystery as well. Sylus, as well as others who had fought them, guessed they were similar to roaches or other insects. Based upon this, they tried to strike organs that they would expect a large roach to have. More often than not, those efforts proved fruitless. The dwarves had found no organs. There was no spot on the lurker's body where a single stab would result in death. Severing the head worked, but even when the dwarves had managed to take a lurker's head, the beast would continue to run around and attack for minutes, lashing out with its terrible claws just as dangerously as before.

To make it worse, the claws themselves seemed to be formed by some unknown material that was capable of piercing most armors worn by the dwarves. Only mithril could stop the tip of the lurker's claw, and even then the force of the blow itself was still dangerous.

Sylus stroked his beard and leaned against the wall near the opening. He knew his restlessness must stem from his lack of understanding his foe. The unknown threat was always more dangerous than the known and understood enemy. Sylus sighed and watched as the dwarves continued their work.

Soon the baskets were heaping with piles of addorite and the surface of the chamber was looking more and more bare by the minute. Within another hour the dwarves were hauling the baskets out of the chamber and setting them into handcarts. It appeared that Sylus' concern had been in vain.

A miner on the opposite side of the chamber gave a mighty chop with his pickaxe and a hunk of stone fell out of the wall that was larger than he was. The miner jumped out of the way as the boulder rolled over to reveal that there were several addorite crystal growths on the back side.

"Found more," he called out. He then bent down to inspect the cavity and pointed inside. "A lot more in here too!"

Didger bounded over happily and smacked the miner on the back. "Well done, Hasim." Didger turned and surveyed the baskets, beaming from ear to ear when he saw that there were none left with enough space for the newly found pocket of addorite. He turned to the king and shrugged with a gaping grin. "As I said, much more than what we needed."

Sylus nodded and started walking over.

A great *crrrack* sounded on the other side of the wall. A fissure ripped through the stone and from deep within the mountain poured out a fiery red glow. Didger turned and put a hand up over his eyes.

"What in the name of Volganor is that?"

A thunderous rumbling echoed through the chamber and shook the floor so violently that the dwarves fell to all fours. *Crrrrack! BOOM!*

An explosion of rock and light erupted into the chamber. Sylus barely caught a glimpse of Didger's broken body flying limply through the air before a fiery hand reached through the massive hole in the wall and seized the miner by the throat. The hand squeezed and the dwarf's neck snapped in less than a second.

"To arms!" one of the soldiers cried out. The miners fled to the back of the chamber and waited with their pickaxes in hand as the soldiers rode in upon their cavedogs. A great beast stepped through the opening and roared terribly, emitting a wave of heat so intense that Sylus had to shield himself with both arms. When he could finally look at the invader once more, he realized this was something much more dangerous than a lurker.

The fire demon stepped confidently into the chamber, its twin tails swishing angrily behind it as it walked. In its left hand it held a sword of crude iron, while its right hand wielded a large, spiked mace. Four horns crowned its head, one on either side just above the temple, and two sticking out the front of its forehead that curled up. Its chest was easily four feet across, and however tall it was, it had to stoop over to maneuver under the thirteen-foot-high ceiling.

One sweep of its right hand obliterated a fair number of dwarves and their cavedogs. A few got in close and swiped at the demon's legs, but it moved so quickly with its sword that it swept the attackers away, killing several of them. It then roared again, issuing fire from its mouth.

"Dismount!" King Sylus shouted over the din of the angry demon. "Let the cavedogs fight on their own."

The soldiers obeyed immediately, rolling off their mounts as the cavedogs sprang into action quicker now that they didn't carry any burden upon their backs. The dwarves shifted to using crossbows with mithril bolts, something they had started carrying in response to their battles with the lurkers. A few of them managed to let fly their bolts before the demon let out another wave of fire.

Sylus couldn't tell if any of the shafts hit their mark. If they did, the demon certainly wasn't slowed by them. It stomped and crushed cavedogs as it moved in with its mace and sword. Dwarves circled around it, refusing to offer the demon a single direction to focus his attacks.

King Sylus watched the demon for several moments, learning its movements and timing its reactions. Dwarves moved in, jabbing and striking at the demon's legs. The demon deflected most with its own weapons, but others it countered with its twin tails, snaking out around the dwarves and slapping a few across the chest and another in the head.

The cavedogs darted in and around the demon's legs, biting and snarling. Even their attacks were having little effect. A few gashes opened on the demon's legs, but nothing serious enough to bring it down.

Then the unthinkable happened.

The demon ignited its own body and covered itself in a living armor of fire. Three cavedogs had their heads and mouths scorched. A dwarf was encircled in flame and ran away from the fight, screaming in agony.

Sylus couldn't wait any longer. He took his hammer in hand and sprinted in as soon as the demon turned to the right and exposed his left side to Sylus. The dwarf king moved speedily, and silently. He kept his eye on the prize he wanted. He flipped his hammer over so as to strike with the spike on the back. He moved in, ducking under a wild swing of the demon's sword that *whooshed* a couple of feet above Sylus' head. Then he spun and put every bit of strength he had into his attack.

The spike sailed in, arcing for the front of the demon's left knee. Neither the flames, nor the patella, could withstand Sylus' blow. The spike drove in, breaking through the kneecap with a gruesome *snap!* The demon howled in pain and moved back, but Sylus held his weapon in place, letting the spike linger in the space inside the knee joint.

Another dwarf ran in and leapt up. He too wielded a hammer. As he sailed through the air, he wound up an overhead chop and came in with a savage yell. The hammer connected with Sylus' hammer, driving the spike through the demon's leg entirely, and nearly ripping the left leg in half.

The demon shrieked so loudly that all of the cavedogs winced and shied away. Even several of the dwarves had to cover their ears. Then, the demon let out a devastating attack. Fire spewed out from its mouth, bathing nearly a dozen dwarves in flames. The sword came down hard on the left. Sylus was swift enough to dodge it, though he had to leave his hammer stuck in the demon's knee. Three other dwarves were not as lucky. They were all cut down in the blow. Four more took the brunt of the spiked mace and were squished in a sweeping attack that smashed them into the wall.

Then the demon lost the strength lent to it by its anger, and it fell as it tried to put weight upon the left leg. Sylus bent down and took a spear from a fallen dwarf. He and several others rushed in to finish the battle. The demon raised its sword, and with a flick of its wrist it stabbed two dwarves as they charged. Its right hand released the mace, the spikes still stuck in the wall, leaving the weapon to hang there with the dwarf bodies like a grotesque tapestry before it struck out with its flaming fist, crushing a few more dwarves. Cavedogs rushed in and, despite the flames, leapt up to bite at the demon's chest. In return, it lunged down and bit one of the cavedogs in the neck.

However, in leaning down, the demon exposed its own neck.

The Wealth of Kings

Sylus sprinted the last few steps and put all of his weight behind the spear thrust aimed at the side of the demon's neck. The weapon went in much easier than the hammer. Flame and bright, orange light seeped out around the shaft of the spear, but Sylus drove it in as far as he could, unflinching from the heat. The dwarf king then hung from the spear as the demon tried to rise again. The demon let out a gargled cry and bent in pain toward Sylus.

The mighty dwarf king held fast, pulling and jerking on the spear with all of the strength he could muster, widening the wound in the demon's neck. The demon fell to the ground, and a trio of dwarf soldiers moved in to hack and stab at the neck as well. Within moments, the head rolled free of the neck, and the flames surrounding the demon faded.

The dwarves stood, stunned and heaving for breath as they stared at the demon's corpse.

"What in Hammenfein's name was that?" one of the soldiers asked.

Sylus turned and surveyed the area. There were only seven soldiers left. Three of the cavedogs remained, though Sylus took heart and smiled when his lizard approached him proudly and stood next to him. About half of the miners survived. Most of the others had been taken by the many fire attacks. Some had been mortally wounded by the shattering rock when the demon had first entered the chamber.

"This addorite better be worth it," one of the miners said.

Sylus looked up and saw another miner slapping the one who had spoken, harshly criticizing him for questioning the king.

The dwarf king went to retrieve his hammer, and then he went to the miner who had murmured against him. The other dwarves stood rigid, but the miner who had spoken stood tall, as if preparing to let Sylus know what he thought of the attack and the dangers presented in the deep mines. However, instead of chastising or punishing the miner, Sylus stretched out a hand and put it on the miner's shoulder.

"I share your concern," he said. Sylus glanced around the chamber and then locked eyes with the miner. "I will go and speak with Tu'luh. Mark my words, if I ever, for one second, think that we are wasting our lives needlessly, I will close the mines."

None of the dwarves spoke.

They stood silently, watching as Sylus went and mounted his cavedog. The dwarf king motioned to the chamber with a sweep of his hand. "Gather our fallen kin. When the reinforcements arrive, take them up and prepare for the funeral rites." Sylus then looked to the gaping hole from whence the demon had come. There was no light coming from beyond the chamber anymore. It was dark and silent. "Blow this chamber. Seal it off."

*****

Sylus yanked his dented armor off and threw it on his bed. He didn't even bother cleaning himself before he went out to the tunnel that joined his room to a large balcony that served as a platform for Tu'luh to land upon. He stormed out, hammer in hand and fuming mad as he had ever been in his life.

He went to the large pedestal on the balcony and uncovered the crystal sphere sitting atop it. He spoke the ancient words passed down from the first king of the dwarves, and the crystal awoke. At first it was a tiny, yellow glow deep within the crystal, but it quickly grew into a thick shaft of light that streaked up into the night sky and pierced the heavens.

There was no way for Sylus to know how long it would take the Ancient to respond. Sometimes it was minutes, at other times it took several days. He knew only that he needed to know more about the addorite in the depths of the mountain. As far as he was concerned, his continued obedience to Tu'luh was staining his hands with the blood of his kin. It was one thing for soldiers on the battlefield, but it was another matter entirely to command miners and engineers to march into the depths knowing that it could spell their doom.

Fortunately, Tu'luh arrive within the hour. It was fast enough that Sylus could appreciate the Ancient's answering the summons on short notice, but also long enough that he had managed to cool his temper just enough to remember his manners when speaking to the mighty dragon.

Large, strong wings of scarlet beat upon the air as the dragon slowly lowered its massive body to the large, flat platform of stone. Tu'luh's massive head turned so that his eyes could watch Sylus carefully. It occurred to Sylus that perhaps the dragon had expected this particular conversation.

"You have found the addorite?" Tu'luh asked in a mighty voice that echoed off the mountainside.

Sylus nodded. "We found nearly a ton, but we found something else as well."

"More lurkers?" Tu'luh asked. Sylus had mentioned the beasts the last time he had spoken with the dragon, but Tu'luh had offered almost no insight.

The dwarf king set his hammer's head down on the ground and rested his hands atop the upside-down handle. "A demon that commanded fire," Sylus said. "It killed a great many dwarves, and cavedogs besides. It broke through a solid wall of stone to ambush us."

Tu'luh nodded slowly. The Ancient emitted a deep, throaty growl and then snorted, shooting wisps of smoke out its nostrils. "Yes, I thought there might be a chance you would meet the demon."

"Why didn't you warn me?" Sylus asked. "I could have prepared better. I could have ordered an army down into the mines. We could have prepared weapons for the demon."

Tu'luh shook his mighty head. "I was not sure you would encounter it. I believed that the mine would have to be much deeper before it would penetrate into their realm."

Sylus was taken aback. His throat caught for a moment, but it was soon replaced by hot anger. "Their realm?" he echoed in a sharp yell. "You mean there are more of them?"

Tu'luh grunted and nodded once. "The bowels of Terramyr are a dangerous place. However, the magical fields below Roegudok Hall should suppress the demons. I thought they would be much deeper in this area, for they do not thrive where the Mystinen operates." Tu'luh let out a short growl. "It appears I have made an error in my calculations. For that, I am truly sorry."

Sylus felt the heat of rage boil up within him. No longer could he sit behind the tradition of reverence when faced with such incompetence and apparent apathy. Before he had a chance to think about his next words, he let them tumble out of his mouth.

"How dare you tell me you are sorry!" Sylus shouted as he moved toward Tu'luh, his hands ripping the hammer up from the ground and holding it in front of him. "I have fought for you when you asked me to. I defend humans who are too weak to defend themselves from the orcs that invade from the south. I have sent men to die in the mines, when we have more than plenty lining our pockets. What is this greed that drives you to waste the sons of the mountain?"

Tu'luh moved lightning fast. His snout stopped inches in front of Sylus' face and his hot, fetid breath washed over Sylus. The king stiffened, but he did not shrink away. The dragon snarled, curling his scaled lip up to reveal long, wickedly sharp fangs. Tu'luh growled and then pulled his head up, standing at his full height, towering over the dwarf. His right hand moved out and a black, curved talon rested its point on Sylus' chest, pressing the skin in ever so slightly.

"You are no son of the mountain," Tu'luh corrected. "You exist only because we, the Ancients, have formed you. You were created separately from all the other races of dwarves on Terramyr. Icadion gave us permission to create you, so we used the same method we utilized on Kendualdern. We formed you from the rock of Roegudok Hall." The dragon snorted and flames shot out angrily from its nostrils. "Don't you for one moment forget that you are sons of the Ancients. The mountain is your home, but we are your creators."

The talon angled downward, sliding the dangerous point away from Sylus and leaving the back side of the claw pressed against him. Tu'luh then flicked his claw and Sylus was thrown to the ground. The dwarf king landed hard on his back. He heard the talons scrape the stone platform next to him as Tu'luh set his massive foreleg down nearby and scratched the stone.

"You would kill me?" Sylus asked, some of the fight gone from his voice now.

Tu'luh bent his head down and growled. "I would remind you of your place," Tu'luh said diplomatically. "You are the people of the Ancients. You are chosen to protect the Middle Kingdom. That requires sacrifice on your part, but it is for a greater good."

Sylus rose to his feet and set his hammer down once more. "Then tell me what greater good is served by mining addorite in the depths below Roegudok Hall. Tell me why my people must sacrifice themselves to demons and giant bugs that would eat us."

Tu'luh's tail twitched and thudded against the stone as the dragon considered the dwarf king's request. Then, he bent down once more, bringing his face closer to Sylus. "The addorite is being used in Valtuu Temple by the Ancients. Hiasyntar'Kulai, the Father of the Ancients, needs the crystal to read the deeper wisdom found within an ancient tome called the Infinium. Without it, the book cannot be read entirely."

"What is so important about this book?" Sylus asked.

Tu'luh shook his head. "It is not for me to disclose," he said. "My father has forbidden it. If you want to know, you will have to ask him."

"Then bring him to me," Sylus said.

Tu'luh laughed and smoke came out in puffs. "A dwarf king can light the summoning beacon, but he cannot command the Father of the Ancients."

Sylus sighed. "Then at least tell me how much addorite you need. Once we have enough, then I can close the mines and protect my people."

Tu'luh came within a few inches of Sylus and turned his head so that his large, right eye peered deeply into Sylus' eyes. "We need every ounce you can find."

Sylus stepped back and shook his head. "Then, why not go with us?" Sylus asked. The dwarf king gestured out beyond the large balcony to the valley below. "You have fought beside us beyond the mountain before. I know your strength. You can help us. We can widen the tunnels and—"

"No," Tu'luh said flatly. "You know I cannot do that. The Mystinen that flows deep below Roegudok Hall is toxic to dragons. I cannot go into the tunnels with you.

"But you can handle addorite?" Sylus asked.

Tu'luh nodded. "The crystal formed below the mountain is not toxic to us, though it would be to humans or elves. Your folk are immune to both the Mystinen and addorite. That is why you were created. There is no other place on Terramyr that has the conditions necessary for addorite to form. Roegudok Hall itself was pushed up from the ground by this unique field of Mystinen."

"So there is nothing you can do to aid us?" Sylus asked. "You would have me throw all of my folk into the mines, knowing the dangers below?"

Tu'luh nodded. "I assure you, your sacrifice will aid us Ancients in avoiding a much larger danger that will threaten all of Terramyr, including your people." The dragon's voice softened. "I understand your anger. Therefore, I will forget your outbursts. However, if you return to your chamber and read from the first book of kings that your great grandfather wrote, you will see that even in his time we Ancients told him we could not tunnel into the bowels of the mountain. Your miners know this as well."

Sylus relented with a nod. "Can you tell me anything of the demons?"

Tu'luh nodded. "Though the lurkers were something we did not know of, the demons that live within the bowels of Terramyr are something we have seen before. Use mithril arrows…"

"We have," Sylus said. "My soldiers fired several mithril crossbow bolts into him. It did nothing."

Tu'luh grunted. "I wasn't finished," he said pointedly. "Use mithril arrows that have been coated with a special poison made from addorite and bloodgrass. Listen closely, and I will instruct you how to make it."

Sylus looked up to Tu'luh. "I'm listening," the dwarf king said.

Tu'luh looked into Sylus' eyes once more and the dwarf went rigid. The dragon formed a telepathic connection with Sylus and showed him how to mix the correct proportions of bloodgrass and addorite to form the poison. Then, when the lesson was done, the dragon broke the connection and pulled away.

Sylus stumbled forward a step, weary from the spell.

"Do you understand?" Tu'luh asked.

Sylus nodded. "I can replicate the process you showed me."

"Very well. Now listen to my final instructions for the night."

Sylus nodded and looked up, leaning upon his hammer for support.

"Most of the addorite will be shipped to Valtuu Temple. Ensure that no one takes the crystals from you. Orcs or thieves may try to steal it, mistaking it for treasure. However, not all of it needs to go to Valtuu Temple. Keep ten pounds on hand in the mountain at all times. This will ensure you have enough to create the poison you need to defeat the demons. Then, for every thousand pounds you mine, send one hundred pounds to Bendor's Cave to the southwest."

"Why there?" Sylus asked.

"That is not for you to know," Tu'luh said sharply. "Now go. Do not call me again until you have a sustainable flow of addorite moving to each location."

Sylus grudgingly bowed his head and the Ancient leapt into the air, stirring up dust and wind with his magnificent wings. Tu'luh let out a mighty roar that shook the very ground

Sylus stood upon, and then the dragon turned to the southwest and flew away, disappearing over the top of the mountain.

The dwarf king stood on the large platform for several minutes, wrestling with himself about the fate of his people. Finally, he decided he would try Tu'luh's poison. If it worked, then Sylus would do as he was told. However, he also set his mind that if the fighting in the mines grew much more costly, then he would collapse the tunnels. If he had to, he would sever Roegudok Hall from the Ancients. Tu'luh himself had already explained that the Ancients could not enter Roegudok Hall due to the Mystinen, so there would not be much they could do to him or his people should they hide inside the safety of their mountain.

CHAPTER 9

Year 3,711 Age of Demigods, Early Autumn.
2nd year of the reign of Aldehenkaru'hktanah Sit'marihu, 13th King of Roegudok Hall.

Al stood in the throne room, waiting for the others to arrive. He studied the portrait of King Sylus, wondering what it was the ancient king had done to usher in an era of prosperity. How was it that the summer had passed and the autumn had come without so much as a cart-full of gold or silver to show for all of the mining efforts Al had put into place? He had thought the chamber with the lava tube would yield something substantial, but the gold vein was shallow and only a handful of low quality, clouded diamonds had been extracted. What was he missing?

The door to the throne room opened and in walked Alferug.

He was flanked by two other dwarves, but they were not part of the council; these were engineers that Al had summoned himself.

The dwarf king peeled himself away from Sylus' painting and then went to the engineers. Gimil, an engineer with centuries of experience, pulled a rolled parchment from a wooden cylinder and held it out for Al.

"I drew the plans as you requested. Please let me know if I have made any errors."

Al took the parchment and unrolled it. He could see Alferug trying to sneak a peek, but Al positioned it away from

Alferug. "This is a surprise, Alferug," the king said.

Alferug nodded and continued on toward the council table.

The king studied the schematics and then glanced to the north wall of the throne room. He then grinned and rolled the parchment tightly and handed it back. "How soon can you start?"

Gimil took the parchment and slid it into the cylinder. "We can start immediately. I have already put the necessary laborers on standby."

"Excellent," Al said. "How long will it take?"

Gimil scratched his head. "Oh, not long at all. We have already moved the bulk of the equipment into place. Now it is just a matter of the wall. That was why I wanted to come to you and triple check that you were sure you wanted it done."

Al nodded. "I am more than sure." He clapped Gimil on the shoulder and sent him away.

The two engineers exited the throne room just as Kijik, commander of the Home Guard, entered the throne room. Al nodded at Kijik and motioned for him to join Alferug at the council table.

Kijik offered a short nod and walked by quickly. Over the last several months, Kijik had seemed to adapt to his new role quite well. The Home Guard was still smaller than Al wanted, but recruits were in training and the current members of the Home Guard were receiving practice drills. More than that, Kijik had squads of his men rotating in as guards in the mines.

Fortunately, no more incidents had occurred since the time when the five miners were attacked by a yet unknown creature in the depths. Al could only hope that they had destroyed whatever had attacked when they collapsed the lava tube in that chamber where Tareggh and the others had disappeared.

Al made his way to the head of the table and sat down. Over the next ten minutes, he watched as ten more dwarves came into the throne room. Seven male dwarves and three females. Each of them had advising responsibilities. Some were still new to the council, having only been appointed within the last two weeks, but all of them were extremely motivated and dedicated to their work. Moreover, none of them had served in positions of authority under Threnton's rule. Al waited until the last of them had seated themselves and then he started the meeting.

"Thank you all for coming, we have a lot to get through in today's meeting. We'll start on my left, and then go down the line in order." Al turned to Alferug and motioned to him. "Alferug, do you have anything to share with the group?"

Alferug stood in his place and addressed the others. "The people are still mixed on the subject of the Ancients. Many welcome the rededication to follow our traditions, others reject it. However, there is peace in Roegudok Hall on this matter. There have been no incidents." Alferug then sat down.

"Have any dragons returned to Roegudok Hall?" Dvek asked.

Alferug shook his head. "No, not yet. But I believe they will one day come."

"Have any been spotted in the Middle Kingdom at large?" Dvek pressed.

Alferug shook his head again. "Not that I have been told." The old counselor turned and directed his gaze to Hento, a middle-aged dwarf who had been appointed as Liaison to King Mathias. "Have you heard anything?"

"No. I have not heard anything on this subject," Hento said flatly.

"Very well," Al said. "Let's continue."

A sharp impact hit somewhere on the other side of the north wall that caused some of the dwarves to jump in their seats. They turned and looked for the source of the noise, but the dwarf king held up his left hand and then pointed to Benbo. "Please, let's continue."

Benbo's brows shot up but he quickly regained his composure and turned back to the group. "The army is strong.

Over the last several weeks, we have sent roughly half of our soldiers out into the Middle Kingdom. They, in conjunction with some of our best engineers, are helping some of the destroyed towns and settlements in the south rebuild. From everything I hear, the effort is going well."

Hento cut in. "Yes, King Mathias sends his most sincere thanks for the help. He has applauded our efforts, and hopes for more cooperation between our peoples."

Al nodded and stroked his beard. "Mathias may soon get the chance to help us as well," he said. Then, he motioned for Benbo to continue.

"That is all, Sire," Benbo said. "In other news, we have guards patrolling the mines as you ordered a couple months ago. There have been no new incidents."

Al nodded. "Kijik, anything from the Home Guard?"

Kijik opened his mouth to speak, but was interrupted by another loud thunking sound that echoed through the chamber.

"Ignore that," Al said with a half-grin on his face. "It is work I ordered."

"With respect, perhaps they can wait until we are finished," Alferug whispered as he leaned in toward Al.

The dwarf king laughed. "No, I asked them to do it."

Alferug frowned.

Kijik cleared his throat and sat rigid in his chair as he began his report. "We have two hundred recruits in training at this moment," he said proudly. "Otherwise we are practicing drills, and we are taking rotations with the regular army down in the mines."

"And your contribution is much appreciated," Al offered.

"Thank you, Sire," Kijik replied with a respectful nod.

Dvek didn't wait to be called upon. He leaned forward, elbows on the table and hands up with fingers entwined a few inches away from his face as he turned and directed his gaze to the king. "I regret to say that we are no better off now than we were at the beginning of the summer.

Our crops have not yielded a harvest that will sustain us through the winter. We are still draining our reservoirs for culinary water, as we have found no new wells. This fact in and of itself prevents us from growing cave-rice. Furthermore, our mines are still not producing. We are, for lack of better words, running out of time."

Al sighed and looked to Mitgar, a young, black-haired dwarf who had been appointed as the Agricultural Advisor. "How much did the harvest yield, exactly?"

Mitgar shook his head and pulled a small, leather-bound book from a pocket and began to read. "We have butchered seven hundred sheep. We have fished fourteen barrels of mountain trout. We have harvested—"

"Mitgar," Al interrupted. The dwarf looked up from his list with a slack mouth and knit brow. "I don't need all of the details. Just give me a summary, or your best estimate for how long the food supply will last us."

Mitgar closed his mouth and nodded. His eyes scanned over the pages and he moved his fingers in the air next to the book as he quickly mumbled. Then he looked up to Al and said, "Two and a half months, perhaps three."

A heavy silence fell over the table. No one had to spell it out for any of them. Roegudok Hall wouldn't last through the winter. In fact, the food would run out before winter arrived. Al tapped a finger on the table and then skipped over to Hento with an arched brow.

"Hento, what of aid for Roegudok Hall? What can King Mathias spare?"

Hento rose to his feet, but he did not look anyone in the eye. He kept his gaze down to the top of the table. "Senator Mickelson informed me that the king has no stores to spare."

"How is that possible?" Al asked. "We have sent our own people out to help rebuild." Al shook his head and pounded an angry fist. Hento jumped nervously and glanced at the king's hand before looking away again. "We sacrificed our lives in the war with Tu'luh and the orcs! How can he abandon

Sam Ferguson

us now in our time of need?"

Hento shook his head. "Mickelson said that the king has used what stores he had to resupply Fort Drake, various other military encampments, and also the towns in the south." Hento clasped his hands in front of his waist to keep them from shaking from his nerves, but he could barely look in Al's direction before his voice cracked. "Mickelson said that Mathias has been able to feed our kin who are helping rebuild, but he has nothing extra to send to Roegudok Hall. I do have other connections. Let me speak with them. I am sure we can come to an arrangement. Perhaps we can offer to barter with credit. Roegudok Hall has never defaulted on any of its financial obligations."

"Actually, that is not entirely accurate, Hento," Dvek cut in. He stood again and address Al. "It won't do any good to look to other merchants. We failed to pay the Greenband in full. They have levied sanctions against us. Unless the king offers us food, we have no other options other than continuing to expand our mines and hope they start producing. Even if the Greenband wasn't levying sanctions against us, it appears that the other merchant guilds have kept a close hold on their goods, especially food. I would say that the guilds are hiding large stores of food so they can drive prices up by creating scarcity."

Al nodded. "I would agree, Dvek."

Benbo leaned forward, his mouth opening to say something, but then he glanced around the room and closed his mouth, furrowing his brow and leaning back in his chair.

"Don't be shy, Benbo," Al said. "If you have something to say, then come out with it."

Benbo shook his head. "No, it was an irrational idea, Sire. It isn't worth discussing."

"Too late now, Benbo. My curiosity is piqued and I must know what it was."

Benbo hesitated, and then leaned forward and turned toward Al. "I thought, only for a moment before my senses came to me, that perhaps we could take a group of cavedog riders and…"

Al laughed as Benbo's words faded into the air and the commander of the army made a shrugging gesture. Benbo blushed and sat back in his chair, obviously embarrassed to have the thought out for all to hear. "I like your tenacity," Al said. "However, it would do us little good to become a band of brigands and thieves."

"If the merchants withhold their goods only for the sake of driving up prices, it may call for some sort of measured response," Alferug said.

Al shook his head. "No, we will not police the merchants in the Middle Kingdom. We will gain nothing by stealing from them and giving it to our folk. It would destroy relations with Mathias."

"I could propose the idea to Mickelson that we could help search for the rumored stores," Hento said.

Al shook his head. "No. That wouldn't work much better. We may as well tell King Mathias that he is not running his kingdom properly and offer to take it off his hands." Al sighed. "No, we will find another way. If trade is what is needed, then let us discuss what we can produce." Al pointed to Akmei, a beautiful, young, green eyed dwarf who had recently been appointed as the Mining Advisor. "Do we have anything?"

Akmei stood and swung her long, red braid of hair up and over her shoulder. "No, my king. We have found a lot of that bloodgrass, but no new gems or ore sources, precious or otherwise. It is only a matter of time though."

Al smiled as she sat down. He liked her optimism as much as her beauty. He let his eyes linger upon her face for a moment longer before nodding and turning to Kangas, who oversaw textile operations.

Kangas was an older gentleman, finely dressed in a sleek long coat over a neatly pressed red shirt. He reached up to shift the glasses on his nose and then smoothed his silvery beard. "As a result of butchering all of the sheep that Mitgar spoke of, we have more than enough wool to produce many goods. We are currently weaving large rugs and tapestries of a similar pattern and quality as those we sold out in the human cities before trade relations were severed by King Threnton. Additionally, we are holding much of our supply in reserve so we can take orders from without the mountain."

"Estimated total value?" Al asked.

Kangas shrugged. "Hard to say until we have used our supply of wool." The dwarf cleared his throat and hummed for a moment as he took in a deep breath and narrowed his eyes on the table as he thought. "I should say we have currently an inventory worth several hundred gold crowns. The tapestries and carpets currently being made would add to that, and the custom orders could range anywhere from a few hundred silver pieces, to several hundred gold, depending on what kind of orders are received."

Al nodded. "That is good," he said. "That should go a long way toward purchasing food, then."

Hento raised his hand. "I am afraid that will not go as far as you think, my king."

Al arched a brow. "Explain."

Hento stood and shook his head. "The normal price for a block of cheese has traditionally been stable at three silver pieces. However, in the wake of the destruction of the war, and the food shortage claimed by the merchants, that same block of cheese has now risen to one gold, or even twice that in some of the villages."

"That's outrageous!" Dvek howled.

Hento nodded in agreement. "A bushel of apples can cost as much as one gold crown."

Al couldn't believe what he was hearing. With prices like that, the merchants would be bleeding most families dry. There were few he knew in Buktah that could ever afford those prices well enough to eat beyond a meager subsistence level. What it meant for the dwarves was even worse. Unless they could find a productive mine, there would be much suffering in Roegudok Hall.

Helmi, a portly she-dwarf stood and gave her

accounting next. "In terms of inventory, we have nothing to sell unless the mines produce more ore. We have a few bracelets and the like, but nothing fancy enough to catch a human's interest."

Pikari, Helmi's sister, added her thoughts. "It doesn't sound like most humans will have the means to buy jewelry or fine crafts anyhow if they are struggling to buy apples."

Al nodded and leaned forward. "A good number of Mathias' citizens live and work on a nobleman's land. Normally, that nobleman can produce enough for the people on his land. So, it is still possible to find areas where trade can flourish."

A heavy pounding echoed through the throne room and everyone turned to the wall just as a large hunk of stone fell in and slammed onto the floor, chipping and breaking into pieces as bits slid out from across the polished floor of the throne room.

"What is the meaning of this?" Alferug gasped.

Al stood and pointed to the wall. "Everyone, I want to show you my short term plan for augmenting trade."

None of the others spoke.

As the moments ticked by, bits of stone fell out from the wall until a rough passageway was opened to a chamber that none but Al knew existed. Al motioned for the others to follow him to the wall.

"Ferrick has told me that we do have an ample supply of iron, so I thought we could create items needed outside Roegudok Hall." Al turned to Ferrick and pointed at the Smithing Advisor. "You did say we had roughly three tons of good quality iron, correct?"

Ferrick nodded. "Yes, and as you and Benbo suggested, we are busy working the metal into nails, latches, hinges, and braces to be used in rebuilding the human settlements."

"Are you suggesting that we withdraw our offer of aid and start charging Mathias for the supplies?" Dvek asked.

Al shook his head. "No, nothing like that. However, I

have chosen three smithing apprentices to work with me in my personal forge. We will craft weapons and armor. Having seen firsthand the destruction of the war with Tu'luh and the orcs, I know that the Middle Kingdom could use more armaments. We will sell those. I have redirected one ton of iron to my forge, and with it we can create enough arms and armor to purchase much more food than we could otherwise." Al looked to Kangas. "When you produce textiles, you must pay your workers. This means that most of the money you said could be made from the endeavor will not come to the royal treasury. While it will help some of your workers and their families, it won't address the overall food shortage we face."

"What are you proposing?" Alferug asked.

Al beamed ear to ear and waved to his forge. "I was never meant to be a king, at least, that is what I told my father. I not only completed smithing training, but I became one of the finest smiths Roegudok Hall has ever seen."

Ferrick nodded. "It is true. The king's name still hangs in the Smithing College as the second best smith to ever graduate. His quality of workmanship, and the speed with which he can produce, are currently unequaled."

Al took his hammer in hand. "When I am not otherwise engaged in official duties, I will be in the forge. The items I produce can be sold, and all of the profit can be used to barter for food. The people of Buktah know my name well. Beyond that city, I am known throughout many places in the Middle Kingdom. They will pay for my weapons and armors."

Alferug stepped in close to Al so that none else could hear. "What of the Wealth of Kings? We must spend our free time looking for the way in."

Al nodded. "I can't beat the riddle by sitting at my desk. I do my best thinking when I am manipulating metal and swinging my hammer. I will solve the riddle, but I must do so while helping our people."

Dvek stepped in and gently moved Alferug aside. Al turned to the man and saw a small tear forming in the Commerce Minister's left eye. "I have not seen a king so willing to devote himself to his people. After working under your brother, may I say that it is an honor to serve you now."

Al took Dvek's outstretched hand and smiled back at him. "We'll get through this together," Al said. The dwarf king then took the council through the forge, showing them his equipment and letting them inspect the operation. Then, he sent them out with a charge to continue their efforts and assuring them that they would solve Roegudok Hall's shortage before winter came.

*****

Hiasyntar'Kulai, stood watch over the ruins of Valtuu Temple from a hill a few hundred yards away. Several priests worked near the rubble, building a new home for their order. The sound of pickaxes and hammers working the stone rang out melodically as the hot sun bore down from overhead.

With the former prelate dead, and the Keeper of Secrets missing along with Lady Dimwater, the new prelate had decided it best to reestablish the temple so that Hiasyntar'Kulai would have a place to rest and recuperate as he resumed his duties watching over the people of the Middle Kingdom.

Hiasyntar'Kulai smiled as he caught sight of Sissil in her flowing, white dress. She exited the stone building and was pointing to the rubble. A couple of priests with her were nodding their heads and then they moved toward the ruin. Sissil then turned and waved at a group of twenty young men and women seated on the ground nearby before walking toward them and speaking. Hiasyntar'Kulai couldn't hear what she was saying, but he knew she was teaching the new initiates. The dragon thought that Sissil was doing very well as the new prelate.

The golden dragon thought of his son, Tu'luh the Red. His happy heart grew heavy and he set his head down upon his forelegs. Tu'luh had been defeated, and the orcs had been driven back to the south, but there were still dangers that threatened the fragile peace within the Middle Kingdom. With

Master Lepkin disappearing, nobles were again jostling for favor with the old king, hoping he might name them as his successor in the event of his death.

It was also possible that other orc tribes could attack from the south. The Middle Kingdom had suffered a great many losses, and could ill afford to fend off another assault just yet.

Still, despite all of this, there was hope. Nagar's Secret had been destroyed, and the threat it brought with it was vanquished. If only he could find the addorite that Tu'luh had stolen, then perhaps he could make more headway.

Hiasyntar'Kulai suddenly became aware of a presence near him. He turned and saw a stranger standing on the grassy hill with him. The Father of the Ancients did not know him by name, but he knew his order.

"Do you come bearing grave news?" the dragon asked in his low, deep voice.

The stranger pulled back the green hood on his cloak. "I am here seeking answers," he said. "I recently visited the dwarf king, and thought that perhaps I should come and visit you as well."

The dragon emitted a soft, throaty growl. "It has been a long time since I have seen one of your order. I had hoped never to set eyes upon you again."

The man in the green robes smiled and nodded knowingly. "All things move in turn," he said. "Still, I am not here to discuss that. I came to pay respects."

"An interesting sentiment, coming from you," Hiasyntar'Kulai said. "Still, if you wish, hospitality is not dead among dragons. I can prepare a feast for you."

"No," the man said. He waved his hand and floated up to be at eye level with the Father of the Ancients. He locked his blue eyes with Hiasyntar'Kulai and the two remained silent for many moments as they stared into each other's eyes. The Father of the Ancients could feel the man sifting through his memories and reliving them in a matter of moments. Then, the stranger broke the spell and nodded with a slight smile. "I will be going now."

"Do you have what you need?" the dragon asked.

The stranger refused to answer as he disappeared like an extinguished flame into the ether.

*****

Several hours after the council had been dismissed, Al was walking into his bedchamber. He greeted the two guards and pushed into his room, closing the door and locking it behind himself. It had felt good to finally be working a forge again. His arms throbbed from the pounding, and his clothes smelled of sweat, dirt, and smoke. He lifted the leather apron from his chest and laid it over the back of the chair at his desk. Then he took off his boots and shoved them next to the chair.

His hand went to his belt and he found his hammer tucked safely at his waist. He pulled it up and twirled it in his hand before letting the solid head fall and thump into his other palm. He still felt the weight of the crown upon his head, but it somehow felt lighter now. It wasn't just the work of the forge, it was the smells, the sounds, and the heat all combined in a way that invigorated the dwarf king. He no longer had the war to fight alongside Erik and the others, but while fashioning weapons and armor, he could reclaim his purpose, and regain his sense of self.

Al peeled off his socks and wiggled his toes upon the cold stone floor of his room. A cool breeze rolled into the room from the outside. Al sniffed and narrowed his eyes on the door. He was certain he had closed it. Ever since that stranger in green robes had appeared on the balcony, Al had always ensured the door was locked except when he wanted to go out onto the balcony.

The dwarf king gripped his hammer tightly, ready to pulverize the tall invader if he had dared to come back.

CHAPTER 10

Year 3,711 Age of Demigods, Early Autumn.
2nd year of the reign of Aldehenkaru'hktanah Sit'marihu, 13th King of Roegudok Hall.

"I hate to say it, but I wasn't sure you could get us this far," Delmecian said as they approached the landing that Threnton said led into the hallway near the king's chambers.

"One should never underestimate a dwarf," Threnton replied evenly. "I found this tunnel shortly after my brother tried to depose me the first time. Had it not been for my cousins, he would have died afterward."

"How did you find it?" Delmecian asked.

Threnton stopped and smirked. "My guards told me that my brother had come through a large mirror. I couldn't open the passageway from the inside, so I figured the best way to find it would be to retrace my brother's steps. It wasn't that hard to find."

"The moonstone you spoke of, is that it?" Delmecian asked as he pointed to a glowing blue stone on the side of the cliff face.

Threnton nodded. "That was the hardest part about this whole thing," he said. "Figuring out that the passage was sealed by a moonstone took me a couple of days, but I did find it." Threnton grinned and motioned for Delmecian to keep up. "I will take us in, and then I will kill my brother."

"I am sure the Blacktongue will see to that,"

Delmecian replied.

Threnton shook his head. "It takes a lot to catch my brother off guard. I am willing to bet the Blacktongue will fail." He sneered and then added, "I am going to break that arrogant pig's nose."

"Remember," Delmecian cautioned. "If you want to look like him, then I need to see him before you change the way his face looks."

Threnton nodded and the two moved toward the rock below the glowing moonstone. Threnton placed his hand below the moonstone. "I Threntonsirai Sit'marihu, command the door of kings to open and allow entrance to Roegudok Hall."

"Will it work?" Delmecian asked. "Isn't your brother the king now?"

"Ah, but I was the king, and shall be again," Threnton said confidently.

The mountain groaned. Shale and pebbles bounced and vibrated away from the landing they stood upon as the rock itself came alive, sliding and scraping as it writhed before them. A massive, arched slab of slate and granite removed itself to the side and revealed a shallow cavern that covered a glowing blue doorway, covered in runes and designs of stars and moons.

Threnton led the way inside without hesitating. He reached up to the side of the cavern, grabbing a brass tube.

"What is that?" Delmecian asked.

"It is the secondary key," Threnton replied dryly. As the dwarf twisted the brass tube, a stream of light emerged from the end and shone upon a small spot on the door. Satisfied that he had adjusted the light correctly, Threnton walked forward to the door.

"I kept the last key," Threnton said as he moved toward the door. "I bet Al has been beating his head trying to get back inside here."

"Why would he?" Delmecian asked.

"It holds the secret of the Wealth of Kings," Threnton

said. After I locate it and show the dwarves the vast wealth of the mountain, they will beg to have me back as their king."

"Indeed," Delmecian said. "Just, don't forget about our deal."

"I never forget a debt," Threnton promised. He traced his finger in the empty space where the jewel should be and let the light from the brass tube dance upon his skin for a moment. Threnton then pulled a pink gem from his pocket and placed the stone into the empty mount on the door and took a step back.

The silver light from the tube refracted in the pink gem, splitting its light and sending rays to the several other blue stones in the door. The runes sang in answer to the light and the door glowed brighter as each of the jewels soaked in the light.

"It isn't opening," Delmecian said.

"Patience," Threnton said. "There is yet a third key."

The dwarf stood waiting as the door grew brighter and brighter. As the brilliance grew, Delmecian shielded his face from the intense light. As the entire cave danced with the dazzling colors emitted from the stones, a pattern became visible in the center of the door. A golden dragon's face glowed in the stone itself.

"It is a reminder of the Ancients, those who would have subjugated us under their heels and kept us as slaves," Threnton stated sharply. "It is also the third key." He stepped forward and put his forehead to the image of the dragon's head, locking eyes with the glowing eyes in the stone. A yellow light emerged and created a conduit between Threnton and the image in the door. The light was warm, and inviting as it entered his eyes gently. The whole ordeal lasted only a few seconds before the light pulled back and the golden dragon turned white. Then the door vanished, allowing entrance into the great dwarven kingdom.

"Incredible," Delmecian said.

Threnton turned back and smiled. "Dwarves are a clever folk."

The two walked through the corridor until it came to an end. The wall was smooth and flat. There was no hint of a door anywhere.

"A fourth key?" Delmecian asked.

Threnton shook his head. "No, the keys are only used at the entrance. This door is hidden and opened by the use of a secret button." He moved to the left side of the wall. "I can find it, just give me a moment." He ran his hands over the surface and grinned when he found a small hole. He wiggled his pinky finger in and depressed the button inside. A series of clicks and snaps were heard. Then the sound of a heavy chain winding around a windlass echoed through the cave above the din of the stone slab sliding up into its sheath.

Threnton stepped through first. Delmecian followed only a moment later. The round chamber was filled with overturned bookcases, and books and tomes were strewn about the floor. Only the large desk on the far left of the chamber stood in place.

"What happened here?" Delmecian asked.

Threnton ignored the question. He wasn't about to tell Delmecian that he had already tried to search the library for the location of the legendary treasure only to come up empty-handed. It didn't matter though, for Delmecian was soon looking up and awestruck by what he saw.

"The ceiling is filled with glowing stones," he said.

Threnton glanced up to the cupola and nodded. "Dwarf craftsmanship," he said. "Now keep your voice down. We need to move quietly."

The dwarf didn't miss the fact that Delmecian was nearly drooling when his eyes spied a large chest near the desk. Threnton just urged the nobleman along and they exited the area quickly. They walked to the other side of the room where a large window was fitted into the wall with a hefty golden frame around it. Only, it wasn't a true window. The foggy glass let in light from the hallway beyond, but Threnton knew that from the hallway it appeared to be nothing more than a mirror.

"Ready?" Threnton asked.

Delmecian pulled a thin, long dagger from his belt and nodded.

Threnton reached out and pulled the jeweled handle on the glass door.

The heavy door moved silently on perfectly hung hinges. The two of them stepped through. The hallway was clear. No one was around. Delmecian held the door open while Threnton bent down and placed an old book into the doorway to keep it from sealing shut.

"Very clever," Delmecian whispered.

"Come, let us pay my brother a visit," Threnton said as he pulled his hood up over his head.

*****

Al stepped out from the short tunnel leading to the balcony and looked around. There didn't appear to be anyone there. Cautiously, he moved toward the ledge some fifteen feet away and looked down. The sheer cliff went down for hundreds of feet. So sheer was its face that even the mountain goats avoided it. He felt silly for even thinking someone might have climbed it.

There had been the stranger in green, but he had obviously used magic.

Al turned around, half expecting to see the stranger again, but there was nothing there. The mountain walls around him rose up, continuing toward the peak in a sharp incline. The tunnel stood open and clear.

Perhaps a servant had opened the door.

Yes, that must be it. Someone was cleaning and opened the door to air out the room.

Al wiggled his toes on the cold stone and then started for the tunnel.

The hairs on the back of his neck stood on end. Had it not been for the full moon at his back that night, he might not have caught a glimpse of the moving shadow approaching him. So faint and quick was its movement that he wasn't even sure what he had seen. Still, after his adventures with Erik, he knew better than to second guess his instincts.

Al dropped down to his knee and spun around, hammer in hand.

A glinting blade slashed through the air just over his head, close enough that he felt the displacement of the air as the assassin moved.

Al struck out and caught the human in the right knee. The joint buckled inward with a resounding *crack!* As the would-be assassin stumbled, Al recognized the tell-tale tattoos and shaved head of a Blacktongue assassin.

The dwarf launched a left handed punch into the Blacktongue's stomach, doubling the assassin over. Then he came up with the top of his hammer and struck the Blacktongue in the jaw as the assassin was falling. The jawbone shattered and the assassin fell unconscious to the ground.

Al jumped up and turned to shout for his guards, but another form was leaping down from above the tunnel. Al barely had time to roll to his left as a hatchet came spinning down at him. The blade chipped into the stone balcony, clanging loudly as it bounced out over the edge and fell. The second Blacktongue landed a moment later, swinging a wickedly curved sword in his right hand.

Al backpedaled out of the way as the tip of the sword whooshed by. The Blacktongue was sneering evilly, licking his lips and flexing his pectoral muscles as he stalked in closer.

The dwarf king had dealt with Blacktongues before, but never had they been so bold as to come to Roegudok Hall. Then it clicked in his mind. They had come because Threnton had sent them. Why else would they hunt him here? How else would they know of the king's balcony?

This thought gave Al a burst of strength that flowed through his body. He swung his hammer, the head connected with the Blacktongue's sword and the blade broke in three places. Sparks shot out as the metal fell to the stone.

The Blacktongue dropped the handle and went for a dagger, but Al was upon him and landed a devastating blow to the Blacktongue's ribs. The bones cracked and broke inward. The Blacktongue was thrown several feet to the side, gasping for breath.

Al knew the ribs had managed to puncture the Blacktongue's lungs when a stream of blood burst out from the assassin's mouth as he exhaled sharply. The assassin moved to attack, but winced in pain and recoiled.

The dwarf seized the opening and threw his hammer. It spun gracefully end over end until the head slammed into the Blacktongue's skull. The bone broke inward, leaving a grotesque, bloody dent in the human's forehead. The assassin fell to the ground, dead.

Al retrieved his hammer and turned back to finish the first Blacktongue.

The assassin had come to, and was pushing up to his feet.

"You should stay down," Al said as he readied to charge.

The Blacktongue never gave him the chance. The assassin turned and hopped on his good leg for the cliff and then leapt out into the night.

Needing to be sure that the fight was over, Al went to the edge and peered down.

He saw the flailing assassin tumbling through the air, falling to his death.

The dwarf king turned and made haste for his bedroom.

He called out for his guards.

The doors burst open, but it wasn't his guards who came in.

A hooded dwarf and a tall man wearing a dark blue cloak came inside and bolted the door from within. Al knew immediately that Threnton was hiding his face under the hood, but he didn't know who the human was. He recalled the stranger that had found him on the balcony before, but the man in green robes was much taller than this man, and their faces were different.

"Nice to see you, Brother," Al said derisively. "Couldn't make it on the outside?"

Threnton reached up slowly and pulled back his hood.

Al smirked when he saw the gray overtaking Threnton's naturally dark hair and beard. He recalled the time when they had fought before. Threnton had used stone shell, a special spell the dwarves of Roegudok Hall could employ but once in a lifetime due to its tremendous cost as it consumed half of a dwarf's life force.

"The throne is mine," Threnton said. "As is the Wealth of Kings."

Those last words hit Al the hardest. His eyes went wide and he cocked his head to the side. "Did you open the library again?" Al asked.

Threnton snorted. The deposed king turned to the human and gestured with his head toward Al.

The human brought his hands up and weaved a pattern in the air. A golden sphere of light formed in the air and shot out toward Al. The dwarf king somersaulted out to the right, managing to take cover beside his large bed. The golden orb crashed into the wall behind him and sizzled as smoke wafted up from the stone.

"Come on, Al, don't make this harder than it has to be," Threnton teased.

Before Al could think of a plan of action, the human circled out around the bed in a wide arc, maintaining a good distance between them as his hands weaved another spell in front of him. Al jumped up to his feet and charged the human.

Another sphere shot out. This time, Al was unable to dodge it entirely. It snagged his left arm and then it turned silver as the orb seemed to freeze in place. Al's arm was stuck. His skin was compressed and held still, but it wasn't very painful. Al tugged against the spell, but couldn't free his arm.

"Don't waste your time," Threnton said. "It's pointless to struggle now."

The human prepared another spell. Al raised his hammer and threw it. The weapon spun end over end, flying in

Threnton's direction. The other dwarf easily ducked under the hammer. The weapon flew into the door and smashed heavily into it before falling to the floor.

Then a flash of gold enveloped Al's body from his neck to his toes and started to squeeze him. Al struggled to breathe. The pressure came in from all sides. He was now trapped. He moved to yell, but a red orb hit him in the neck, and his voice was taken from him. Any time Al opened his mouth to call for help, a barely audible wheeze was all that came out.

"I need your face free so I can study it a moment," the human said as he moved in close to Al. "Then, when I am done, we can finish this nasty business and you will be free."

Threnton moved around and laughed at Al. "By free, he means dead, just in case that wasn't clear."

Al tried to move, tried to yell at his brother, but there was nothing he could do. The spell held him fast, suspended in the air and entirely helpless. The human moved in and placed his fingers on Al's forehead. He ducked in and around his own arm, studying Al's face for several moments.

Then, the human turned and muttered something Al didn't understand.

Before Al's very eyes, Threnton turned into an exact physical copy of Al. Everything was identical, down to the last hair.

"Marvelous, isn't it?" Threnton asked as he spun for Al to see. "This way, I can rule from the throne and none of them will need to know it is me. Soon, I will bring back the dwarves that are loyal to me. Eventually I will remove the mask, of course, but by then it will be too late to stop me. Your rule is over."

Threnton then turned to the human. "Go and get the bodies. We can't risk them being seen."

The human quickly moved out of Al's limited field of vision. When he returned, he was dragging the two guards along the floor. He took them out to the balcony through the tunnel.

"Don't worry," Threnton told Al. "We will take you out to join them next."

Al couldn't believe it. Everything he had been through with Erik and Master Lepkin. Fighting dragons, orcs, and wizards, and now he was outwitted by his brother. His mind flashed back to the fight they had had in the throne room.

Threnton came in close. "I bet you are wishing you had killed me when you had the chance," he whispered. "That is where we differ, brother," Threnton continued. He pulled a dagger and moved to stab Al, but a knock came at the door.

"Sire, are you alright?"

Al knew the voice at once. Judging from the scowl on Threnton's face, he had recognized it also.

"I am fine, Alferug, go away."

Al smiled. He couldn't scream, but his mouth still could move. He gathered as much spittle as he could and then he launched it directly into Threnton's face.

"Gargh!" Threnton yelled as he stepped back and wiped the liquid from his face.

"My king?!" Alferug shouted from the other side of the door.

"I'm fine!" Threnton shouted, but it was too late. The door was already opening.

Threnton rushed in, sheathing his dagger and reaching out to push Al back toward the bed. Al tried to struggle, but the spell held fast.

He landed hard, but with his face pointed under the bed. He couldn't warn Alferug, and Alferug was too late to see him.

"Forgive me, my king, I thought I heard you struggling." Alferug came in through the door and Al could see his blue leather shoes. They took three steps into the room. "Are you certain everything is alright?"

"I am fine," Threnton said, impersonating Al's voice rather well.

"I see," Alferug said. "I came because I wanted to discuss tomorrow's meeting."

"Let's talk about it in the morning," Threnton said.

"Of course," Alferug said. His feet turned and Al felt fear grip his soul. If Alferug left the chamber without discovering the danger, then all was lost. Al summoned all of his strength to shout, but nothing happened. He remained trapped in the spell. He watched helplessly as Alferug walked back toward the doorway.

Then the blue shoes stopped. After a moment, Al saw a hand reach down and pick up the hammer he had thrown. Al smiled. There was yet hope. Alferug knew how important the hammer was to Al. He would know that it would never be cast onto the floor.

"My king," Alferug started. "It appears you dropped your hammer. Shall I place it in its box?" Alferug asked.

"That isn't necessary, I'll do it," Threnton said.

Al could hear Threnton moving around the bed.

"It's alright," Alferug said. "I don't mind. Tell me, is the box still in the desk drawer?"

Threnton's footsteps stopped. "As you say," he replied.

Alferug's feet turned to point back into the room. They took two steps and then there was a *whoosh* through the air. A second later there was a heavy *thump*. Threnton fell to the ground, moaning.

Alferug rushed in, stepping heavily.

"Sire!" he shouted as he rounded the bed and came to Al.

Al felt himself turning over. He tried to warn Alferug about the human, but his voice still didn't work. Alferug frowned as Al tried to work his mouth. The advisor glanced out to Threnton and shook his head. "If not for your hammer, I wouldn't have suspected anything. This is some dark magic indeed!" Alferug worked his hands quickly, trying to tug at the solidified silver globs holding Al in place.

Alferug then went for his mithril dagger. "Hold still," he whispered. The advisor then stabbed into the material and worked his knife. To Al's surprise, the tactic worked. Alferug cut away hunks of the silvery stuff only to have each piece sizzle and evaporate as it was separated. Alferug worked at Al's right arm first, then his left.

As soon as Al had his hands free, he reached for the dagger and pulled it out of Alferug's hands. Al's left hand went up to his throat, feeling for where the red gob had struck him. He found a lip under the material and then plunged the flat of the knife in, sliding the side between his skin and the spell that sealed his voice.

"Careful, now. Let me do this part," Alferug demanded. He took the handle, pushing Al's hands away. He gently cut through the material, careful not to injure Al. All at once the stuff broke in half and fell like pieces of shattered clay.

"Threnton!" Al said quickly. "It's Threnton, and there is a wizard."

Alferug froze, his brow knit together and his eyes flashing hot. The advisor turned, but then his body went rigid and he groaned. Al looked up and saw that the human had snuck up behind Alferug. The old counselor let out a savage yell and rose to his feet, head-butting the wizard in the chest and driving him away.

Al furiously hacked at the spell holding his legs. He ripped and pulled the pieces apart. As soon as he was free, he was up on his feet and running to help his friend.

The wizard threw Alferug off of him and then followed up with a fireball. Alferug took the spell in the chest and lunged in. He managed to tackle the wizard to the ground, but there was no strength left in him to block the quick double-thrusting attack of the human's knife afterward.

Al made it to them just as the wizard pushed Alferug's body off of him and rose to his knees. Al drove Alferug's mithril dagger into the base of the human's skull, yanking it up into the man's cranium and ending him.

The dwarf king looked down to his gasping friend as he dropped the lifeless wizard.

There was nothing he could do for Alferug. Al leaned

Sam Ferguson

down and held his friend as the last gasps of air left his body. As the light dimmed in Alferug's eyes, Al heard another deep, loud breath.

He looked up to see Threnton coming back to consciousness.

Al gently laid Alferug back down on the floor and moved to Threnton.

The former king was clutching his chest as he turned to see Al walking toward him. "Remember," Threnton said. "You aren't like me."

Al gripped the mithril dagger in his hand and set his jaw. "Goodbye, Threnton," Al said.

Threnton's eyes went wide as the blade plunged into his heart. The dwarf convulsed twice and then went still.

Al rose from his brother's corpse and then left his room. If Threnton had gained access through the library, then maybe it was still open. Al would find out now if it was, and then afterward he would allow himself to mourn Alferug.

The dwarf king took his hammer in hand and made his way down the hall to the large mirror on the wall. As he hoped, he found it slightly ajar, propped open by a book. Al yanked the door open and hurried through to the library. What he found only gave him cause for grief. Books littered the floor and everything was tossed around haphazardly. It was obvious that Threnton had already been here, looking for clues to the Wealth of Kings.

Al wiped a streak of dust off the back of an overturned bookshelf and rubbed it between thumb and forefinger. Al yelled and bent down to strike a fist on the back of the wooden shelf. The wood split apart and Al beat it again and again. His cries echoed out from the small library and down the hall, but he didn't care. His frustration had boiled over what he could contain. He lifted the broken bookcase up and tossed it into a wall. He tore through the room like a whirlwind of fists and rage. Incensed, the dwarf king began picking up books and throwing them as well. The pages flittered and flapped through the air until they struck the wall and fell back to the floor.

He moved to the desk, grabbing one of the ends and hoisting it up to his waist. It was heavy, built of extremely dense wood, but Al didn't let it stop him. He shifted into a deep squat and then launched the desk over its end, sending it crashing into the wall.

Crack! The desk split in two. The top half tumbled to the ground, creaking and thumping as it rolled awkwardly down to the floor. Al rushed over, grabbed the broken half and heaved it across the room as he erupted in a feral yell.

The bank of drawers split apart upon impact with the stone. The top of the desk-half flipped up and then ricocheted out. The drawers split and shattered, and the wooden frame of the desk came entirely apart. As it did, a book shot out from what Al had previously thought was a solid wall in the desk.

The binding was made of green leather, the same type of binding used in Sylus' book of kings.

Al's fury vanished.

Had he finally found Sylus' other book?

The dwarf king clambered through the messy hall and bent down to scoop the tome up. It was sealed with a band of leather, but it was easily undone. Al opened the book and read the dark runes on the first page aloud.

"I, King Sylus Magdinium, pen this tome by mine own hand. If you have found it, then I suspect the bloodgrass has returned and you are searching for the Wealth of Kings. Read on, and I will explain everything, but know this, in the year the bloodgrass returns, there shall be much sorrow and suffering. Beware that you do not squander the lives of our kin in searching for that which is cursed."

CHAPTER 11

Year 3,499 King's Era.
299th year of the reign of Sylus Magdinium, 5th King of Roegudok Hall.

King Sylus stood pouring over a map of shaft 37. A mug of stale ale left its ring on the wooden table as the king ignored the drink. His back faced the large, mithril portcullis that he had erected in the tunnel as a final precaution. Around him and through the tunnel were camped one thousand dwarven soldiers. There were seven hundred cavedogs as well. Beyond the great mithril portcullis were another two thousand warriors. Those two legions were commanded by Sylus' sons, Ravik and Thorin.

"My king, come quickly!" a dwarf shouted as he ran toward Sylus from the other side of the portcullis.

Sylus looked up from his map. Dwarves were hopping into motion all around him. A pit formed in his stomach. Without even turning to see the runner, Sylus knew that the day he feared was upon him. The dwarf king turned and saw what he had hoped he never would.

The dwarf was running, nearly stumbling as he crossed beyond the mithril gate, and clinging to his left arm with his right hand. Blood streaked down from the left shoulder and ran over the dwarf's right hand. Sweat and blood matted the runner's hair. He cried out again as he fell to his knees.

"Come quickly, sire, we are under attack!" The dwarf's eyes were wide, and his chest heaved for breath. A few medical officers ran to him, but the runner collapsed to the floor, his skin ashen-white. His breathing slowed until his last breath escaped.

Sylus didn't bother checking the runner himself. He knew the look of death when he saw it. There would be nothing he, nor any of the medical officers could do to bring the runner back.

"To arms!" Sylus shouted. The army moved into position as quickly as they could. Sylus' cavedog zipped up next to him and he launched atop his saddle. He strode toward the gate and pointed to a group of seven dwarven footmen. "You seven stay here. Once we have passed through the gate, you close it."

"My king, you would be trapped inside."

Sylus nodded. "If I come back, you can reopen it. But it ends today. No more dwarves are allowed into this tunnel beyond this point. Close it. That is an order."

The dwarves nodded solemnly.

Sylus urged his mount onward. Soon he was joined by the sound of hundreds of claw-tipped lizard feet sprinting down the tunnel with him. They covered the three miles to where his sons had camped in less than twenty minutes, but by the looks of the battle, it was at least twenty minutes too late for most of the soldiers.

The mining chamber in this section of the tunnel spanned a mile across and was two miles long, tapering toward the end of the hall. The ceiling arced more than fifty feet overhead, with large spikes and columns of addorite stretching downward. It had taken ninety-two years to develop the mine, and the dwarves had fought lurkers and demons every step of the way. However, once they reached this massive chamber, they found more addorite here than even Tu'luh had imagined possible. Over the last year, they had concentrated solely on extracting the addorite from this chamber. If all had gone well, they would likely have been able to stop mining the pink crystal after this area had been mined out.

Seeing the destruction now, Sylus wished he had never

agreed to mine for the cursed crystal.

The glistening, pink crystals adorned large swaths of the chamber's walls. They hung from the ceiling above as well, but now their color was tainted by black smoke and crimson blood. An army of lurkers was cutting through the dwarven ranks furiously, backed, or perhaps led by a dozen demons.

Bodies lay everywhere. Miners made up the majority of the corpses heaped upon the ground, but there were well over a thousand dwarf soldiers lying dead upon the stone as well. Sprinkled throughout the heaps of dwarven bodies were dead lurkers and a few fallen demons, but the odds looked to be very much against the dwarves. Sylus feared the worst for his sons. He could not see any sign of them or their flags anywhere.

The dwarf king led the charge for a pair of demons that were busy crushing a battered group of soldiers two hundred yards in front of them.

"Crossbows!" Sylus shouted as they rode into the battle.

Bolts were pulled back into place as the soldiers prepared to fire. The cavedogs snarled and growled ferociously. The group of dwarves fighting the demons turned and ran toward Sylus, cheering at seeing reinforcements arrive. Sylus took aim with his double-bolt crossbow and fired at the closest demon.

The giant creature roared as the bolts closed in. A pair of brown, shiny wings wrapped around the demon like a cocoon, shielding it from the bolts. The second demon, seeing the first protect itself from the barrage of crossbow bolts, uttered an arcane spell that summoned a sphere of yellow energy around itself which deflected the crossbow bolts.

"They have magic!" one of the soldiers called out.

Sylus set his jaw and pulled Murskain, his mighty warhammer out and prepared for melee.

The others put away their crossbows and pulled axes, swords, and spears.

Sylus was the first to reach the winged demon. He

darted under the wings and struck out at the demon's leg with his hammer. To the dwarf king's satisfaction, the front of the demon's leg was not made of the same, shield-like skin that formed its wings. The shin split open and a river of blood coursed down the demon's shin. It pulled its leg up and launched into the air, taking flight with several hundred crossbow bolts protruding from its wings.

"Fire again!" Sylus ordered.

It took a few seconds, but a group of fifty dwarves pulled their crossbows out again and fired at the demon's belly. This time, the shafts struck true and the poisoned bolts worked their magic. The demon cried out in pain and convulsed uncontrollably as its wings collapsed and it crashed to the ground. In a larger turn of fortune, the demon crushed several lurkers beneath its weight, killing them as it twitched and writhed on the floor while the poison continued to work through its system.

"Look out!" someone shouted from behind.

Sylus turned to see the other demon casting yellow and orange fireballs out at the dwarves. The magical spheres exploded on impact. Some hit the floor and walls, spewing sparks and shards of stone and crystal, while others hit their target and obliterated dozens of dwarves and cavedogs, sending bodies rocketing through the air.

Sylus turned to engage the demon, but a lurker jumped over a pile of bodies and blocked his way. A massive, deadly claw streaked in front of Sylus, but it missed him. The lurker then swung with its other claw. This time, Sylus was forced to duck under the deadly, white appendage. Unfortunately, the lurker also launched a savage kick with one of its forelegs that caught Sylus' cavedog. Sylus fell to the stone as his cavedog skittered and bounced across the stone, squeaking and sprawling as it reached out with its claws.

The dwarf king looked up and saw both white claws coming down toward him. He held up his hammer and barely managed to stop the assault before the tips of the claws reached his face. The lurker snarled and leaned its weight forward. Sylus grunted as he struggled to keep the claws up with his hammer. The shiny, black scales along the lurker's underbelly shone a dark red as they were smeared with blood from the battle. The long, wicked fangs dripped with a mixture of blood and saliva as the beast opened its mouth and roared.

Sylus knew he was trapped. The lurker needed only to strike down with its mouth, and everything would be over.

The creature arched backward, preparing to strike with its terrible fangs. It snarled once and opened its mouth as wide as possible.

Then, a gleaming arrow flew into the lurker's mouth and exploded out the back of its head with a great spray of the nasty, yellow goo the lurkers had inside of them. A second later, a pair of dwarves rode in. The first struck the base of the creature's neck with his axe. The weapon bit through the scales, but failed to sever the head entirely. The second dwarf finished the task by driving his weapon into the gaping wound. They then turned and leapt from their cavedogs. The giant lizards lunged up, knocking the thrashing lurker body to the side and freeing Sylus.

The dwarf king rose to his feet and turned to see his son Ravik. Sylus nodded proudly at his son.

Ravik smiled and leapt atop a cavedog, riding it toward the fireball-throwing demon. He was one of the few dwarves to ever wield an actual bow. Most of the soldiers preferred crossbows, but Ravik had been blessed with arms long enough to wield a compact re-curve bow forged by the elves. It allowed him to fire upon enemies from a much greater distance than any crossbow-wielding dwarf, but that didn't mean Ravik was useless at melee combat. Quite the opposite was true. Ravik slid the bow over his shoulder and pulled a large, curved scimitar out from a black scabbard and charged the demon.

Sylus ran to his cavedog, and upon seeing that the animal was not injured save for a few scratches, clambered atop the saddle and charged in to help his son.

The forty-foot-tall demon had dropped its sphere, likely so it could continue to throw fireballs. It kicked and thrashed at the dwarves who came in close, squishing any slow enough not to evade his furious stomps. Ravik joined four others and they went for the left leg.

Sylus charged in, but from his vantage he saw something the others did not. The demon was squatting down, preparing to jump. Everything seemed to slow as Sylus called out to his son. Ravik never heard the warning.

The demon launched into the air before Ravik or the others could reach the leg. The gigantic creature sprawled out in the air, holding each hand out toward the ground as it tucked its feet up under itself. Two large cyclones of fire shot out from the hands. One whirled down and consumed seven dwarves and their cavedogs. The other snaked downward toward Ravik.

Ravik turned his cavedog away, but the force of the firenado was too strong. The four dwarves behind Ravik were pulled into the fire first, screaming and flailing as they flew up to be swallowed by the fire.

Ravik held tight, but his cavedog could not keep them on the ground. The two of them went up, tumbling backward in the air until the fire consumed them.

Sylus cried out, but he was helpless to stop it. He dropped his hammer and went for his crossbow. Other dwarves must have had the same thought, for several hundred crossbow shafts flew up and bit deeply into the demon's face and neck. The fires flamed out and the demon fell to the ground, shaking the immediate area around itself.

The dwarf king rushed in, but Ravik was gone. Nothing was left of Sylus' eldest son.

The dwarves swarmed in around him, fighting off a dozen lurkers that had advanced on their position. Screams and terrible cries of agony rose up all around Sylus, but none were as loud, nor as gut-wrenching, as his. The dwarf king ranted upon the ground and screamed his son's name over and over.

It wasn't until he felt a tug at the back of his armor that Sylus regained some of his senses. He turned around to see his cavedog pulling at him, urging him to rejoin the battle. Sylus looked around and saw his soldiers fighting and dying. He looked up to curse Tu'luh, but that was when he saw a score of lurkers crawling across the ceiling. Their black fur helped them blend into the shadows, but he saw them nonetheless.

"Lurkers on the ceiling!" Sylus shouted. "Lurkers on the ceiling!" He knew that if his soldiers didn't react quickly, the lurkers would drop down behind them.

Fortunately, several dwarves heard Sylus' warning and the shouts spread through the ranks quickly. Crossbows were pointed up and fired. A couple of lurkers fell to the ground, but most continued on. A couple hundred dwarves moved back, leaping off from their cavedogs and letting the lizards run toward the back of the chamber. By the time the lurkers dropped, the dwarves and cavedogs had prepared, and the lurkers were cut down with minimal losses.

Sylus pressed across the battlefield. He saw another two demons die by his warriors' hands, but the dwarves were being cut down by the score at the front of the field. The remaining demons spewed fire, conjured lightning, and used massive weapons to obliterate the dwarf lines.

The dwarf king called out orders, sending his warriors in to flank the lurkers and hem them in as much as possible. For ten or fifteen minutes, the battle seemed almost even. Lurkers died in tens and dozens. Dwarves fell just as fast, but the cavedogs were running through and around the lurkers, helping to cut the enemy down.

Another demon fell, a crossbow bolt protruding from its third eye in its forehead. A second demon died shortly after, but then the battle took a turn for the worse.

A winged, fire-breathing demon launched into the air. It spewed fire out over the battlefield and in one swoop killed at least sixty dwarves, as well as many cavedogs that had been in the fire's path. A group of dwarves moved in and lined up their crossbows, but the winged demon dropped to the ground and took cover behind a row of lurkers. The giant, bug-like monsters charged forward, spitting their vile slime at the dwarves, blinding several of them. The crossbows managed to take down two of the lurkers, but the rest pressed forward until the two groups clashed in battle.

Sylus shook his head as the lurkers ripped through the dwarves and then pressed in to attack another group. A few more dwarves fell before a small group of cavedogs moved in and evened things out by killing three of the lurkers. Sylus then stared with his mouth open in horror as the demon launched upward again and showered the area in a flood of lightning bolts. The purple and blue streaks blasted through the dwarves, dropping them in seconds. Then the demon spewed more fire, killing the lurkers and dwarves unfortunate enough to be caught by the flames.

Sylus urged his cavedog onward. He held Murskain firmly in hand and prepared to attack the cursed demon. A lurker lunged in from the side, but Sylus knocked its head clean off with his hammer and continued his charge toward the demon. The great, brown-winged beast hovered in the air above the field. The flames had ceased to issue forth from the demon's mouth, but it continued to send out bolt after bolt of terrible lightning.

The dwarves cried out in agony, none of them able to get in close enough to kill the demon.

Sylus charged in from the demon's left. The king's cavedog darted in a zig-zag pattern, carefully to keep Sylus in the demon's blind spot. Then, when they were close enough, Sylus flipped his hammer over and launched it through the air. As he released his weapon, he uttered a prayer, not to the Ancients, but to Icadion, the God of Terramyr.

The weapon flew true and the spike on the back of the hammer sunk into the demon's neck. It shrieked in horror and fell to the ground, wings flapping furiously as dwarves swarmed in and finished it off. Sylus continued to urge his mount forward so he could retrieve his hammer, but a heavy slap hit his right side. A moment later, another, heavier force knocked into him. His armor held, but he was thrown from his cavedog. He slid across the stone, his armor screeching along until he stopped. Sylus looked up and saw a lurker looming over him.

The two claws went up into the air.

Sylus had no hammer. He had only his daggers, and they were not going to be able to block the large, menacing claws.

A dark form leapt up and ran along the lurker's back. The lurker jerked around, snarling and hissing. The dwarf king watched in amazement as his very own cavedog clawed its way up the lurker's back and sank its teeth into the monster's neck. The lurker howled and swung its claws at the cavedog, but the lizard was not in a spot it could reach. The cavedog tugged and pulled at the lurker's neck. Sylus got up to his feet and pulled his daggers. He studied the lurker's movements, looking for an opening to rush in and stab it in the chest.

When he thought he saw his opportunity, he sprinted in. The lurker must have seen him though, for a leg lashed out and kicked Sylus in the chest, sending him back to the same spot on the stone where he had landed before.

The cavedog used the distraction to claw higher onto the lurker. It bit twice, and then ripped the head free from the neck. The lurker's body began to spasm and flail about. Sylus got to his feet and motioned for his cavedog to return to him. The obedient lizard leapt down from the lurker's back and ran toward Sylus. As his cavedog ran in from of the thrashing lurker, the monster's left claw came down and cut the lizard's back third off. The cavedog grunted and slumped to the ground. A moment later, the right claw dropped down, piercing the cavedog through the spine. Then the lurker's body went limp and collapsed on the stone.

Sylus stood frozen, mouth agape and eyes staring at his cavedog. He turned in anger, looking for an enemy to chase down, and that was when he saw his other son.

Thorin was sprawled upon the ground. His eyes open, but dull. Blood seeped from a gash in his head. His left arm was severed just above the wrist. The hand still fiercely gripped his sword. His armor was dented and a large hole had been ripped into the breastplate.

Sylus ran to his son's body and cradled it in his arms as he wept openly. He forgot about the battle around him, surrendering to the pain and agony he felt inside his tearing heart. He bent low and pressed his head to Thorin's, crying and shaking as he rocked on his knees, holding Thorin's broken body.

There he remained for another half an hour. The fight raged on around him. The sounds of swords clanging against lurker scales and hammers splitting bone resounded through the chamber, but he no longer paid them any mind. The dwarf king also ignored the shouting of his warriors, and the snarling cavedogs that continued to fight.

Only when the din calmed, and the fighting ceased, did Sylus look up from his son. He looked around, surveying the grotesque field of desolation and blood around him. He saw no movement whatsoever. The shouting and yelling was gone as well. Sylus slid Thorin's body down gently and he rose to his feet. He spun around, looking for any sign of survivors. He saw none. Worse still, there was no groaning of wounded dwarves. There were no snarling cavedogs. Everyone was dead.

Sylus let his hands fall back to his daggers as he stood, stunned. He didn't see any enemies either. He looked up, but there were no lurkers upon the ceiling. Everything was dead. He was all that was left. He turned back and let his eyes linger upon Thorin once more, and then he turned to look for his hammer, Murskain.

As he picked his way through the corpses, he heard a rustling sound a short ways off to his right. He turned to see a demon slowly pushing itself up to its knees from the ground. It appeared to be winged, but its left wing was missing, perhaps torn off in battle. Blood ran down its right arm from a gash in its shoulder. A row of horns crowned its head. Fiery, red eyes blinked twice and then narrowed on Sylus. The demon grinned wickedly, revealing a mouth full of jagged teeth. It pushed up to its feet and stood a full twenty feet tall. It bent down and picked up a long, curved sword with its right hand and started moving toward Sylus.

The dwarf king took in a breath and pulled his two mithril daggers out. As he watched the demon move, he channeled his anger and pain. His mind conjured both the image of his broken Thorin lying upon the stone, and of Ravik being consumed by fire.

"It ends now," Sylus growled. He ran forward, jumping over corpses and limbs as the two closed in on each other. The demon predictably led off with a diagonal swing at Sylus. The dwarf king spun out and around the blade, then continued in toward the demon's legs. He flipped his left dagger over in his hand and launched it through the air. It spun quickly and then sunk deep into the demon's thickly-muscled thigh.

The demon recoiled and came in with another swing of its sword, but Sylus had expected that. He dove down, taking cover next to a dead lurker. The demon's sword cut through the lurker, but only barely grazed Sylus' armor. The dwarf king rose to his feet and sprinted in. The demon lifted its left foot and moved to stomp on Sylus.

Sylus darted for another dead lurker and slid down beside it, grabbing the long, white claw with his left hand and turning it upward. The foot came down. Sylus was knocked flat to the ground, but the claw was nearly three feet long. It pierced through the demon's foot and the giant creature howled in pain and stumbled backward.

Sylus regained his breath, jumped up, and ran toward the falling demon. A mere second after the giant monster fell and landed on its back, Sylus clambered up onto its bare stomach, ran up to its chest, and plunged his knife down between the demon's ribs. The demon cried out and shot out lightning-fast with its left hand. The fingers curled around Sylus and a couple of the talon-like fingernails pierced through the dwarf king's armor just enough to scratch Sylus' chest. The demon's claws stung, but they presented no mortal danger. The dwarf king sliced the webbing between the demon's thumb and forefinger. The demon cried out and released Sylus.

The dwarf then sprinted up and lunged for the demon's throat. He plunged the knife in, and the demon was ended.

Sylus removed his armor and set it upon the demon's corpse. He looked down to the holes in his tunic and examined the thin lines of blood starting to flow out from the small puncture wounds. Then he retrieved his knives and jumped down from the demon's body.

He stumbled through the battlefield, clumsily looking for Murskain. After falling to the ground a few times, and walking in a large circle around a pair of dead demons, he found it lying upon the stone, next to a dwarf captain's body.

Sylus picked up his weapon and began the long trek back to the gate. His body ached, and his very soul was numb, yet his fight was not finished yet.

Before he could think of rest, he needed to summon Tu'luh.

*****

Sylus bolted his door from the inside, much to the chagrin of the physician who was still pounding on it and begging to see to the king's wounds. The dwarf king removed his stained tunic and walked out through the tunnel to the large balcony. The pedestal with the summoning crystal stood in its place. As the king removed the cloth, he could feel the crystal mocking his pain.

He spoke the incantation and the sphere glowed bright, firing the column of light up into the heavens as it had always done before. Sylus stepped away from the pedestal and waited, leaning upon his hammer for support.

It was hours before Tu'luh arrived, but Sylus forced himself to stand by the sheer power of will as he waited. Then, when he heard the tell-tale heavy wings beating the air, the king was invigorated by the anger that had been developing within his heart over the years. He looked to the sky and saw the dark form cross in front of the crescent moon. The shadow covered the large platform of stone, and then the dragon dropped down and let out a small, blue flame as it turned to face Sylus.

"Has there been a new development?" Tu'luh asked.

Sylus nodded quietly, staring at the dragon and barely able to contain the hatred he felt roiling in his blood. "We are done," Sylus said.

Tu'luh cocked his massive head to the side. "You have mined all of the addorite?" he asked.

Sylus shook his head and stepped closer to the summoning crystal, letting the light reveal the dried blood streaked down his chest and the two, black holes caused by the demon. "I mean, we are done. There will be no more mining for your precious addorite."

Tu'luh roared and flames flashed between them. "Remember your place!"

Sylus did not back down. "I know my place," he said sternly. "I am King Sylus Magdinium, the protector of Roegudok Hall. I am not a slave to you, or to any winged serpent any longer. Nor shall my people be forced to throw away their lives for your cursed crystals!"

Tu'luh moved in quickly and knocked Sylus down with an extension of his left wing. The dragon then turned and hoisted its massive tail over Sylus, threatening to crush him. "The servant cannot reject the master!"

Sylus pushed up to his feet, his aching muscles fueled by his rage. He spoke in the arcane language used by the Ancients. "Ole mennyt, kiusaaja."

Tu'luh snarled. "What did you say?"

Sylus grinned and repeated his words in the Common Tongue, "Be gone, tormentor."

The tail came down.

Sylus thrust his hammer up, connecting with Tu'luh's tail. The force of the blow pushed Sylus down slowly to his knee, but the dwarf was able to stop the tail from crushing him. "Be gone!" Sylus shouted. He slipped out from under the tail and then came down upon the tail with the spike of his hammer. The spike broke through a scale and pierced Tu'luh's flesh.

The dragon roared and thrashed his tail to the side, flinging Sylus into the stone wall.

Sylus moved as a taloned foreleg came swiping out for him. Tu'luh's claws sent sparks flying as they dug into the stone wall. Sylus knew he couldn't defeat the dragon. Even if his body wasn't fatigued, the Ancient was far more powerful than Sylus could ever hope to be. So, he hit the dragon where it hurt most.

The dwarf king sprinted for the summoning crystal. He raised his mighty warhammer into the air and shouted at the top of his lungs, "Liberty!" Sylus brought the hammer down in a powerful arc. The light shining into the heavens exploded into a bright orb engulfing the platform as the sphere burst into a thousand shards under the weight of the hammer.

The mountain trembled and seemed to groan as the light expanded out and then disappeared into the night. Tu'luh was thrown back by the blast and forced to leap into the air when the platform cracked and the majority of the stone slab tilted and slid away from the mountain. The rocks popped and fractured as the slab jerked and shifted out away from the tunnel. A heavy, dull scratching sound filled the air as the slab fell away from the mountain, carrying with it the remainder of the pedestal that had once held the summoning crystal. Sylus smiled as the heavy slab crashed into the cliff on the way down and broke into many smaller pieces.

Not only was there no more summoning crystal, there was no longer a space for any dragon to land upon Roegudok Hall. What had once been a great, vast platform, was now little more than a stone balcony big enough for a few dwarves. It was a jagged precipice, really. A place from which the dwarf king could survey the valley beyond the mountain and contemplate the circumstances of his people. From now on, any king who sought solace here, would be afforded a private pondering place free from the shackles of the Ancients.

"You are very foolish," Tu'luh said as he slowly beat

his wings to stay afloat above Sylus. "You do not understand the workings of this world."

Sylus looked up defiantly and beat his chest. "I understand the importance and value of my people," he replied.

Tu'luh snorted derisively as a plume of flame shot out from his nostrils. "If you truly valued your kin, you would serve your creators."

"You have brought us only death, and slavery."

Tu'luh let out a throaty growl. "I will leave you with this warning. This is the last year of the Age of Kings. A group of mortals has ascended beyond their appointed station and taken upon themselves the mantle of demi-god. A new era begins shortly, the Age of Demigods. It is only a matter of time before they bring down a destruction upon Terramyr that you could not imagine. Perhaps then you will see the wisdom of the Ancients."

"Be gone, serpent, I will heed no more of your lies and fearmongering."

Tu'luh swished his tail in the air and rose higher as his wings beat stronger and stronger with each flap. "You leave me no choice," Tu'luh said. "If you will not see reason, then I will find a way to force you to dig the addorite up. Mark my words, the next time I light upon Roegudok Hall, it will be with a sore vengeance, and none shall be able to oppose me."

The great dragon turned and flew away, blasting fire and roaring angrily as he disappeared into the night sky.

Sylus turned back to his tunnel. Now was the time he would set things right for his people. He decided in that moment to destroy all of the old records containing the origin of the dwarves of Roegudok Hall. No more would they worship, or associate with the cursed Ancients. More than that, he would seal up the mine, and destroy all knowledge of it and the addorite it contained. Never again would a dwarf lose his life needlessly in the depths of the mountain. It would be enough to mine for gold and jewels in the more shallow parts, far above the demons and the vile lurkers.

CHAPTER 12

Year 3,711 Age of Demigods, Mid-Autumn.
2nd year of the reign of Aldehenkaru'hktanah Sit'marihu, 13th King of Roegudok Hall.

Al sat upon the edge of the king's balcony, his feet dangling over the side. A cool morning breeze gently rose up and caressed his face. He looked down to the green leather bound book resting on the stone next to him. "To think that this very spot used to be a large landing platform for the Ancients," Al said as he stared at the book. "What Alferug wouldn't give to have known something like that."

The dwarf king hadn't slept for days. Aside from overseeing the process of clearing the bodies from his chamber and trying to identify the human, which they were unable to do, he had sent a trio of scouts out to try and identify where Threnton had been hiding. There was a concern that some of the emigrants from the mountain might have linked forces with Threnton, and could be nearby. Benbo had been quick to assure Al that if any rebels existed that intended to do harm to Roegudok Hall, he would handle them swiftly.

Then, Al had helped carry Alferug to the burial shrine. The morticians worked carefully to prepare Alferug properly for the funeral rites which would require three days' preparation.

Afterward, the king had tried to return to his room and sleep, but his thoughts were consumed by the book written by Sylus. He read through it twice before the sun had risen in the east on the third morning after the attack. He hadn't bothered to come out of his chamber in that entire time, except for the few times to receive food brought up by servants, and now to sit upon the balcony and take in some much needed fresh air. Everything Sylus' book had revealed to him had changed Al's perspective entirely.

Still, even with the book's warnings, he couldn't help but recall the voice that had come to him in shaft thirty-seven. Al was destined to find the wealth of kings. But why? According to everything in Sylus' book, the mine should remain closed. Forever. He wished Alferug were still around. Al would very much have liked to discuss the dilemma with him.

As it was, there were only a few hours before the funeral rights were scheduled to happen.

Despite having reading the contents of the book, Al had not called for a halt to the mining. He knew that if he stopped it now, he might avoid waking the demons, but he would also be sentencing his people to starve through the winter.

Al reached over and took a pebble in his right hand. He extended his arm out and dropped the small rock over the edge. It quickly disappeared from view as it sailed downward. Al wondered what it must have been like for King Sylus to face off against Tu'luh by himself. Had he expected to defeat the dragon, or had he assumed he would die? Al was unable to answer that question, but he knew one thing for sure. Tu'luh had remained true to his word. He had come to subjugate Roegudok Hall in the end, not to mention the whole of the Middle Kingdom and the orc nations besides.

Sitting on that ledge, Al couldn't help but wonder what might have happened if Sylus had continued to mine the addorite. Then again, he would likely soon find out for himself. Sylus' book had made mention of other gold and mithril veins down within the last chamber of mine thirty-seven where all of the addorite had formed. Al's people needed the treasure to buy food.

More than that, Al had a better understanding than did Sylus about The Infinium. He had spoken with Erik and Master Lepkin about it many times during the war against Tu'luh the Red. From what he understood, The Infinium was the only book that unlocked the mysteries of the four horsemen, a terrible force the likes of which was unsurpassed in destructive power. To hear Master Lepkin or Lady Dimwater describe them, the four horsemen were beings capable of destroying entire planets, and never before had any planet marked for destruction been rescued from their onslaught. Erik asserted that Terramyr was already set on a path that would bring the four horsemen one day, and they would kill the world, and everything on it. The Infinium promised to have an answer for this otherwise inescapable destruction. It was Terramyr's only hope for ensured survival.

If the Ancients needed the addorite to read The Infinium, then Al was going to try and get it for them. He knew Erik would do the same if he had been presented with the choice.

Al turned and rose to his feet, scooping Sylus' secret book up into his arms and moving back through the tunnel to his chamber. He set the book down upon the desk and moved toward his wardrobe. As officiator of the funeral rites for Alferug, he would need his ceremonial armor. He hated the ostentatious suit. He had even offered to sell it or break down its components for use in bartering for food, but Alferug had rejected the idea outright.

"That is a symbol of our heritage," Alferug had said.

Al smiled weakly as he opened the wooden door to the cabinet that concealed the armor. At least he had found one chest of gold in the library. That would go a long way toward buying his people more time. Still, with the merchant guilds in the Middle Kingdom joining forces to gouge prices for produce and meat, the newfound treasure wouldn't go as far as Al would have otherwise liked.

He stared at the gaudy suit of armor sitting upon its stand inside the cabinet and sighed. "If it were anyone else's funeral, I would wear my smithing apron and black trousers," Al grumbled to himself. He didn't mean it, of course. The funeral traditions were held sacred among the dwarves of Roegudok Hall, but he couldn't help but feel like a stuffed pig on display at a feast whenever he thought of wearing the royal armor.

Al reached into the cabinet and pulled out the first pieces he needed. He could have asked for help, but he didn't want anyone else around him until he had had a few more moments to think by himself. He begrudgingly changed into his royal armor. It wasn't as functional a suit as one he would make for himself. It was meant for occasions such as this, where the show and perception of power was more important than the armor's actual strength or utility. A silver encrusted breastplate with gold inlay around the engraved edges shone brightly in the torchlight of his room. Each masterfully carved rune was traced with a line of gold. Each rivet that attached the layering plates was covered with a cap of ruby or emerald stone. The suit was polished to such a high sheen that Al could see his reflection as clearly as if he looked into a mirror. The greaves were equally as stunning. They were made from black, Telarian steel. Sharp contrasting lines of silver and gold were braided down the outer sides of the greaves, weaving around each other in such a way as to dazzle any onlooker when the armor walked past.

He fastened the greaves first, and then moved to sit in a backless chair to put his boots on. The insides of the boots were made of leather lined with thin rabbit fur to keep the sharp, rigid plates of steel from cutting into him. He barely managed to stuff his feet down inside without falling over backwards off the chair, but he eventually succeeded in hitching them to the greaves with the clasps just below the knee. Al stood up and swung his right leg out. His range of motion was drastically reduced. He would have to walk slowly. He turned and began donning the pads that went under the breastplate and pauldrons before grabbing the outer armor itself. Al slid his hands into the gauntlets afterward. They were longer than most conventional gauntlets, stretching out to cover the forearm up to the elbow joint. Rubies and sapphires studded the wrists of the plated gauntlets, while a great diamond was set in the middle of the forearm so as to look like an eye, outlined in gold. The final piece was the helmet. Al took the open faced helmet in hand and looked at the crown fused to the top. As if the rest of the ensemble wasn't gaudy enough, the crown featured a diamond directly in the center, flanked by two rectangular cut amethysts, which were followed around the rim by a pattern of emeralds, sapphires, rubies, and onyx.

"I still think it needs a unicorn's horn," Al quipped.

He set the helmet atop his head and moved to look in the nearest mirror. It was terrible. He could barely stand to look at himself. He wasn't like a stuffed pig at all. No, he looked more like a prancing, primping peacock with jewels tied to the body. Had he not been going to the funeral rites, he would have torn the ridiculous suit of armor off and kicked it under the bed to hide it, or perhaps tossed it over the balcony outside.

"I'm selling this thing as soon as I can," Al promised himself.

He made his way out and into the tunnel. As soon as he was in the hallway, he was flanked and followed by six guards. When they had learned of the attack, his bodyguards had insisted they would be going everywhere with him. It was a wonder they let him remain alone inside his room over the last couple of days. Both Kijik and Benbo had argued that Al should let them post permanent guards on the king's balcony as well. Al had been able to broker a compromise, but it was still one that he felt uncomfortable with. Any place outside of his own bedchamber, he was to be accompanied at all times by half a dozen warriors. Al figured he would be spending a lot more time in his room, or perhaps he could have them remain in the throne room if he was in his forge with his apprentices.

They moved down through the mountain and into a large shrine that was located a quarter mile to the west of the main hall. It was modest enough, but still displayed the proud dwarven workmanship that so characteristically defined the rest of Roegudok Hall.

Four half-columns were carved from the walls, which were in turn engraved to look as though the shrine was built with stone brick, rather than simply hollowed out from the mountain. A single dwarven rune was carved into each of the half-columns.

Stone pews formed the seating area before the raised dais and granite pulpit. Behind the pulpit, a large mural was painted onto the stone wall showing Hiasyntar'Kulai, the Father of the Ancients. The painting had been ordered by Al's father several centuries before. Al smirked when he saw it. He wondered what Sylus would say if he could see such a mural in place now.

Then his eyes drifted down and he saw the stone casket lying in front of the pulpit. His heart sank. He stepped toward the coffin and rested his hands on the open edge, looking down to Alferug. The deceased, gray-haired dwarf looked as though he were simply resting with his hands at his sides. Al shook his head and sighed heavily.

"The lining should be silk," he said to Alferug. "Forgive me, my friend, but wool is all we can afford at this time. I know it doesn't fit for a dwarf of your stature, but it is the best I can do." Al nearly smiled as he reached up to wipe a tear. "You know," he said half choking on the lump in his throat. "I could have gotten you silk lining if you had let me sell this ridiculous suit of armor." He laughed once, a forced, short lived moment that had the sound of mirth but carried with it none of the joy.

*****

"Hey, boss, I found something," a miner called out as he rolled a large boulder out from a pile of stones leading into a small side chamber that was only a few feet deep and perhaps a yard wide.

The crew leader walked up and whistled as he approached a large mound of pink crystals sprouting up under the heavy boulders. "Alright, clear a bit more of this rubble out of the way and start mining that up," the boss said.

"When do you think this stuff formed here?" the miner asked.

The crew leader shrugged. "Beats me. I would wager that if this patch of crystal had been here before they closed the shaft down originally, they would have extracted it already. Don't know how it could form here, under all this rubble, but this will maybe earn us a dinner with the king, if we're lucky."

A couple of the other miners laughed.

They were quick about moving the stones away and then they set to work chipping the crystals out of the mound.

Lemi, the explosives expert, started making a few bombs, just in case they wanted to try and blow the wall to see if there was anything else out to the side. He set the fuses and pulled his matches out onto his lap as he watched the others collect the pink crystals.

"Is it just me, or does this crystal feel warm?" one of the miners asked.

"Aye, it does a bit, doesn't it," another replied.

The crew leader brought a large sack over and set it down in front of the others and they began putting the crystal inside.

Lemi finished his third bomb and was about to set them aside when he felt a sudden gush of wind. He looked up, and suddenly a large creature appeared atop the mound. Lemi raised his hand and shouted out a warning, but it was too late. A long, white claw ripped through one of the miners. The creature had shaggy black fur along its back and shiny, black scales along its underbelly. It snarled and displayed fearsome fangs.

The crew leader turned and was about to call out for the guards, but at that moment another creature seemed to appear out of nothing from the top of the mound. This second creature was brown, with glowing, orange veins running beneath its skin. A pair of fiery wings jutted out from its back and it held a mighty spear in its left hand. Without hesitation, the demon threw the spear through the crew leader's neck.

Lemi did the only thing he could think of, he lit a bomb and threw it at the demon. The bomb arced over the winged creature and landed on the crystal mound. A moment later, it exploded, sending shards of crystal everywhere. A half-second after the black, scaly monster was obliterated, a large shard of stone pierced Lemi's chest. The dwarf slumped to the side and looked down at his chest. Blood seeped out around the wound.

He looked up and saw that the mound of crystals was now buried in stone. The other miners were dead, but the demon was walking toward Lemi, and it was angry. Lemi's last thought was how far the demon could make it through the tunnels before someone could stop it. Then a massive, clawed foot came down and crushed the life out of him.

*****

Al closed his eyes.

He placed a hand on Alferug's cold chest and then patted his friend affectionately before moving to take his place at the pulpit. The bodyguards took up their protective positions, and began admitting those invited to the funeral rite. Al watched as the other members of the council entered the room, followed by Alferug's immediate and extended family. Alferug's wife had passed on twenty years before, but his children and their families still remained. There were also cousins, nieces and nephews, and a host of grandchildren, great grandchildren, and other descendants. The room filled within minutes.

Al looked down, hoping somehow that Alferug would yet rise from his coffin and apologize for causing everyone to worry. He knew that wouldn't happen, but he couldn't help but wish for it.

The doors closed then, echoing throughout the shrine

and signaling that it was time for Al to begin.

He looked out at the crowd and then he turned his eyes to the four half-columns. He then glanced down to Alferug and offered a sincere smile to his departed friend.

"As king," Al began. "It is incumbent upon me to give a rote speech during the funeral rites. I am to talk about how we were formed from the stone in Roegudok Hall, and thus when we die we shall return to what gave us life, thereby completing a cycle. However, when I look at Alferug, my dearest friend inside the mountain, I cannot recite the words. They feel hollow, and I think all of you would agree with me when I say that that wouldn't be good enough for Alferug Henezard." Al pointed to the four half-columns. "Look to those columns and you will see a single rune carved into each one. Honor. Truth. Courage. Duty." Al took a breath and nodded his head as he let the crowd glance at the pillars for a moment.

"Alferug Henezard exemplified each of those traits. He lived his life with honor. He sought for, and cherished the truth. His sense of duty was unfailing, as I can attest, having seen him when he was exiled. He remained close to Roegudok Hall even then, when my brother shunned him and banished him from the mountain. He did this because he truly cared about each and every dwarf in this mountain. No one can question his courage either. He not only helped me confront Threnton, but he also gave his life for mine when Threnton and a group of assassins attacked me in my bedchamber."

Al felt a tear fall from his eye, but he made no move to wipe it from his face. "I am proud to have called him friend. I am honored to have benefitted from his mentoring. I am hopeful, that I will live up to his legacy. I would go so far as to say we likely all feel the same way."

Al reached into the shelf at the back of the pulpit and pulled a crystal bell.

"It is said, that this was the first crystal mined from Roegudok Hall. If we are to believe the books of the kings, this crystal was found the day the first prince was born in

Roegudok Hall. It was fashioned into a bell, to be rung whenever a dwarf dies in Roegudok Hall." Al rang the bell once. It's sharp, delicate sound reverberated through the chamber. "We ring the bell to announce to the mountain that another dwarf's body is returning home to the womb that created him." Al rang the bell again. "We ring the bell to announce to Nage that a noble dwarf spirit is ready to cross over the rainbow bridge and take his place in Volganor, the Heaven City." Al rang the bell once more. "We ring the bell so that the departed may know we have not forgotten them."

The adults in the audience produced small, brass bells of their own. In unison, they repeated the ritual with Al. They rang their bells the first time, the sounds and pitches mixing and mingling. They spoke the same words Al had spoken. When the ritual was completed, the dwarves rose and filtered out of the shrine.

Al placed the crystal bell back onto the shelf and waited until all of the others had exited the shrine, then he moved down and closed the stone casket. A team of dwarves led by the mortician, all dressed in black robes, pushed a long, four-wheeled cart.

"We are ready to move him into the catacombs," the mortician said.

"Rest well, my friend," Al told Alferug. "Keep a watchful eye on us from above."

Al stayed in the shrine for a couple of hours after they had wheeled Alferug's body away, sitting on the first pew in the room and staring at the mural painted on the wall behind the pulpit. He would have stayed there for the remainder of the day, except there was a terrible commotion that erupted outside the shrine.

Al rose to his feet, but the bodyguards were first to the door.

"What is it?" Al asked.

One of the body guards signaled for the others to protect Al, then he turned to the king. "I will go and see, Sire. Please, stay here."

The bodyguard disappeared out through the door, but it didn't take long for Al to understand what was happening. He heard a loud, terrible roar that nearly shook the stone walls of the mountain.

"We have woken a demon," Al said. He looked to his guards, "Come, we must protect our people!"

CHAPTER 13

Year 2, Age of Demigods
301st year of the reign of Sylus Magdinium, 5th King of Roegudok Hall.

Sylus coughed and pulled the wool blanket tighter around his shoulders as he struggled to keep his hand from shaking. He had to finish writing his book. It had been over two years since he had last seen Tu'luh. The dwarf folk were recovering slowly from the heavy casualties they suffered in the deeper mines, but there was prosperity to be had for all.

Mine thirty-seven had been closed off with the large mithril portcullis and the tunnel leading to the giant chamber had been collapsed by the hand of a dozen explosives engineers. The bloodgrass had died and was no longer growing in Roegudok Hall. The lurkers and demons no longer assaulted the dwarves, and the tunnels that remained open were safe.

Yet Sylus was plagued by dreams in the night.

He saw the bloodgrass returning. He saw a future king opening the mithril portcullis and reawakening the demons sleeping in the great depths of the lower tunnels. He saw blood and destruction returning to his people. For this cause, he penned a special book. In it, he spoke of his plight with the demons and lurkers. He warned against trusting the Ancients, and he all but forbade reopening the lower mines.

Sylus sighed as he pulled his shaking hand back from the page. He set his pen down into the inkwell and reached for a cobalt blue bottle with a cork stopper. He pulled the stopper free and drank half of the bottle's contents. The cool liquid tingled as it slid down his throat. Then, a few seconds later, his stomach burned. Sylus gripped the edge of the desk as the burning spread through his entire body. He hated the medicine, but he knew it was the only thing keeping the tremors at bay. As the burning moved into his arm, his hand ceased to shake. His mind cleared, and he was once again able to create the delicate runes of the dwarven language.

It had taken him the better part of a month to write about the dangers of mine thirty-seven. As he finished describing the horrors he had witnessed, he began to have a new kind of nightmare. He saw the well go dry, leaving the dwarves of Roegudok Hall without water. Then he saw the gold, silver, mithril, and gems disappear from the mines. He saw the aftermath of a great war in the Middle Kingdom. Worse than that, he saw that the only way for Roegudok Hall to restore its wealth, and save its people from starvation, would be to reopen the mine where his sons had perished.

He saw the king who would find mine thirty-seven, and noted that bloodgrass would return to the mountain weeks before this future king would stumble into the bowels of Terramyr, and thus awaken the demons. No matter how hard he tried to focus on his visions, he could never see beyond the point that the future king opened the mithril portcullis set deep within the mines.

He feared for Roegudok Hall greatly. Even in his prime, with thousands of warriors under his command and enough treasure to supply every desire, they had failed to conquer the deeper mines. If the future king would rule during a time of famine when the dwarves were recovering from a massive war, how could they hope to prevail?

Sylus finished the book that morning, wrapped in his woolen blanket.

He ended it with a warning.

"Beware not to squander dwarven blood; it is far more precious than treasure," Sylus said aloud as he penned the runes onto the page. He sat back from the book and sighed.

He could only hope the book would survive long enough to reach the king who would need it.

A knock came at the door.

Sylus called out and said, "Come in."

The door opened and in walked a stout, muscular dwarf with black hair and a long beard. "You wanted to see me, Sire?" the dwarf asked.

Sylus smiled and nodded his head. "I do indeed, Kizpa."

Kizpa moved into the bedchamber and bowed to his king. "What can I do for you?"

Sylus stood slowly upon his feet and pushed the chair away. He slid the blanket off of his shoulders and moved to the right side of his desk. His left hand went down, grasping the handle of Murskain. He lifted the hammer with a bit of effort and held it out for Kizpa.

Kizpa looked to him with a furrowed brow, his green eyes glancing from the king to the weapon. His mouth opened to ask a question, but Sylus spoke first.

"Your father served me well as a captain in the army," Sylus said. "He served valiantly until the great battle with the demons."

Kizpa nodded reverently.

Sylus continued. "Your brother serves me now, making medicine that keep my body strong after the demon's poison entered my blood from the wounds I received in battle. Without his aid, I would have died weeks ago."

Again, Kizpa nodded.

"And then, there is you," Sylus said with a smile on his face. "You remind me of my son, Ravik. You act like him, and you think like him." Sylus pressed the hammer into Kizpa's chest. "Take it," Sylus commanded.

Kizpa took Murskain in his hands and studied the weapon. "It is magnificent, my king," he said.

Sylus nodded. "It is the symbol of the protector of Roegudok Hall," he said. "As I am without any sons, and you are without father, I am hereby adopting you into my line."

Kizpa's eyes widened and he shook his head. "Sire, there are dwarves better than me—"

Sylus shook his head and narrowed his eyes on Kizpa. "You have been my personal servant since the battle with the demons. You know everything about ruling the mountain. You accompany me to court. You have seen how to govern the needs of the people. You shall succeed me when I die. I have already announced this to the counselors." Sylus pulled a rolled parchment from his pocket and held it out for Kizpa. "Kizpa Sit'marihu, you shall be the sixth king of Roegudok Hall. From that day forward, the crown shall be passed down to your heirs. I expect you to train them well, as I have trained you."

Kizpa nodded, but the expression on his face displayed his lack of confidence. "Sire, I don't think I can do this. I have been with you only a short while. It would take much more time to prepare me for this."

Sylus stretched his hand out and placed it upon Kizpa's shoulder. "I have constructed a secret library down the hall. There, I will place all of the knowledge and resources you shall need to rule effectively. Moreover, it will serve as an excellent means of tutoring your heirs and preparing them to one day take the crown." Sylus turned to his left and indicated the book he had just finished. "I will place this in there as well. It is a book describing the mines, and the dark omens preceded by the bloodgrass. I want you to promise me that you will ensure it is kept safely in the library."

Kizpa nodded. "I promise."

Sylus nodded back and smiled. "Promise me two more things," he said.

"You have only but to ask, and I shall do anything," Kizpa replied.

"The first, is I would have you promise to place a stone tablet in mine thirty-seven. I want it displayed in front of the mithril portcullis, so that any who find the gate can plainly see the warning."

"What shall I write upon the tablet?"

"Beware not to squander dwarven blood, it is far more

precious than treasure," Sylus said.

Kizpa nodded.

"The second demand I have is that you ensure our people are never enslaved by the Ancients again. Throw out their traditions and religion. We can never go back to cowering under their wings, do you understand."

Kizpa hesitated at this, but he nodded his head and promised to do as the king instructed.

Sylus smiled and then looked back to the book. "Take this book. Read it. Once you have finished reading it, we will place it in the library."

Kizpa moved to reach for the book and took it in hand. He read the rune on the cover. "The Wealth of Kings," he said aloud.

Sylus held up a finger. "That rune on the cover also has a second meaning," he said.

Kizpa cocked his head to the side and nodded. "Duty," he said. "The Duty of Kings."

Sylus nodded. "The king that seeks for the treasure in the mines below must weigh the need for treasure against the duty to protect the dwarves of Roegudok Hall. That is why I chose this particular rune. Be sure that your heir understands this."

"Of course, my king."

For the next forty-eight years, Kizpa shadowed Sylus everywhere, learning all he could about ruling Roegudok Hall. When Sylus finally succumbed to the demon's poison in his veins, Kizpa took the throne with every intention of following Sylus' instructions to the letter. However, as time passed under the reign of the sixth king of Roegudok Hall, the library Sylus built was sealed away. The book he wrote, The Wealth of Kings, was secreted away inside a large desk in the library. Kizpa thought it wiser to hide the knowledge of the book, rather than tempt any future king with the rumored treasures in mine thirty-seven.

The truth of The Wealth of Kings faded into legend. Then, over the centuries that dragged on into eons, legend became myth, and myth faded to rumors until all within the mountain forgot the truth of mine thirty-seven.

CHAPTER 14

Year 3,711 Age of Demigods, Late Autumn.
2nd year of the reign of Aldehenkaru'hktanah Sit'marihu, 13th King of Roegudok Hall.

It had been several weeks since the demon had managed to launch a surprise attack in the main hall. The Home Guard was left with twenty dwarves, including Kijik, barely enough to patrol the main hall for any sign of trouble. The dwarf king still replayed the events in his mind over and over. If only he had prepared better. If he had been able to create the poison crossbow bolts he had read about in Sylus' book, then they could have put the demon down before it destroyed most of the Home Guard. He knew it wasn't his fault. There hadn't been enough mithril on hand at that time to create the shafts, and Sylus had explicitly said the powdered poison needed to be applied to mithril. As it was, Al had been fortunate that Benbo had been marching a contingent of cavedog riders back in from practicing maneuvers in the valley outside of Roegudok Hall when the demon attacked. Had they not been as near the main hall as they were, many citizens would be dead now in addition to the slain Home Guard members.

Ever since that attack, the army had been put on its highest alert. Two thirds of the warriors were down in the lower tunnels. The other third was split into two groups, one that would remain in the main hall, and one that would accompany Al to a strange, mithril gate the miners had recently reached in mine thirty-seven.

Before this day, Al had not been properly prepared to lead the charge.

He had spent the last several weeks creating a new set of armor for himself during whatever down time was left after issuing orders to Benbo and Kijik. Fortunately, the two officers were highly capable and needed little direction. Essentially, they sought only to confirm their plans of action and receive the approval of the king. Al was thankful for that. It was hard enough to calm the folk of the mountain as it was. It also freed him to work on his armor, which was what he was supposed to be focusing on now.

His hand went down, beating the rim of metal into place. He tried to focus on his work, but his mind pulled him back to the tragedy with the demon in the marketplace. Al shook his head, forcing himself to think of something positive. At least the investigation into Threnton's treacheries seemed to have gone well.

No groups of rebels had been found in the forest or valleys beyond Roegudok Hall. Benbo and Kijik had even managed to root out a couple of Threnton's spies that had tried to escape from the mountain. More than that, the captured spies had given up the location of Threnton's hideout. It took only a week for Benbo to clear the hideout and bring the traitors down. As for the majority of the emigrants, they had dispersed throughout the Middle Kingdom, so Al ordered that they should be left alone. All things considered, it had worked out about as well as any scheme involving Threnton could have.

He then thought of the new well that had been discovered adjacent to the existing well that had dried. Gemma had been on one of her rounds, inspecting the pipes and hoping to find water rising in the old well, when she saw water seeping in through the walls. It took little effort to connect the new well to the existing plumbing. Food was still being rationed, and would run out within a couple months if nothing changed, but at least they had fresh water again. It appeared

Sam Ferguson

that the shifting of the Mystinen had not depleted the first well so much as it had diverted it into a different shaft. As that shaft began to spill into a small chamber, the water had eventually worked its way through the rock.

Al set his hammer down and looked at the new breastplate he had created. The base layer was made of iron, but he had fused iron with the metal from his ceremonial armor to improve its durability and create a second layer to cover the base layer. The outer layer was what he was most proud of, as well as slightly ashamed of. If Alferug had seen what he had done, there would have been much wailing and shouting. Al smiled to himself as he held up the breastplate. It was, perhaps, a bit sacrilegious, but it was appropriate as well. Al had been so distraught and frustrated by his lack of preparedness for the demon that had attacked the marketplace, that as soon as the battle had ended, he had stormed up to his forge immediately. He hadn't planned on doing it, but when he saw King Sylus' armor on the pedestal, an idea struck him and he acted on it. Sylus had beaten the demons before. So now, Sylus' armor was removed from his pedestal in the hall of kings before the throne room. Al had melted down and reformed everything but the Telarian steel greaves, those were perfect as they were.

The purely decorative parts he had, of course, set aside to be sent to the Greenband. However, the resulting outer layer for this new armor was extremely efficient. Despite the many layers, the armor was lighter, more maneuverable, and much stronger than anything else Al had at his disposal. The entire suit of plate mail armor appeared black to any other observer. Only Al knew of the second and third layers underneath. He called out to his apprentices and they put down their hammers and approached him.

Al slipped into the thick leather pads and then held his arms out.

His apprentices began attaching each piece of armor on him, starting from the black boots, all the way up to the helmet. The entire process took twenty minutes, as there were

186

several smaller joints and plates that had to be attached separately. Al had designed this suit of armor with utility in mind, foregoing the added artistry and fine details that would normally be present in a king's suit of armor in exchange for speed, and maximum protection and mobility. Still, this morning he had woken to find four runes etched into the breastplate and lined with some of the silver that Al had set aside after melting down his ceremonial armor.

His apprentices had used the dwarven runes that Al had spoken of during Alferug's funeral; honor, truth, courage, and duty. He would have normally beaned an apprentice with a lump of coal to the back of the head for touching his work, but in this case, he made an exception and thanked them for the gesture. When Al looked at the suit of armor now, it was as if he was being guarded by both King Sylus and Alferug.

When he was finally suited up, he made his way out of his personal forge, through the throne room, and out into the hall of kings. His eyes lingered upon each of the pedestals he passed as he thought of the great heroes that had come before him. He stopped when he saw Sylus' now empty pedestal. He pointed to the wall.

"My hammer will not do for this battle," Al told his bodyguards. "Fetch me Murskain. By Sylus' own hammer shall I vanquish the demons below."

When he was handed the weapon, it was almost as if Al could feel a connection with it. The metal seemed to vibrate ever so slightly, as if it was a living thing. The dwarf king gave it a slow practice swing and admired its perfect balance. It was solidly built, yet Al's strong arms manipulated the weapon easily.

He smiled and then they descended the stairs to the main hall.

Five hundred dwarves waited next to their cavedogs for Al. They saluted him upon sight, slapping armored fists to their chests with a loud cacophony of clanking iron. Al held Sylus' hammer over his head. The soldiers looked to him expectantly, as if waiting for some motivational speech, but Al had not prepared anything of the sort. He was used to playing the part of the soldier, and not that of a king. He stood there, surveying his fellow dwarves, trying to think of something he could say. What words could he offer that would give any of them more courage than they had already shown?

As the seconds passed, women and older dwarves drew near from the marketplace, watching their king.

Al frowned behind the visor of his helmet. I should not have stopped. Now they really expect me to say something.

But what could he say that would offer the wives and mothers any confidence that their sons and husbands would return? He took in a deep breath as he lowered Sylus' hammer. He set it down upon the stone floor and rested his hands across the bulky head of the weapon. He surveyed the crowd, and for a brief moment he thought he could see Alferug standing in the crowd.

Al reached up and lifted his visor to get a better look, but the apparition had disappeared. Al searched the crowd, trying to recapture the brief glimpse he thought he had seen. Then, in the back of the crowd, he saw a faint, silvery glow. Alferug stood in the air. Next to him floated Al's father. Behind them stood ten other dwarves. All of them were caught in an other-worldly mist that none of the other dwarves seemed to notice.

One of the floating dwarves stepped around Al's father and pointed to Al. "You are destined to find the Wealth of Kings," the familiar voice said. Al knew at once it was the same voice he had heard before in the tunnels. The spirit then waved his hand in the air and Murskain felt warm in Al's hands. "My hammer shall guide you as you protect our people."

Al realized then that he was seeing Sylus.

"My king, is everything alright?" one of the bodyguards asked with a slight nudge to Al's right side. Al turned to nod at the guard.

"Yes, everything is fine," Al said. He turned back to look at his father and the other past kings once more, but they had vanished from sight, returning back to their plane. Al sighed, wishing he could call them back and ask them for strength and guidance.

Murskain grew warmer in Al's hands. In that instant, he knew that the kings of old *were* with him. His eyes were opened and the veil between the realm of the living and the plane of the dead was rent in twain. He saw thousands upon thousands of dwarves he did not recognize. Each of them were gathered around the warriors waiting for Al. In that instant, Al knew that there were far more allies with him than the demons below could possibly withstand.

Al lifted the mighty Murskain in the air and shouted out through the hall, his booming voice echoing off the walls. "Let us not fear death, for death is only the doorway to a new life. Instead, let us go down with fire in our hearts to cleanse the invaders from our halls. Our battle is not one only for Roegudok Hall, but also for all of Terramyr. The world may never know of our struggles here today, but if the gods themselves only knew what it is we fight for, they would bow to us in reverence." Al swung the hammer up and then slapped it down into his open palm. "Your ancestors are with you today. They give you strength. Welcome that strength. Use it. By the Ancients who created us, I declare that we shall overcome the darkness lurking within the bowels of this mountain. In purging that darkness, we shall find the means to overcome a much greater foe. Some of you know of what I speak, the rumored four horsemen that have been whispered about in the wake of the war we fought in the Middle Kingdom. When Tu'luh fought against us at Fort Drake, he came as the harbinger of the four horsemen. We now, the dwarves of Roegudok Hall who were formed of the very stone of this mountain, shall gain the means to repel the cursed horsemen, and in so doing we shall win life and liberty not only for ourselves, but for all of Terramyr."

Al hopped down the last several stairs and leapt onto his cavedog. "We ride!" he shouted.

The dwarves shouted and cheered around him as they

fell in behind him. Al led the army down through the tunnels. They rode for miles through shallow descending tunnels and around the winding shafts that branched out below the mountain. It took them hours, even upon their cavedogs, to reach their destination.

When they finally met up with the other two thousand dwarves, they were met with cheers and cries of excitement. Al surveyed the warriors and smiled when he saw the preparations they had made. There were ballista launchers, hedges of stacked stone, and side tunnels that allowed for dwarves to retreat out or attack the enemy flank should any demon somehow make it up this far. Some of the engineers had balked at Al's insistence, but Benbo was quick to bring the others around to the idea after Al explained not only how they could have been used in the market to kill the demon, but also how big Sylus had reported some of the demons to have been in the final battle which Sylus had waged in the great cavern which was supposed to lay at the end of shaft thirty-seven. Al expected trouble, a lot of it.

Al saluted the dwarves as he rode to the front of the long line of encamped soldiers. Only when he saw Commander Benbo standing near a shining, mithril gate did he slow his pace.

Benbo saluted the king and gave a bow of his head as Al drew in close. Al set the officer at ease and leapt down from his cavedog to inspect a broken tablet of stone on the wall. He walked to it and brushed a layer of dust away with his hand.

"Beware not to squander dwarven blood, it is far more precious than treasure," Al read aloud.

"A warning against greed," Benbo commented.

Al turned around and shook his head. "Only partly," he corrected. "It is also a call to action." Al pointed up to the mithril gate. "Do you see those runes?"

Benbo looked up and made a puffing sound as he shook his head. "I hadn't noticed those before."

Al nodded. "This is the way to the Wealth of Kings," Al said. "However, look at the rune they used for 'wealth' and tell me what you see."

Benbo shrugged. "It's an older rune, but that makes sense given the fact this gate was built under Sylus' reign."

Al chuckled. "I was going through some of Alferug's books over the last couple of weeks. He had quite an extensive history on our language, its origins and mutations." Al pointed to the rune that symbolized wealth. "This particular rune is hardly ever used now, but that is because it has a double meaning."

"Something other than wealth?"

Al nodded with a smile. "It means duty," Al said. "This gate opens the way to the *Duty* of Kings."

"What duty?" Benbo asked.

Al glanced back to the stone tablet on the wall. "I imagine Sylus meant the duty of the king to protect the people of Roegudok Hall. A king should not waste the lives of his citizens. However, looking at the whole picture, it appears that the duty I must face, is the responsibility of opening the gate in search of something more valuable than mere treasure."

"The addorite," Benbo said. "I received your letter a few days ago.

Al nodded. "Good, then you understand why we must lead an assault."

Benbo shrugged. "We can open the gate, but the tunnel beyond is still filled with rubble and stone. It will take some time to clear it."

"See that it is done as quickly as possible," Al commanded. "I will settle the reinforcements in. Let's open this gate and see what lies beyond."

Al ate his supper from a plate sitting atop a mostly stable boulder while he listened to the music of explosions and pick-axes breaking apart the rubble and forging the way forward. A long line of miners carried the rubble out of the tunnel in handcarts they pushed and dumped into several of the side chambers further up the mine shaft. The soldiers were all on alert. They lined the walls, standing ready to pounce at the first sign of trouble from down the line.

It was hours before the first alarm went up through the camp. When it did, the soldiers reacted so quickly that Al was unable to reach the battle until it was over. He found forty dwarves gathering around the bodies of a pair of lurkers that had sprung from an opening in the wall created by one of the explosions. The warriors swept the small chamber and found a lava tube. Moments later, explosives engineers were preparing to collapse the lava tube.

Soon, a loud, terrible explosion rocked the mine as the lava tube was blocked up by a pile of broken hunks of stone.

"Any losses?" Al asked.

Benbo shook his head. "When we saw the hole in the wall we sent up the alarm. The miners ran and the soldiers rushed in. The lurkers never knew what hit them."

"Your training over the last several weeks has served you well."

Benbo shook his head and deflected the compliment. "Without the pointers you offered me that were written in Sylus' book, we would not be as efficient as we are now."

Al nodded, smiling pleasantly. "Let's keep it up."

Benbo nodded. The commander then turned to a pair of mining crew leaders. "Go ahead and fill this chamber with rubble from the main tunnel."

"As you command," one of the miners replied.

For the rest of the day, there were no more attacks and the dwarves made excellent progress through the last couple of remaining miles.

Early the next morning, Al was standing in front of the last few feet of piled rock that separated shaft thirty-seven from the large chamber containing the addorite. Through cracks and openings he could feel a cool, musty air flowing out toward him. The dwarves worked hard clearing the stone, setting lanterns, and watching for any sign of predators.

Al fidgeted inside his armor as the last of the rocks began to fall away and the light from their lanterns pierced into the darkness of the open chamber beyond. The dwarf king took a torch from one of the miners and walked toward the waist-high pile of rubble. He threw the torch into the chamber. The torch spun end over end as the flames roared in protest. The light spun up, then down with each revolution of the torch, illuminating the depths of the darkness until it struck the ground where the light flickered and nearly went out before it stabilized.

"By the stars above and the stones below," Al said as he looked to the light.

All around the torch he saw piles of bones. Most were either from dwarves or cavedogs from the looks of it, but there were also giant bones sticking up out of the piles in some places. Black scales also littered the ground, along with rusted swords and axes.

"It's bigger than I thought," Benbo commented with awe as he stepped closer to the dwarf king.

Al turned and clapped him on the shoulder. "Let's get the last of the rocks out of the way and then move in and form a defensive perimeter."

Benbo nodded, but his wide eyes never left the piles of bones in the great chamber beyond.

After the path was cleared, Al waited a few yards inside the chamber as the army marched in. With every new torch and lantern that was brought into the chamber, Al felt his heart sink a little more as he was able to see more clearly how vast the battlefield truly was. Had it not been for the vision of deceased ancestors he had witnessed in the main hall, he might have ordered the tunnel to be recollapsed and sealed off forever.

He knew he couldn't do that though. This was a dangerous place to be, and their activities here could very well awaken something far beyond what the dwarves could handle, but if they could get the addorite to Hiasyntar'Kulai, then it would be worth the risk.

Al knew all too well from his time with Erik that the four horsemen were far more than legend. They were very real, and they were coming. He didn't know when, but he knew it was a near certainty that they would come. When they arrived, they would destroy Terramyr. The only known information that could shed some light on how to stop the horsemen was contained in The Infinium. The idea that even the Ancients needed help reading the book was not something Al liked to think about. The possibilities of what might happen to a great dragon if they tried to read the book without the help of the addorite crystal was enough to keep the dwarf king awake at night.

Still, he couldn't help but wonder how the addorite actually assisted the Ancients decipher the book. If he lived through this ordeal, he would have to ask one of the Ancients.

As he thought on the subject, he saw a group of miners move in close to a section on the wall that was bursting with pink crystals. He moved to them and looked at the crystal formation.

"Is this it?" a miner asked.

Al didn't know how he knew, but he was certain the crystal was addorite. He nodded. "That is it. Wait until we have secured the chamber before we start removing it. For all we know, the explosions might not bother the monsters. It might only be when we try to take the crystal from the mountain. A shift in the Mystinen perhaps."

The miners nodded and carefully set their pickaxes down on the ground while they waited.

Al moved to join one of the forward patrols. The old bones beneath their feet clicked and snapped like twigs underfoot. Dust popped up from the ground as the group disturbed the endless mound of bones and scales. Al and the others moved to cover their mouths and noses as they continued to scout through the chamber. They moved slowly, using their torches to scan the area for any sign of hostile life. The group picked its way toward the outer wall where the bones were thinnest as they passed around the largest heap of bones and debris.

"This must be where the fighting was the worst," one of the soldiers said.

"Can you imagine climbing on a growing hill of bodies

to fight your enemy?" another one called out.

Al silently surveyed the pile, following the patrol and recalling the words Sylus had used to describe the horrors of this particular battle. He didn't dare share that information with any of the soldiers around him now. He saw little use in making them soil themselves before they had even begun to fight.

A shout rose up from somewhere off in the distance. Al and the others quickened their pace around the large mound so they could see what the matter was. As they rounded the pile, they saw a great creature, the likes of which they had never seen before. It had thick, bony plates along its back, with spikes jutting out the sides. A short, thick neck protruded out from under the covering of bony plates and held a round, scaly head that ended in a stubby snout filled with large fangs. It walked upon all fours and was fairly slow as it came out from under a pile of bones and tried to escape from the dwarf patrol chasing after it. As it emerged from the bones, Al saw the long, massive tail that was tipped with a round knob of solid bone.

No sooner had the tail come free from the pile of bones the creature had been hiding in than it swung out to the side and swept two dwarves off their cavedogs. They flew through the air and landed far off in the mess of bones.

"Come on!" Al shouted.

He led the charge from their side toward the strange creature. The patrol group that was nearest the beast circled around it, waving their swords and keeping it from escaping. The dwarf king shouted to let the others know that he was on the way. He quickly realized he had made a mistake. A pair of wings erupted out from the bones immediately in front of Al and a long, slender body rose into the air directly in front of them. Al and the others around him slid to a scratching halt as the bones beneath their feet scraped along the stone. The flying demon was maybe seven feet from head to foot, with a long, spike-tipped tail thrashing wildly behind it. Long, curved talons jutted out from its feet. It lashed out with one foot, scratching, but not piercing, Al's breastplate. Al retaliated quickly by driving the spiked end of Murskain through the flying creature's thigh. The thing screeched in a terribly shrill voice that all but pierced the dwarves' ears, but Al held firm and kept the monster from flying away.

Two other warriors lunged in and plunged swords deep into the creature's abdomen. It fell to the ground, crying and screaming in pain. Its white, blind eyes were opened horridly wide, revealing blood-red eyelids as it thrashed about. Al pulled the hammer free and then came down with a savage blow of Murskain's heavy side. The creature's skull was crushed as easily as an egg beneath a boot. The group then continued to ride on to help the others.

By the time they reached the large, four-legged animal, it was bleeding from its head, neck, and two hind legs. The dwarves were bringing it down piece by piece. Al moved in with his hammer and tried to close in on the beast's head, but every time he came closer the animal turned to the side and presented its tail. A couple times it brought it down just inches away from Al and his cavedog. Splintering bone fragments exploded in every direction as the tail whomped down time and time again.

Ultimately, a lucky crossbow shot to the eye put the beast down.

After it was dead, several other patrol groups arrived to look at the thing.

Benbo ignored the animal and moved next to Al. "We have finished sweeping the chamber," he said. "We found a few strange flying creatures, but we put them all down."

"Losses?" Al asked.

Benbo replied, "Less than a score in total." He turned and pointed out away from the bone-plated animal. "Additionally, we found two of our comrades over there. They looked like something had crushed their chests. Now that I see this animal, I think I understand."

Al nodded. "It has a wickedly powerful tail." He turned around in his saddle. "What else?" he asked. "Where are the exit tunnels?"

Benbo shrugged. "That's the thing. We didn't find any tunnels leading out of here."

Al looked at Benbo with disbelieving eyes. "What do you mean there aren't any other tunnels? Were they sealed up?"

Benbo shook his head. "This giant chamber is a dead end. There are no tunnels other than the one we used to come in."

Al shook his head. "That can't be," he said. "There must be something."

Benbo sighed and frowned. "There is nothing here. It looks like this was the final resting place of the demons King Sylus fought."

Al narrowed his eyes and looked around. "No, there was something," he said. "Sylus believed they invaded from somewhere else. He details that they mined here for quite a while before they were attacked. There must be a tunnel somewhere."

"There isn't," Benbo replied flatly.

"Have the patrols look again." Al looked up to the ceiling. "Have them inspect the ceiling too. Whatever it takes. We must find the source of the demons before we can begin mining the addorite."

Benbo nodded. "It is possible the mountain has shifted. After all, we are miles below the surface now. It could be that whatever ancient tunnel let the demons in has been sealed off by the mountain itself."

"I suppose," Al mused.

"We did find gold veins on the far wall," Benbo said pointing out to the east. "There looks to be enough there that we can alleviate our food shortage if we begin mining."

"We can't mine until we find the tunnels that Sylus spoke of," Al replied. "If you can't find obvious tunnels, then have the miners clear these bones off to one side of the chamber. Maybe there is a tunnel leading down. Have them set metal remnants of armor and weapons in a second pile. Maybe we can reuse the material."

"As you command sire," Benbo replied. "What if we find no tunnels, what shall we do then?" he pressed.

Al thought for a moment. He could hear the exasperation in Benbo's voice. He knew that he could not justify waiting to extract the gold unless there was a clear and present danger. If there really were no tunnels, then perhaps Benbo was correct. The mountain could have sealed them off. "If there are no tunnels, then set up the best defenses you can and let the miners get to work."

"By your command," Benbo said.

Al watched the commander ride away and bark out orders to the patrols. The dwarf king couldn't help but feel as though something was missing. There was an uneasy feeling in his stomach that the demons would come as soon as the dwarves mined the addorite.

*****

Hiasyntar'Kulai was sitting in the large, crystal-walled chamber deep within the ground beneath his castle nestled in the mountains when the three dragon spirits returned from their quest to find the missing addorite.

The three spirits settled upon the floor and bowed deeply.

"Have you found it?" the Father of the Ancients asked.

The middle dragon, a large, strong spirit with blue scales lifted its head and looked to Hiasyntar'Kulai with its black, penetrating eyes.

The golden dragon formed the telepathic connection with the blue dragon and relived the memory of discovering the addorite through her eyes.

The cave was found exactly where Tu'luh had said it would be. The three dragons entered the cave and swiftly floated through the winding passages. They heard strange noises echoing through the caves, but there was no sign of any life. They wound their way down long, dank corridors. The deeper they went into the cavern network, the more tunnels seemed to branch off in every direction.

The three dragons split up.

The blue dragon, whose memories Hiasyntar'Kulai was watching, chose a tunnel that led deeper into the mountain. She floated through quickly, not needing to worry about the physical constraints of the tunnel as her ethereal form easily passed through the solid stone walls and stalactites that would have prevented her from navigating the tunnel had she been alive and in her physical body.

That was why Tu'luh could never recover the addorite, Hiasyntar'Kulai thought to himself as he watched the memories. The tunnels were far too small for any dragon to infiltrate.

The tunnel came to a large chamber with an underground pool of water. Green, thick algae grew along the top of the pond and stretched over the stone banks. There were several piles of bones as well. The blue dragon moved closer to inspect the bones, and realized that they belonged to goblins.

She moved on. Something moved in the shadows in a tunnel off to the right, so she followed after it. Quiet footsteps padded along the cave a short ways in front of her. She increased her speed and discovered a hulking, hunch-backed figure with green skin dotted with cysts over the left shoulder. It turned and narrowed its gray eyes, seemingly looking right at the blue dragon. It snarled, revealing a set of crooked, jagged teeth. Then it turned and hobbled through the tunnel, shifting its weight from foot to foot.

The blue dragon followed the deformed creature until the tunnel opened into a large chamber filled with torches and fire pits that illuminated the entire area. The hulking creature moved in and went to a large, iron cage filled with goblins. They shrieked and jumped to the back of the cage as the deformed creature approached. It opened the cage and reached in, seizing one of the goblins by the wrist and yanking it out.

The goblin fought wildly, screaming and shouting, but

the hulking creature held it firm with one hand and then used a massive club to bash in the goblin's forehead. The goblin went still. The hunch-back dragged the lifeless body to a large, black cauldron and tossed the body inside, clothes and all. He then added wood to the fire and stepped around the cauldron to pick up a pile of white bones. It carried the bones up through the blue dragon's spirit and back up the tunnel the dragon had just left, presumably to toss the bones on the other piles near the pool.

The blue dragon looked around the chamber, and soon saw several more hunch-backed creatures coming in and out of the large chamber. Some carried wood and placed it atop a large, central pile of logs, others carried stones. The rest were either removing bones or throwing goblins into pots to be cooked.

A gong rang out from a different tunnel and the blue dragon watched as a procession of strange, hulking creatures entered the chamber. They resembled goblins, except they were twice as tall, with oversized heads, lanky arms, and thick legs. Their beady eyes flicked to the cauldrons many times as they took up positions around the chamber and sat down upon the floor.

A gong rang out again, but this time only one figure emerged from a tunnel on the far side of the chamber. This one was like the others, but even taller and thinner. It was the only one that wore a full set of clothes; a long, brown robe that reached down to its ankles. The robes were open, showing the creature's red shirt and black pants. Its long, green feet were bare, with yellow toenails that curved under the toes.

It spoke in goblin tongue, and all the others listened to it. When it ceased speaking, the hunch-backs returned and began pulling the boiled goblins out of the cauldrons and serving them to the other creatures.

The blue dragon moved toward the leader of the tribe, and noticed a small, pink crystal held in a wire setting that dangled from a leather strap around the leader's neck. The blue dragon knew at once that it was addorite.

The dragon waited until the meal was finished and the leader disappeared through the tunnels again. She followed him, winding through several tunnels until they came to a small chamber that was filled with books and various sundry objects lined upon a stone shelf in the chamber.

The blue dragon saw a large crate and moved to it. Except for a small amount of pink dust, there was no addorite left.

Hiasyntar'Kulai broke the connection and thanked the blue dragon.

"They consumed it all," he said with a sigh.

"And it changed them," the blue dragon spoke. "Those hunch-backed creatures and the taller ones used to be goblins, I believe. I think that their use of addorite changed them, and warped them into a dark and disgusting race."

The golden dragon nodded.

"Leave me please," he said. The dragons obeyed and he was left alone to contemplate how to ask Al, the King of Roegudok Hall, to reopen the addorite mines deep under the mountain.

Fortunately, he did not have to contemplate the idea for long. A familiar spirit approached him with a large smile on his face.

"My king," the dwarf spirit said. "I have good news from Roegudok Hall."

"What is that?" Hiasyntar'Kulai asked.

The dwarf spirit stopped and bowed politely before speaking. "The king of the dwarves has reopened mine thirty-seven. They have already encountered demons and lurkers, but they are not deterred. They are set upon vanquishing the foe and mining not only the gold and other precious ores and gems, but they are determined to find and mine the addorite."

Hiasyntar'Kulai grinned slyly. "Tell me, King Sylus, why would they do that?"

Sylus' spirit smiled back. "I may have given him some encouragement."

"And has he found your book?" Hiasyntar'Kulai

asked.

Sylus nodded. "He does not know everything concerning the addorite, but he is figuring it out."

The dragon rose to his feet and bowed his head to Sylus. "It is good to have you with us once again, King Sylus."

Sylus bent low and then indicated with a nod of his chin to the private study chamber that held The Infinium. "Had I known more about that, I would like to think I would have made a better choice during my lifetime."

The dragon smiled. "Go, lend strength to King Sit'marihu when you can. I will fly to Valtuu Temple and have them build a store house for the addorite. The new prelate there can use her magic to contact me when it is filled, and then I can bring the addorite here to continue my research."

Sylus bowed and the two went their separate ways.

CHAPTER 15

Year 3,711 Age of Demigods, Early Winter.
2nd year of the reign of Aldehenkaru'hktanah Sit'marihu, 13th King of Roegudok Hall.

Al strolled through the large chamber, now affectionately known as Demon Spring, for the twentieth time since he had finished lunch. Miners and soldiers were braking for dinner, forming lines that stretched out from the food carts and kitchen equipment that had been set up in the last half of autumn and first couple weeks of winter.

The others seemed to be reveling in their good fortune. The gold vein had led the miners to a vein of mithril, and from there they had discovered pockets of diamonds and silver deposits as well. The Greenband debt had been paid in full and the sanctions against Roegudok Hall had been lifted. The food shortage was over. The smell of pork-and-beans as well as roasting beef filled Demon Spring. Al had also received reports from the council that the main hall was flourishing again. In a few short weeks, the dwarves of Roegudok Hall had gone from rationed food and water to having a surplus of both.

Al folded his arms and stopped as he turned to look at the miners. Some of them were teasing each other, stealing biscuits from plates when heads were turned, only to throw the food back in their companions' faces. The dwarf king marveled at how quickly food had gone from precious to little more than a toy to be tossed and wasted in the eyes of the people.

That wasn't what really nagged at him though. No, it wasn't the fact that they rejoiced in their fortunate turn for better, or even that they wasted food. It was the fact that none of them seemed to be concerned about the demons anymore. He heard a few of them talking just before starting this last round through the area.

"The demons are long gone now," one miner had said.

"Aye, if any still remained, they would have shown themselves already," another agreed. "It's been weeks, and things have been quiet as a grave."

When Al had heard those words, he needed to walk away from the group of miners, or else he might have lost control and smacked the careless oaf. The fact was, Demon Spring *was* a grave. It was where thousands of dwarves had lost their lives. More than that, Al knew that Sylus had enjoyed years of plentiful mining from this very spot before the final clash with the demons.

He had tried to tell as much to the miners and soldiers every chance he got, but with each passing day, they lost their sense of caution. None of them had outright called him mad, but he could see the sentiment in the blank stares or blushing glances they shared with each other when he now spoke.

Al huffed angrily. He felt a nuzzle at his leg. Al looked down to see his cavedog standing with him. "At least you understand," Al said. Then he swept an arm out toward the many sleeping cavedogs, lazily sleeping upon the stone floor throughout Demon Spring. "Even the other cavedogs ignore my concerns," he said.

The lizard looked up and flicked its tongue out into the air and blinked.

"Now I am talking to a lizard," Al said with a shake of his head. "Why had all of the spirits shown up to encourage me if there was no danger? It makes no sense!" Al grabbed a rock from the ground and threw it away. It sailed through the air and landed several hundred feet away, bouncing across the stone floor toward a patch of addorite crystal that formed a small mound. The stone bounced up over the crystals, and then it vanished.

Al scrunched his brow together and cocked his head to the side. "Now, I'm seeing things," he muttered to himself. He picked up another stone and launched it at the same patch of addorite. This time his aim came much closer to the mound, but the rock landed short, bouncing and skipping across the stone floor as had the first rock. It popped up, in nearly the same trajectory as the first, but then it fell and landed in the crystals, breaking a piece off and creating a small plume of pink dust.

"Hey!" a dwarf miner shouted as he jumped up from the other side of the crystal patch, rubbing the top of his head. "Who threw that rock?" The dwarf turned back and pointed angrily at a trio of dwarves who were passing a wine skin around. "Daggidy, I know it was you! Fess up, or I'm gonna break your nose!"

Al smirked. The thought crossed his mind to call out to the dwarf, but frankly he didn't care enough to worry about a fist-fight between miners. He walked along the eastern wall toward the north where the large chamber ended in a smooth, unbroken wall of stone. His cavedog walked a few feet behind him, silently flicking its tongue out, tasting the air as it followed the dwarf king. Al walked the length of the eastern wall and didn't turn toward the west until he was faced with the curved wall that marked the end of Demon Spring.

He placed his armored hand along the smooth surface of the stone. His eyes traced the wall up and inspected the ceiling above him. The miners had been quick to erect large mounds of stone that had allowed them to fasten lamps and torches near the top of the wall so that the ceiling was very well lit. In doing so, they had shattered Al's theory that the demons had entered through tunnels in the ceiling. There were patches of addorite there, but nothing else.

Al skirted along the northern wall for several minutes before he came to a patch of addorite in the floor. Like the one he had hit with the rocks, this patch of crystal formed a mound that rose about waist high on a dwarf. Al glanced back to his cavedog and then looked at the addorite.

"I wonder..." Al reached over his shoulder and retrieved his hammer. He walked toward the addorite and stuck the hammer out over the addorite. Nothing happened. He inched closer and kicked the nearest addorite crystal. It shattered apart, but again nothing happened.

"Stonebubbles!" Al cursed. He angrily stomped up to the peak of the small mound, about to smack the crystals with his hammer when the light around him vanished. The hairs on the back of his neck rose to stand on end as a cool breeze swirled around him. He looked down and saw a faint pink glow in the darkness. The addorite was the only source of light he could see.

Something metallic scraped against stone, scratching along as it moved in the darkness.

A flash of light exploded in the distance as fire erupted from some sort of stone vent. Near the fire, Al saw moving bodies. They weren't lurkers, for they had no scales, and they walked upon two legs. Al could only guess that they were demons, for they matched the descriptions in King Sylus' book.

He crouched down low to the patch of crystals in case any demon was nearby. Another vent of fire erupted, this time off to the left. Al turned his head to look at it and saw a large, winged creature standing next to the vent, breathing in the yellow smoke issuing out with the fire. The thing was at least forty feet tall, with legs thicker than an oak tree. Next to it sat a large lurker, curled up near the vent and apparently sleeping.

Al heard a faint sound behind him, like shifting gavel. He turned and tried to focus his dwarven eyes on the darkness. A large flash of light erupted from somewhere in the strange cave and illuminated the form that was approaching him.

A seven foot tall, two legged demon with horns poking out in a ring around each shoulder stared back at him with icy, blue eyes. It cocked its round head to the side and narrowed its eyes as it curled its upper lip back in a silent snarl. From the stomach down, it was covered in white fur. It lifted its right arm, and a web of yellow lightning began to form between the fingers. Al knew he had to act quickly. He swung Murskain with all of his might at the demon, but he missed.

The hammer sailed back through the rift and Al followed after it, tumbling back down the mound of addorite crystals and crashing into his cavedog. All around him the area was bright again. He had found his way back to Demon Spring.

"My king!" Benbo shouted excitedly. Where did you come from?"

Al looked up from the ground and saw that he was surrounded by an entire patrol of dwarves. "Benbo, there is a portal, a rift! It leads into the demons' plane. I don't know how I passed through, but I did."

The other dwarves glanced at each other with stares of disbelief.

"You must believe me, Benbo, it's the truth!" Al got to his feet and pointed to the mound. "I walked up the mound and then I was there. I saw them, many of them."

"I believe you sire, but, are you injured?" Benbo asked quickly.

Al shook his head. "No, I saw a demon sneaking up on me from behind, so I swung at it, but somehow I fell back through the rift."

"Sire, how long were you in there?" Benbo asked.

"I don't know, maybe a few minutes, why?" Al noticed the slack jaw on his commanding officer's face as Benbo turned to look at the others. "Benbo, what's wrong?"

Benbo shook his head and turned back to Al. "My king, your cavedog came and basically dragged me back here to find you."

"Ah, well, that's loyalty for you," Al said with a smile.

Benbo dismounted and stepped in to grab the dwarf king's arm. "No, you don't understand. He dragged me back here to find you over a week ago."

Al balked and pulled his arm free from Benbo. "What are you saying?"

Benbo pointed to the mound of crystals. "What was only a matter of minutes for you, has been a week for us. We have been searching the tunnels for you. You disappeared. I only stayed at this mound because your cavedog wouldn't leave it."

"Did you try walking up the mound?" Al asked with a derisive snort. "If you had, you would have bumped into me. Watch." Al bent down and grabbed a stone. He tossed it over the mound. A frown pulled at the corners of his mouth when the rock sailed over the mound uneventfully.

"Sire," Benbo began.

"No, I was *there*. I know I was," Al said. He bent down and picked up a black stone. He tossed it over the mound. This time, the stone disappeared.

The dwarves began to whisper and Benbo froze with his eyes wide.

"There! See?" Al shouted satisfactorily. "Now come on, we have to figure out how these things work so we can close them off."

Benbo held his hands up. "Sire, I think you just did."

"What are you talking about now?" Al asked.

Benbo poked Al's armor. "What is this made out of?" he asked.

"It's a blend of steel, ferrokortanite, and ferrotantilite," Al replied. "It was used to help give the armor its black color, and it is a bit lighter than some of the other iron blends we had available when I needed to make a suit of armor."

Benbo bent down and picked through a few rocks until he came up with another black rock. "Sire, this is ferrokortanite."

Al noted the black, metallic shine and nodded. "I know what it is, Benbo."

Benbo patted the air and stepped around the dwarf king. He tossed the stone over the same spot and it too vanished. Benbo smiled, bent down, and picked up several more stones.

"This is just a hunk of granite," Benbo said. He threw

it as well, but instead of going through the portal, it sailed over the mound of crystals and landed on the ground. "Look, every bit of stone that has ferrokortanite seems to go through. Your armor has some ferrokortanite in it, and it also goes through." Benbo turned to one of the dwarf patrolmen. "Go and fetch me a lurker's scale, now!"

"So, everyone needs to wear armor made of ferrokortanite?" Al pressed.

Benbo shrugged. "I have been examining this mound since your disappearance. I knew your cavedog wouldn't sit here, refusing to move, unless this was where you disappeared. My first thought was to break apart the crystal and see if there was some sort of tunnel underneath, but your cavedog stopped me. It dragged me over the mound several times. So, after a while, I thought perhaps there was some sort of portal here."

"How did you figure that?" Al asked incredulously. "My lizard takes you over a mound of crystal and you assume there must be a portal to another world?"

Benbo smiled. "Before I joined the army, I too had another area of interest that called to me. I wanted to study magic. My father, of course, forbad it, but I never gave up the hobby. When I stood atop the crystals I could feel a difference in the air. I even thought I heard a humming noise during different times of day. It seemed as plausible as anything else. I mean, we don't know much about the Mystinen that creates the addorite. We also could never find any tunnels that brought the demons here for the fight with King Sylus. So I figured there had to be a portal."

Al nodded slowly. "Who else knows of this?"

Benbo shook his head. "I kept it to myself. I didn't want to create hysteria without knowing I was right. Then, when you came tumbling out of thin air before my eyes, I knew I had been right."

At that moment, the patrolman returned with the lurker's scale. He handed it to Benbo.

Benbo held it up to Al's armor and nodded. "Look, it has a similar sheen to it. If it has some of the same elements as ferrokortanite, then it could explain why their scales are so tough to pierce." Benbo turned and tossed the scale up over the mound.

It vanished as well.

"I'll be a toad's lover," Al said.

"What?" Benbo asked as he frowned at Al.

Al waved him off. "It's an expression I picked up in Buktah," he explained.

"A bit crude at that," Benbo remarked.

Al nodded. "Humans aren't known for their elegance," Al replied.

"So what do we do now, my king?"

Al shrugged. "Now we know where they are. What I don't understand is why they don't come after us."

"Maybe the lurkers are the key," Benbo suggested. "Perhaps they hold the way open to let the demons through?"

Al shrugged again. "Your guess is as good as any. Either way, it does us little good. If I am the only one who can cross over, then we are nothing more than sheep corralled in a pen while the wolves encircle us about."

Benbo stood silently, arms folded over his chest and eyes fixed on the pink crystals.

Al was silent as well. If he had ever needed Alferug's wisdom, now would be the time.

"Who else knew I was gone?" Al asked.

"Just your bodyguards and these soldiers here, sire," Benbo replied. "We thought it best to keep that quiet."

Al nodded and tugged on his beard. "We need to pull the miners out," Al said.

"What? But you said we need to mine the addorite for the Ancients."

"I know what I said. But, we are sitting in the open. We don't know if the demons I saw can traverse the rift at will. We need to pull back."

"Do we blow the mine?"

Al shook his head. "No. Create mounds of stone around the patches of addorite on the floor. Maybe that will at least close off a few entrances to our world. Then, we fall back to the mithril gate, and we reinforce it. Maybe we can mine enough ferrokortanite to make armor for everyone, then we can march into their world and take the fight to them."

Benbo nodded. "Why mine ferrokortanite sire?" Benbo asked with a sly grin. "Why not just take all of the lurker scales he can find and use those?"

Al smiled wide. "Faengoril was right about you." Al nodded and waved his hand. "Go and make it happen. Once we are prepared, then we march against the enemy."

CHAPTER 16

Year 3,711 Age of Demigods, Winter.
2ndyear of the reign ofAldehenkaru'hktanah Sit'marihu, 13th King of Roegudok Hall.

"Sire?" Benbo called out as he approached Al's personal forge just off of the throne room.

Al looked up from his work to see the commander. "The idea to use the scales was a stroke of genius," Al said. "They become pliable once heated up, but then after they are cooled, they are nearly as hard as steel. I dare say the army will be well prepared to face down the demons when we are finished."

Benbo moved in and rapped on a finished suit of armor with his knuckles. "It seems tough."

"Tough as steel, but even lighter than mithril," Al said with a hearty smile. "Speaking of mithril, I have added a thin layer of it to the inside of my armor. I thought to add some of the lurker scales, but I decided against it. The ferrokortanite already allows me passage through the portal, so there isn't any reason to waste the scales on me."

Benbo was unusually silent. Al stopped and frowned.

"Well, spit it out, is something wrong?"

Benbo shook his head. "There is a dragon outside the front gate. He is asking for you, Sire."

"A dragon?"

Benbo nodded. "Said his name was Hiasyntar'Kulai."

Al nearly stumbled backwards. "The Father of the

Ancients is here!" Al started to wipe his hands on his apron and looked around as if he had forgotten something. "Good heavens, why didn't you say so from the beginning?"

Benbo shrugged. "Shall I tell him you are coming then?"

Al shook his head. "Come with me if you like, but I am going straightaway to him. He's out front you say? Out by the main entrance tunnel?"

Benbo nodded.

Al whistled sharply. A second later he was saddled atop his cavedog and zipping through the throne room, down the grand stairs, and from the market place, through the three-mile-long tunnel to the front of the mountain. He left so fast that he had barely succeeded in taking his apron off.

When he reached the outer gates, the sunlight hit him hard in the eyes. He balked at it, raising a hand over his face until his eyes adjusted. Then, once he was no longer blinded, he saw the large, golden dragon lying less than fifty yards from the entrance. The end of his tail flipped back and forth, and he had his long, serpentine neck curled around toward his body so he could rest his head upon his forelegs. When the dragon saw Al, he smiled and raised his head slightly.

"It is an honor," Al said as he dismounted from his cavedog and walked toward the dragon.

Hiasyntar'Kulai emitted a low rumbling sound deep in his throat and nodded slightly. "The king of Roegudok Hall, I should say you are every bit as impressive as Erik led me to believe."

Al bent down and knelt upon a knee. "We have been shipping addorite to Valtuu Temple," Al said as he lifted his head.

Hiasyntar'Kulai nodded. "Yes," he began in his thunderous voice. "But in the last few weeks, the shipments have stopped."

Al nodded knowingly. "I should have sent a messenger, I apologize."

"You have found the demons, haven't you?"

Al nodded.

"King of Roegudok Hall, if you will permit me, I would connect our minds, so that I may see what you have seen. Would you permit this?"

Al cocked his head to the side. "What would I need to do?"

"Only look into my eyes, and say that you permit it. I can do the rest."

Al nodded twice. "I am ever at your service," Al said.

The dwarf king looked into the dragon's eyes and a great warmth latched onto his face, holding him still. A cool, tingling sensation penetrated Al's eyes. It wasn't painful, but it was not exactly comfortable either. The tingling stretched through into his mind and then it was as if Al was aware of a presence in his memories, rifling through them as if they were books on a shelf. Al was able to continue his own thought process, but simultaneously he saw hundreds of memories play out in his mind in a matter of seconds. Then, as quickly as it had been established, the link was severed and Al stumbled forward to the ground.

"You will regain your strength presently," the Father of the Ancients promised. "I have seen your deeds, and I am more proud of you now than I was when I first learned of your discovering the addorite."

"We have not yet beaten the demons," Al said.

"No, but you have a better plan than any that has been tried before."

"If we fail," Al began slowly, "then the demons will be free to enter this world more fully won't they?"

The dragon nodded. "If they are able to break through your defenses, then yes, they could spill into the Middle Kingdom after they destroy those within the mountain. However, I will stay here until the battle is finished. If you should fail to destroy them, then I will protect the Middle Kingdom as best I can from the demons. Although, I should say, I believe you will win."

"How can you be so sure?" Al asked.

"I have already seen a world pass on and die. There were few on Kendualdern who possessed the courage and strength to fight. However, when I look into your soul, I see what was so sorely lacking on my home world."

"Is there truly no other way to access The Infinium than with the use of addorite?"

Hiasyntar'Kulai's eyes turned downward in a sad, distant stare. "I had many sons," he replied. "One of them found The Infinium before we fled from Kendualdern. Despite The Aurorean's warnings, my son tried to read The Infinium in its entirety, without the assistance of addorite. The powers of the book were too much for him, and they drove him mad."

"Tu'luh," Al guessed.

"No," Hiasyntar'Kulai corrected. "Tu'luh has never read more than the unsealed portion in the beginning of The Infinium, though I did recently uncover the fact that he had hidden away a significant supply of addorite to attempt to do just that. Tu'luh lost his way, believing that forcing people to do his will and suppress their freedom to choose would result in a less corrupt world. He hoped that would stop the four horsemen from ever coming."

"Are we sure they are coming?" Al asked.

Hiasyntar'Kulai let out a soft growl. "I am. I have already been visited by one of their judges. You met him also, I see. He was the tall, human-like stranger in green robes who magically appeared on your balcony. He met with me also."

"And he will send the horsemen?" Al asked.

The dragon shook his head. "I do not believe the time has come yet, but I also do not think it far off. In any case, the son who read The Infinium is known to you as the Patron of Chaos. He is the twisted black dragon who beguiled Khullan into forming the cursed races during the creation period. His name was Gorensikdar. He was killed a few centuries ago during a great war far to the west from here."

"I am sorry for your loss," Al offered.

The golden dragon let a tear fall to the ground. "I lost

my son when he read the Aurorean's book. You see, the power within the book is so great, that without the addorite to absorb some of the energy from The Infinium, the book will warp even the mind of an Ancient. We had been instructed, in order to read the book, to crush the crystal into a powder, then to heat it with dragonbreath in order to create a thick smoke in the room where the book will be read. Only then will our minds be protected from The Infinium's harmful energies. There is not a day that goes by I do not wish my son could have shown the patience and forbearance necessary to wait until we could have come into possession of sufficient addorite to read the book safely.

"By the time we had been instructed by the Aurorean on how to access the knowledge in the Infinium, it was too late for our world. There was no time to search for the Mystinen nexus there, but we did have hope of finding a new world where the nexus could be located, and addorite extracted. However, Gorensikdar had been driven to the brink at the loss of our world. He sought a way to exact revenge, not merely to prevent future loss of life, and went to The Infinium in a moment of recklessness before we met Icadion. I made a mistake in bringing him with us, for I thought someday I might be able to cure his mind, but I never was able to. Part of me still clings to the hope that I may find some answers in The Infinium that would enable me to bring my son back."

"That would explain why you continue to need more addorite," Al commented.

"Yes, it consumes quite a lot of crystals in the process. I have made excellent progress so far with what you have sent, but I will need more to finish my work."

"Does The Infinium truly hold the key to defeating the four horsemen?" Al pressed.

Hiasyntar'Kulai nodded. "The Aurorean himself created The Infinium. He was a dragon made of light itself. He embodied all wisdom and knowledge. He was the creator of the sun that gave birth to us of Kendualdern, from whom remain only those you know as the Ancients here upon

Terramyr. He then formed Kendualdern, and all of the dragons that inhabited that world. All of his knowledge was transcribed by his own hand into The Infinium. If there is a way to defeat the four horsemen, he would know it."

"But you aren't sure?" Al asked incredulously.

"I am not certain, but I am confident the answers will be found there."

Al nodded. "Alferug, and King Sylus' book explained that Roegudok Hall is the only place on Terramyr where addorite can form, is this true?"

Hiasyntar'Kulai nodded. "The Mystinen force forms a powerful nexus beneath Roegudok Hall. It converges with ever-present geological pressures to create the correct conditions for addorite to form. There is no other place on Terramyr that is the same."

"Then, I should go. I have demons to slay."

"Before you go, you should know that I have found an answer for you within the pages of The Infinium."

Al stopped and nodded his head to show that he was listening.

"I have read a section about the Mystinen. Apparently it is an energy that comes into being when a seed crystal is created at the moment a plane of Hammenfein is connected to a new world. The seed crystal is released into the world, where it burns deep into its depths, and creates a new plane from which a nexus of Mystinen flows into the new world. When you travel through the portal, you are going to a new plane. It is smaller in scale, but is the home to this powerful crystal, and the creatures which are born of the mountain and the Mystinen. The crystal itself gives birth in each world to a fearsome guardian. The Infinium speaks of a three-headed demon. If you slay this demon, you can bring the crystal back through the portal to our plane of existence. In doing so, all of the portals that link our world with that of the demons will close. However, the Mystinen will still flow on our plane until the power in the crystal fades. Thus, you will be able to mine addorite without fear of any lurkers or demons appearing from the other plane."

"How will I know this crystal?" Al asked.

"The Infinium describes it as a blue, pearlescent crystal that is smooth and spins in the air. It will likely be in some sort of shrine, as it also is the source of the demons' magic. Take the crystal, and the demons will not only be sealed off, but they will lose their magical powers."

"And then the mine will be safe?"

Hiasyntar'Kulai nodded. "This doesn't eradicate all demons throughout Terramyr, of course, but our concern is the small, alternate world that has formed a nexus with our own. Take the crystal, and that link will be broken."

"And you are sure this is accurate?" Al pressed. He was slightly worried that the large dragon might grow intolerant of his questions, but the golden dragon continued to smile softly and nod his head as he explained it for Al.

"The Infinium detailed that this particular nexus is formed with every world, but that each world links to its own alternate plane. Think of it as a shadow. I have a shadow and you have a shadow, but the properties of our shadows are the same. Thus it is with this alternate plane that is linked to a world through the Mystinen. It is a force that begins during a world's creation, and while each world has its own alternate plane created by its own Mystinen, the properties of that plane, and the crystal within the alternate plane, as well as the large three-headed demon, are all the same."

"Is it true you can't come into the mountain?"

Hiasyntar'Kulai nodded once more. "Though I am the strongest of my kind, the Mystinen is toxic to me. Until it is gone, I cannot go inside Roegudok Hall."

Al nodded and turned back to look at the open gate. "I had better go and finish our preparations then."

"Fortune be with you, King of Roegudok Hall," the dragon boomed.

CHAPTER 17

Year 3,711 Age of Demigods, Winter.
2ndyear of the reign ofAldehenkaru'hktanah Sit'marihu, 13th
King of Roegudok Hall.

Al stood quietly as he surveyed the warriors gathered
in Demon Spring. There had been enough lurker scales to
forge three hundred sets of armor. It wasn't nearly as many
soldiers as King Sylus had during his final battle with the
demons, but Al hoped it would be enough. Knowing that there
were twenty addorite mounds where the portals would be
functioning, the army was going to be divided into twenty
groups of fifteen. The previous night, Al and Benbo had
selected eighteen captains to lead eighteen groups of fifteen
warriors each. Benbo would lead the nineteenth group, and Al
was commanding the twentieth.

Each group had been briefed on the mission. Get in,
sneak around if possible, slay anything that tried to attack
them, and above all, get the crystal out of the alternate plane.
He also stressed the importance of leaving the tunnel as a
group once someone had the crystal. Anyone who didn't jump
back through the portal before the crystal was brought into
Terramyr would be stuck in the alternate plane forever. Al had
tried to describe the alternate plane to them as best he could,
but even still he knew it was going to be a difficult fight. There
was no way of knowing exactly where the crystal would be,
other than looking for the three-headed demon
Hiasyntar'Kulai had spoken of.

That was to say nothing of the lurkers. Al had no idea how many of them might be hiding in the darkness. To make matters worse, the cavedogs were unable to go through the portals. The three hundred warriors would have to go it alone, and on foot. Then there was the matter of time. For every minute they spent in the alternate plane, a day would pass in Terramyr. They would have to be quick.

The dwarf king took in a deep breath and glanced up to the tunnel leading out of Demon Springs. He took comfort knowing that the mithril gate was closed, and defensive traps had been set in place. If any demons or lurkers managed to come into Terramyr, the remaining warriors would deal with them.

Al looked at the pile of stones encasing the mound a few yards in front of him and his warriors. He nodded to them and gave the signal. The warriors began slowly dismantling the makeshift barrier. As the dwarf king watched them work, he caught a glimpse of something glowing just beyond the soldiers in his group. He stepped around the stone barrier and saw Alferug, King Sylus, and his father standing a few feet in the air above the ground. They smiled at him, and then they vanished. Al took comfort in seeing the spirits.

He walked back to his warriors and encouraged them. "Our ancestors are with us this day," Al said. He adjusted his armor once more and held Murskain at the ready. As soon as the last stone was removed, he made for the mound of crystal. He walked up to the apex and then took one more step. As had happened before, the lights around him vanished and he was in darkness. He quietly looked around, searching for any sign of lurkers or demons.

A vent erupted just thirty yards away, illuminating much of the area around the dwarf king. Seeing nothing, he moved off the mound. The other warriors streamed in one after another. Al signaled to them with a silent wave as another blast of fire erupted from the nearby vent.

They moved along a stone embankment that skirted around a much softer, clay-like substance that had built up around the waist-high vent. When the fire erupted, the dwarves crouched low. Al caught sight of another group of dwarves moving along in the darkness. He silently wished them luck and then continued on.

The air in the alternate plane smelled of sulfur and something akin to rotting flesh. Moisture hung in the air, but there was no visible fog or mist. It was a sticky humidity that soon matted Al's hair under his helmet. There were strange sounds as well. The vents were familiar with their exploding *whoosh!* Yet there were other noises, like clicking nails against stone, guttural grunts and gargled shrieks the likes of which Al had never experienced before. There were also the more familiar sounds of heavy footsteps, growls, and whimpering cries that came from deeper within the tunnels.

Having no other information to go on, Al tried to use the sounds to navigate. He reasoned that if there was a three-headed demon guarding a large crystal that was the source of their power, then that shrine might be located in the midst of a large gathering of demons or lurkers.

The prospect of trying to sneak up on either of those types of creatures was beyond intimidating, but Al let the warm energy flowing from Murskain steady his nerves. He was destined to find this place. That is what Sylus had said.

He would soon discover whether that sentiment was true.

Another flash of fire shot out from a vent nearby and Al signaled for his warriors to crouch low. A lurker moved along the shadows seventy yards away from them, but it didn't notice them. Al began moving again as soon as the light died down.

Then everything took a turn for the worse.

A blood-curdling scream tore through the otherwise peaceful air in the network of tunnels and caverns. Al knew that someone had been slain. The dwarves were now discovered. They would have to work fast to find the crystal before they were all killed.

Dozens of clicking feet scurried in the darkness across

the stone. War cries went up through the air as lurkers snarled and growled. A blue light formed around a winged demon that flew toward the sound of battle and began to blast the area with green lightning bolts.

"Come, we have to move," Al whispered. The warriors at his back hastened their pace as he picked his way across the ground toward a nearby tunnel that led out from the large chamber they had appeared in.

He didn't stop to help the other group of embattled dwarves. He didn't even stop to watch as they were obliterated in seconds by the flying demon and his magic. The dwarf king pushed forward, then turned into a tunnel on his left. In this area there were strange, fungus-like things growing along the wall that gave off faint, blue light. It made running through the tunnel quite a bit easier. With the vent-filled chamber receding behind them, the group slowed to a more silent pace, but not a pace so slow that they might be discovered by the flying demon who would surely be patrolling the area now.

Al's group rounded a corner to the right and then froze when Al held up his left arm. There, in a large dead-end, sat the largest lurker he had ever seen. It was easily twice the size of the other lurkers, and its abdomen was much, much longer. Instead of four legs and two arms tipped with claws, it had six legs and a pair of arms that were only half the size of the other lurkers Al had seen. The claws were made of the same white material, but they were only a few inches long instead of several feet long.

"A queen?" one of the warriors asked.

Al shrugged. He studied the creature carefully. It was lying still on its side, breathing heavily. It hadn't seen them yet, so perhaps they should move out of the tunnel. Al turned to glance around the corner, but one of the warriors in the rear of the group signaled him away.

"Lurker coming in, Sire," the warriors whispered.

Al knew there was only one way to survive. He signaled for the warriors to fan out and attack the queen. They charged in without yelling or shouting, though their plated boots did announce their presence with their loud clanking and slapping. The queen awoke and shifted to rest upon her underbelly. Al prepared for a challenging battle, but the queen proved to be lethargic and hardly worth the warriors' time. She barely turned her head toward them before they hacked into her. Unlike the lurkers they had fought before, her scales were soft, barely sturdier than boiled leather armor. She grunted and wheezed, then fell flat and lifeless.

The lurker that had entered the tunnel was rushing in after them, though. Its clicking feet sped around the curve and it scanned the chamber for the intruders. Al and the others had carefully taken cover behind the queen, poking their heads up and parting the thick fur on her back just enough to watch the lurker in the soft light given off by the glowing mushrooms.

The beast came close, pausing before it stretched its neck out to sniff the queen.

The dwarves came out from their spot and launched a coordinated assault. Al struck the monster across the face with Murskain. Two others hacked off the front left leg. Three more drove spears into the lurker's right side. The rest circled around and attacked the creature from behind. The lurker lashed out with its right hind leg, catching one dwarf in the throat before it was cut down.

Al and the others rushed to the injured dwarf, but there was nothing they could do for him. He convulsed as he bled out in a matter of moments. Al led the group from the tunnel back to the main chamber, ignoring the battle continuing to rage on and searching for another place to explore. A great series of eruptions started roughly two hundred yards away, blasting through several vents, each one closer than the one before and washing the whole chamber in a fiery red light.

Al dropped to his stomach to keep a low profile and used the light to survey the area. In the brighter light, he could see that the network of tunnels was like a hive network. Several smaller shafts branched off from the main chamber they had entered when they stepped through the portal, but there was one wide tunnel that led downward and disappeared into the darkness.

The dwarf king couldn't be sure, but he felt like the shrine would be found in the biggest tunnel.

He signaled for his warriors to follow as he pushed up and moved out across the stone toward the main tunnel. He had gone only a few yards when he felt the hairs on the back of his neck stand on end. He turned to the right and saw a pair of glowing, icy blue eyes staring back at him. A green web of lightning appeared a moment later. Al reacted on instinct, swinging out with Murskain and driving the spike deep into the demon's chest. Two other dwarves rushed in and pierced the demon's neck with their swords, silencing any scream for help the creature might have otherwise mustered.

They moved as quickly as they could while maintaining silent footsteps. Another eruption of fire vents had them scurrying quickly toward the main tunnel, abandoning silence for speed so as not to be seen from a distance.

The tunnel descended so sharply that they almost lost their footing as they went down. They had to move to the wall and steady themselves to keep from sliding along the steep incline. Behind them, more sounds of battle and dwarven screams erupted.

Al could only hope that he was going the right way. To think that all of them might perish without ever laying eyes on the crystal was nearly more than he could bear. This time, the screams and clash of weapons and blasts of spells did not die down quickly.

"They are putting up a good fight," one of the warriors noted.

Al nodded. "Then we should honor their sacrifice by accomplishing our task."

None of the others said a word, but Al knew they agreed.

Another two hundred feet and the tunnel leveled out. It also turned around to the left, curving one hundred and eighty degrees. As they rounded the bend, Al saw yellow light reflecting off the walls some three hundred yards ahead where the tunnel curved out to the right. Shadows danced and moved along the light on the walls.

There was a chamber ahead of some sort. Al was sure of it.

The group crept along the tunnel, glancing over their heads and watching for any sign of danger.

The sounds of battle were quieting as they continued to distance themselves from the main chamber, but the battle itself sounded no less intense. Judging by the number of shouts and cries, Al figured that most of the other dwarves were currently engaged in battle. For all he knew, his was the only group still wandering free and looking for the crystal.

The dwarf king froze mid-step when he heard a howling noise coming from around the bend in front of them. A great shadow moved along the wall. Al studied it and started to smile when he counted three heads atop a large body. They were close.

He doubled their pace, stopping again when they reached the corner so Al could carefully peer around the curve and see what waited for them. He saw a long, rectangular chamber with naturally formed columns and a spring of purple liquid bubbling up in the center of the chamber. Fires burned beyond the alien spring and there, hovering in the air above what appeared to be a stone altar, was the blue crystal Hiasyntar'Kulai had spoken of.

Al smiled and glanced to his group. "This is it," he said. He then turned his gaze back to the chamber. He hadn't seen the guardian yet. He waited for a few moments before a massive, muscular leg stepped out from behind one of the natural columns. Then the body appeared. The demon's alabaster skin was almost painful to look at because of how intensely it reflected the firelight. The three heads were not at all what Al had expected. The center head looked much like an ogre's head, somewhat round, but a bit flattened out as if someone had dropped a boulder on top of the skull and flattened it a bit. The head on the left resembled a large, black wolf head. The pointy ears twitched this way and that as the head stuck its snout in the air and sniffed loudly just before howling. The head on the right looked like a great eagle's head.

Yet, the rest of the body was most definitely humanoid. The bare, extremely white skin rippled with human-like muscles. The demon held a spear in its right hand and an axe in its left. Al waited until it crossed the width of the chamber and disappeared behind another row of natural columns. Then he signaled for his warriors to charge with him.

They ran down the last portion of the hallway leading into the shrine with the crystal as quickly as they could. Al assumed that with the demon's wolf head, it would hear them or smell them coming even if they tried to sneak along, so it was best to charge in and go for the crystal.

Unfortunately, he had misjudged the demon's abilities.

The ten-foot-tall demon appeared out of thin air in the midst of the dwarves. He drove his spear through one of the warriors and cut another down with his axe. Al and the others turned in to attack, but he vanished and the dwarves caught only air.

"Spread out!" Al commanded. "Don't bunch together and give it easy targets."

The group spread out as much as they could in the tunnel and resumed following Al as he made a straight line for the blue crystal.

The demon appeared in the middle of the shrine and hurled his spear with great speed and accuracy. Al managed to jump aside, but the spear skewered two more hapless warriors and carried their bodies several yards to crash into the far wall of the tunnel behind them. The spear then reappeared in the demon's hand and the middle head began to laugh.

Al narrowed his eyes on the demon and felt a rage boil inside of him. Without turning around, he commanded his warriors to each go for the crystal and leave the demon to him. A couple of them protested, but Al wasn't listening. He ran for the demon.

The painfully white creature vanished only to reappear

behind Al. The eagle head screeched loudly while the ogre head laughed and the wolf head snarled and growled ferociously. The dwarf king turned and ducked as the axe sailed over his head. He then jumped up and twirled to the side as the spear struck out at him. Al swung with his hammer, but the demon vanished before the weapon could connect. The momentum of the attack caused Al to spin and lose his balance. He stumbled out toward the wall, but quickly regained his footing and turned to run toward the shrine once more.

The demon appeared in the center of the shrine again. This time it launched the spear and the axe. The dwarves all tried to dodge the flying weapons, but the axe caught one and the spear stabbed another. The weapons disappeared shortly thereafter and the demon vanished as the ogre head laughed again.

Al held up his hand, signaling for everyone to stop. He turned and commanded them all to swing as he aimed for the empty space in the middle of them all. Most of the warriors were confused by the order, so only two others lashed out.

The demon appeared, right where Al had predicted. He drove Murskain's spike into the demon's left thigh while the two who had followed his orders managed to score minor hits on the demon's buttocks. The monster howled and vanished.

"Now throw!" Al shouted. He turned and launched his weapon with all of his might toward the crystal. This time, all of the other dwarves obeyed. Spears, swords, and axes flew through the air. The demon reappeared where he had the previous two times. Murskain pummeled the demon in the chest, while the other weapons pelted the creature with varying degrees of success. The wolf head howled, the eagle head screamed, and the ogre head shouted in an unintelligible language.

Al and the others charged into the shrine, fully expecting the demon to retreat.

Again, they misjudged it.

A blinding light tore through the shrine and a

deafening thunder shook the walls and floor around them. Dust fell from the ceiling as cracks split the stone. When the light faded, there stood three giant creatures, not one. A massive ogre, a black wolf larger than any of the lurkers in the upper chambers, and a gryphon.

The wolf lunged in and seized a dwarf in its massive maw, crunching down on the armor and shaking its head violently. The gryphon launched its attack second, pinning two dwarves against the stone wall and biting at them with its beak.

Two dwarves charged the ogre, scooping up their weapons from the floor and attacking the massive creature's legs. It took the cuts and stabs, staggering back toward the spring of purple liquid. It stumbled into it, flailing its arms as the dwarves finished it off.

Al rushed in and picked up Murskain. He then turned on the wolf and delivered a massive hammer-strike to the creature's ribs. The bones boke, snapping loudly and bending inward. The wolf collapsed on the ground and Al and the others were able to finish it off without much more hassle.

The dwarf king barely heard the flapping wings before a tremendous force knocked him onto his back. He bounced across the stone floor, skidding to a stop just a few feet away from the stone altar below the blue crystal.

"Go for the crystal, Sire! We'll handle this," one of the warriors shouted.

Al looked up to see the dwarves battling the gryphon. He then glanced down to his chest and saw an open gash across the outer layer of his armor. He wasn't sure if the gryphon had managed to cut all the way through, but he also didn't have the time to stop and evaluate it. He need to get the crystal, and then he had to find the nearest portal out of here.

Al jumped up to his feet and ran to the altar. He clambered atop and used Murskain to hook the hovering crystal and bring it down. It wasn't as large as he had thought, just the size of an acorn squash, but it hummed vibrantly with incredible energy. Just touching it invigorated his body and soul. He gripped the middle of Murskain's shaft in his right hand and tucked the crystal into his left elbow.

He started running out of the shrine.

Two more dwarves fell by the gryphon. One had his head bitten off, helmet and all, and the other was cut down by the large talons of the gryphon's front feet. That left only three dwarves fighting the creature. They did their best, hacking and stabbing at it, but Al knew they would not be able to defeat it. The gryphon was so fast and nimble that they had yet to land any hits on the creature.

He ran past, mentally thanking his warriors for their sacrifice.

He heard the gryphon screech out an ear-splitting cry and then a cacophony of metal crashing against stone erupted behind Al. He knew at least one more dwarf had been killed, but he couldn't stop to look back now.

He hooked around the left and sprinted toward the curve leading to the main tunnel. As the light from the shrine dimmed, the crystal he held glowed brightly, lighting the way for him. In a matter of seconds he rounded the next corner and then made the difficult run up the ascending tunnel.

When Al reached the half-way point, a lurker came around the entrance and reared up on its hind legs, snarling and hissing at Al. The dwarf king prepared to launch a savage blow with Murskain, but fortunately a group of seven dwarves tackled the beast a moment later and put it down before Al reached the top of the tunnel.

"My king, this way!" Benbo shouted.

Al was beyond happy to see the commander. The seven dwarves formed a wedge and began sprinting off to the right. The scene around them was not a pretty one. Lurkers and demons swarmed the area. Fireballs and blasts of lightning were zipping through the air. Dwarves were tirelessly fighting through it all, cutting down as many enemies as they could.

A lurker lunged at Al, but one of the seven dwarves with Benbo jumped between them and took the creature's attack for the king. Al had to turn away as the lurker ripped into the dwarf and sent blood spraying out over the floor.

The wedge reformed, tightening due to the loss of a member and pulling Al closer into the center of the protective wall.

Shouts and cries went up through the remaining ranks of warriors as they realized that Al had the crystal. So too, did the demons shriek and wail when they noticed it. In seconds, lurkers and demons were pressing in toward the wedge.

"To the king!" Benbo shouted. "To the king!"

Dwarves did their best to consolidate around the path that Benbo was leading Al over, but it wasn't flawless. A lurker leapt over several dwarves and grabbed the dwarf right beside Al, leaving a gaping hole in the wedge. A moment later, a flying demon of some sort shot through the gap in the wedge and grabbed at the crystal. Al smacked the creature in the face with the top of his warhammer. Blood shot out from the monster's skull and it flopped to the ground as Al wrenched the crystal free and kept it safely tucked in his arm.

"Here," Benbo shouted to Al. "Just a few more yards!"

Al looked through the crowd of thrashing bodies to see a faint, pink glow upon the ground. They had almost reached an addorite mound.

The king knew that if he crossed through the portal before the others, they would be trapped in the alternate plane, and that meant they would be slain by these monstrous abominations. He couldn't have that. "Retreat!" he shouted. "Retreat! Get back into our world!"

Al smiled when he saw two dwarves nearest to the mound leap over it and disappear back to Terramyr. Others gauged how close the king was to the mound before jumping into portals themselves. Benbo, and the other dwarves in the wedge were not about to abandon Al, though. They fought off attacks and pressed forward.

A terrible shriek erupted in the air and Al couldn't help but turn around.

He could see the dark outline of the gryphon flying through the darkness. It shrieked again, but this time there was a force in the scream that knocked Al to the ground. His ears stung and his head rang sharply. A muffled voice called to him and several hands reached down to pull him up. Al shook his head, barely able to cling to his hammer and the crystal as he struggled to make his feet work. His eyes flicked around and noticed that many of the others had been knocked to the ground as well, including lurkers and demons.

The gryphon was closing in fast. Al shook off the sluggishness and forced his feet to move.

Benbo was shouting something, but Al couldn't make it out. The commander pulled and tugged on Al's arm. Another dwarf grabbed Al's other arm, and a third pushed him from behind.

The mound was three yards away.

The gryphon was diving, talons out and beak open as it screeched once more. Al turned to look at Benbo. The commander yanked Al onward and then pointed his sword toward the gryphon and leapt directly into its path.

There was a powerful force that lifted Al from his feet and propelled him forward. He flew through the air, landing hard on the stone floor and losing his breath in the process. His lungs flattened, sticking together and burning for air as Al gasped and sucked for breath. The crystal fell out of his arm and he lost his grip on Murskain.

Something grabbed him and lifted him up. His hearing was still muffled, but his senses were starting to come back to him as he fought against his enemy, swinging his arms and striking out with his fists.

Voices called out to him, but he couldn't make out the words.

Then, his lungs reopened and air flooded into them. He made a horrid gasping sound and everything started to make sense again. He realized there was light all around him. It was then that he knew what had happened. The dwarves protecting him had thrown him through the portal to get him home.

He looked around and saw a group of ten dwarven

warriors standing around him. They had been the ones who had picked him up. Al turned around and saw the crystal lying on the ground. The mission had been accomplished.

The dwarf king then looked back to the mound of addorite. Benbo was still inside, as were so many others. Al turned and reached for the crystal. He scooped it up and started for the mound again. The other dwarves swooped in and tried to block his path.

"No, my king!" one shouted.

"You can't reopen the portal!" another added.

"You'll kill us all!" a third yelled.

Someone wrapped their arms around Al's legs and the dwarf king fell to his knees, just a few short feet away from the mound. Tears filled his eyes and he called out for Benbo.

CHAPTER 18

Year 3,711 Age of Demigods, Late Winter.
2nd year of the reign of Aldehenkaru'hktanah Sit'marihu, 13th King of Roegudok Hall.

A familiar tug came at Al's armor. He looked down to see his cavedog. He reached down and pet the scaly lizard.

"Your cavedog has been loyally waiting for you this whole time," one of the guards said.

"How long were we gone?" Al asked.

"Just under two months," the warrior replied. "I came in only after these others came back from the portal and sent a runner up to me."

"Have you been here long?" Al asked.

One of the other warrior's shrugged. "We came back through the tunnel a couple days ago."

Al nodded and glanced back to the mound of addorite. "It was a struggle for me to get back through," he said. "Come, we should tell the others that it's over. I'll go on ahead and report back to Hiasyntar'Kulai. Bring everyone up from the mines, let's take the next week to rest and mourn for our fallen kin, and leave the mine for a later time."

Al hopped onto his cavedog and rode up to the mithril gate.

The cavedog seemed as excited as he felt while he held the blue crystal in his arms. The lizard zipped along faster than Al had ever ridden it before. As he came within one hundred yards of the gate, the other guards began shouting.

"It's the king! It's the king!"

"He's alive!"

"Open the gates!" Al called out.

The mithril portcullis was raised quickly and Al rushed through, holding the large, blue crystal high over his head for all to see. The miners and guards clapped and cheered as he rode past at a blinding speed, riding straight for Kijik, who was dutifully manning one of the large ballista launchers.

"Hail!" Kijik shouted.

"Hail to the king!" others echoed.

Al stopped his cavedog and held the blue crystal out to Kijik.

Kijik furrowed his brow and reluctantly held his hands out to receive the blue crystal. "Why do you give this to me?"

Al placed it into Kijik's hands and looked the Commander of the Home Guard in the eyes. "You command the Home Guard. That means your highest responsibility is to protect Roegudok Hall. This crystal creates a magical field called the Mystinen. I cannot take it up into the main hall, for it would change the infrastructure of the mountain over time. I also can't give it to the Ancients, for it would harm them. So, I give it to you. I want you and your men to create an iron cage. Line the inside and outside layers with mithril and then bolt the cage down to the wall right there," Al said as he pointed to the wall behind Kijik. "Until the power fades from this crystal, we can continue to mine addorite, and as long as the crystal remains safely guarded inside the metal cage, none shall ever again be able to open the portal back to where the demons came from."

"I understand, Sire," Kijik said. He turned and began barking orders. "You heard the king. Bring me iron, steel, and mithril. We are going to make a cage for this!" Kijik held the crystal high in the air and the others cheered.

Al clapped Kijik on the back. "I will see you tonight in the main hall."

Kijik nodded eagerly and proclaimed, "We should make a feast."

The dwarf king then mounted his cavedog and made haste through the tunnels.

If the cheering had been loud and joyous in the tunnels, it was deafening when he reached the main hall. The entire marketplace came to a halt as merchants and craftsmen stopped to praise the king. He raised Murskain high over head as he urged his cavedog onward toward the exit tunnel and shouted repeatedly, "It's over! The demons are gone!"

As he drew near the gates at the end of the three-mile-long tunnel, his heart was bursting with pride. His excitement amplified as the gates opened and the light of a later winter morning greeted him. He rode out and didn't even mind the cold as he leapt down from his cavedog and walked toward Hiasyntar'Kulai.

The great dragon raised its head and smiled. "The king has returned," he said joyfully.

"I have the crystal," Al said. "I have ordered it to be kept in a metal box near Demon Spring so we can continue to mine in the depths for addorite and the Mystinen shall remain stable."

"Wise," Hiasyntar'Kulai commented.

Al bowed low and then set the head of his warhammer down in the snow. "How long will the crystal remain active?"

Hiasyntar'Kulai emitted a throaty growl and then turned his head to a slight angle. "In the alternate plane, it would have survived for eons, or possibly forever since time is so much different compared to time as we experience it. However, even here it should last for a few hundred years."

"Well then," Al smirked, "I should be able to mine all the addorite you could possibly want."

"It is well," Hiasyntar'Kulai replied. "Now, go inside. Feast and celebrate with your people. A new era of prosperity has begun. I dare say that the glory of Roegudok Hall shall be brightest under the reign of Aldehenkaru'hktanah Sit'marihu."

Al bowed low, and then he bade the Father of the Ancients farewell. He turned and mounted his cavedog once more and entered the long tunnel leading up to the main hall.

The feasting lasted for forty days and nights, ceasing only when the first flowers of spring began to poke through the melting snow.

It was the beginning of the third year of the reign of Aldehenkaru'hktanah Sit'marihu, and the dwarves of Roegudok Hall had never had so many reasons to be joyous since the beginning of time.

About the Author

Well... the truth is that Sam is a very *lucky* guy. He juggles work in such a way that he makes sure to spend enough time with his loving wife and sons. He enjoys bringing his characters to life, and is absolutely thrilled that other people choose to spend their time exploring the constructs of his imagination. Since you are one of those people, thank you very much for your support.

If he can carve out an extra hour for himself during the day, he'll hit the gym to try and regain the body he used to have in his youth (but he eats too much junk food to ever accomplish that goal).

He spent nearly five years serving as a U.S. Diplomat and absolutely loved the experience, but decided to move back home. Outside of the U.S. he has lived in Latvia, Hungary, and Armenia. He speaks Russian, Hungarian, and Armenian. (He used to speak some Latvian too, but he has no one to practice with anymore...)

He has two dogs.

He plays the Elder Scrolls series.

His favorite superhero is Wolverine, but Batman is a close second.

If the kids go to bed at a reasonable hour, he will cuddle up with his wife to watch Scrubs reruns, the Big Bang Theory, Castle, and Burn Notice.

If you enjoyed this book, then join Sam Ferguson's Facebook page, sign up for alerts on his Amazon page, and by all means leave a kind review!